The Village of Dead Souls

ALSO BY

Michael G. Wallace

Eternal Patrol

————

The Village of Dead Souls

Michael G. Wallace

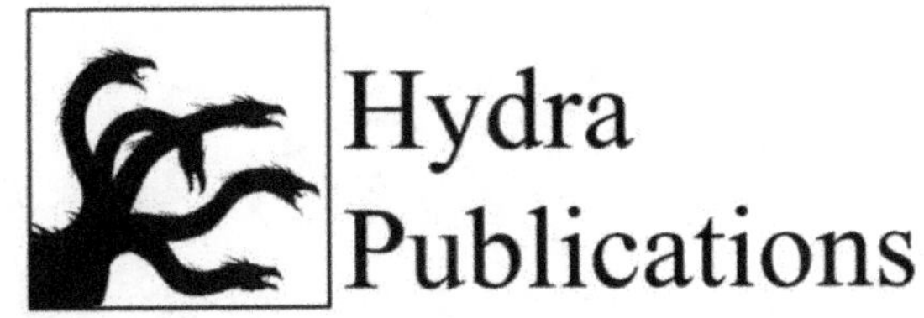

Hydra
Publications

Printed in the United States of America

ISBN: 0996086781

ISBN-13: 978-0-9960867-8-3

Hydra Publications
1310 Meadowridge Trail
Goshen, KY 40026

www.hydrapublications.com

Chapter 1

Scattered voices echoed off the white marble pillars, which surrounded the forum under a cloudless blue sky. Several small groups of citizens in tunics and robes debated various topics, while making grand hand gestures to accent their point. Prometheus stood at the edge of a discussion at the bottom of the bright marble stairs. He noticed a strange scent of dust on the gentle breeze. With the recent rains, the tall Greek man with chiseled features wondered what could be kicking up dust in the city this morning. The elderly man in a flowing robe next to him said, "We have an obligation to remember the dead. We are their descendants and if they disappear from our memories, they will perish entirely. Many of our sons have gone to sea only to have them not return. This is why I give an offering at the Temple of Poseidon each morning." The man noticed his friend did not pay full attention to his words. "Perhaps, the gods will grant us a bountiful catch when the fishermen return."

Prometheus smiled and replied, "Poseidon has favored us for many seasons and I do not see him taking anger with us now. We have built a new temple near the sea, which should only provide him more pride. I talked to good Callius just this morning. He spoke of calm seas and gentle winds for our men."

A woman with long dark hair, wearing a maroon dress, caught his eye as she filled a terra-cotta jug with water from the fountain in the center of the forum. Prometheus stopped listening to his friend and wondered whether he should approach her. It had been many months since he had seen a woman with the stunning beauty she held. Perhaps, he might offer to help carry the jug as a way to introduce himself. He excused himself from the conversation. "I'm sorry, my friend, I must end this discussion for a matter of loveliness has just arisen."

As he turned to walk toward the fountain, distant loud voices caught his attention. They came from several blocks away and sounded like a large crowd in an argument. The yelling seemed to have caught the attention of all in the forum, because the debates trickled to a stop and heads turned in the direction of the noise. The woman, who came for water, set the jug down and turned toward the source of the sound. Prometheus took a few steps closer to her as the voices grew louder. The clink of clashing metal swords mixed in with the commotion. Isolated screams of women and men stood out from the common sound.

A young man from the bakery frantically ran into the forum. Waving his arms, he called out, with panic in his voice, "Spartans! Spartan soldiers are attacking the city."

The people in the forum panicked and ran to the streets, which exited the city center only to be pushed back by the hordes of citizens escaping the advancing army. The city gathering center filled with terrified civilians who ran in all directions, adding to the chaos.

Spartan soldiers burst through the crowd swinging swords and pikes. The unarmed townspeople offered no challenge, and they quickly fell to the army, as their blood trickled across the ground. Several of the men threw rocks at the soldiers, but the military leather and armor simply deflected the useless attempt at resistance. Two Spartans grabbed the woman in the maroon dress next to the fountain. One soldier grabbed onto her long hair when she tried to run off, causing her head to jerk back, as her body slammed to the ground. Running to her aid Prometheus screamed, "Stop!"

He clenched his fist tighter than he had ever imagined. As if it was second nature, he leaped into the air and on the way down, he smashed his fist right between the two face shields of the soldier who held her hair. Blood splattered across his hand and wrist, and he felt the man's nose shatter under his knuckles. The Spartan fell backwards into the fountain. His heavy armor held him on his back underneath the water. A second soldier thrust his xiphos into Prometheus' ribs. Without concern to his fate and with blood pouring from his wound, saturating his white tunic, Prometheus reached down and grabbed the water jug. With a long wide swing, he broke the vessel over the soldier's helmet. As the Spartan fell backward, his sword flailed and it slashed open Prometheus's throat.

The Athenian didn't feel his body hit the ground and the world moved in slow motion about him. The sounds of the battle around the forum disappeared with only the blue sky filling his vision. Into his view, he saw the face of the woman he tried to save. With an expression of deep concern, she caressed the side of his face, while she kneeled over him. As his sight faded to white, another Spartan grabbed the woman by her hair and pulled her away.

Surrounded by nothing but white, Prometheus felt his legs lift him off the ground, but he put no energy toward this movement. He slowly walked through this strange void with confusion racing inside his head. No more pain, no bleeding, and he had the energy of a child which only added to the bewilderment. A few yards in front of him, an image appeared, as if a fog began to settle. He recognized the outline of man in a flowing silk toga. This elderly man with white hair and a muscular build stretched out his hand and said, "Prometheus, come walk with me."

As he moved closer to the stranger, he said, "You know who I am, but I do not know your identity or where we are having this conversation. I would offer gratitude, if you could so kindly inform me of both. Do you know what happened to me by the fountain? I believe my injuries are in need of immediate attention."

The white foggy void settled and Prometheus could see stairs leading to enormous pillars at the front of the largest temple that he had ever seen. It stretched so far into the distance that he could not see the opposite end. Walking next to him, the elderly man replied, "I would imagine with all the temples you have made in my honor that you would recognize Zeus when you met him for the first time."

Stunned to hear those words, Prometheus stumbled through his thoughts to find his next words. "Do you mean to tell me, I am standing on Mount Olympus with the king of the Titans? This truly is a position, I had never expected to be. Perhaps this is only a dream brought about by recent events."

The deity gave a slight smile. "I promise you this is no dream. As you made a valiant attempt to save the maiden by the fountain, you were killed by the soldier who slit your throat."

Prometheus quickly felt his neck where he had been slashed with the blade and found it to be whole, no cuts, and no injuries. The stab wound to his ribs no longer existed. The two beings stopped at the top of the stairs. Prometheus gazed at the elderly man. His mind would not let him believe it could be this easy to stand next to such a powerful god. "I do not feel as if I have died. My condition feels better than it has been in many seasons. The pain in my knees, which has burdened me for years, is no longer present."

With a pat on the back, Zeus replied, "I promise, you have passed from the life, you knew as a mortal. I have chosen you from many who have gone before and after you."

"Your words only offer me more confusion. Perhaps you could offer advice which would clarify my situation."

The ancient divinity smiled and said, "All the gods have come together for a special purpose. It is time to give the human mortals the gifts they need, if they are to continue their growth and evolution. They have reached a point where thought and advanced use of the elements will no longer provide for a sustained existence on your world."

"I see no fault in our existence." Prometheus gazed into the temple and spoke as if he simply debated a friend in the forum. "We have evolved and adapted to provide all we could ever need. Many of our luxuries provide pleasures beyond basic necessity."

"Indeed, you have done well with what you have been provided. However, as you advance and evolve, so does the world that you have yet to discover. Just like the Titan of your namesake, you will take a gift to the mortals, which will help them to inhabit their world. Only this time, it will be given with my blessing."

"A gift?"

"You will collect and process the thread of life inside your new body. When you have obtained the needed amount, your gift will be immunity to all forms of cancer."

"Pardon my ignorance of what you are telling me, but I do not understand what I am to do and what gift I will offer. You speak in words that I feel only the Behemoths would understand. As you have already referenced, I am only a mortal, but a mortal with many questions. These are questions any human man would ask when given this opportunity. How does Apollo pull the sun across the sky without burning up his chariot? If Atlas is holding the earth, what platform do his feet rest upon? Exactly where does Medusa live? I would not want to walk into her lair accidentally. There have been many occasions, where I have altered my course, due to an unknown cave in my path."

As the white void enveloped him, Zeus smiled, but did not answer. Prometheus closed the distance between him and the god while he rubbed his eyes to gain better focus on Zeus. When he opened his eyes, he saw a world he could never have imagined. All around him, buildings as tall as mountains with mirrors for windows. Streets covered with a black as tar type of pavement. No carts or chariots could be seen anywhere. Instead, the roads filled with wagons made of bright painted metal and they moved along the black roads without the use of horses. They made a rumbling sound like distant thunder of an approaching storm. The wheels did not make much noise and were not made of wood. They appeared solid and black, just like the road.

Prometheus took a few steps toward an area with green grass and trees. With all the confusion in his mind, it looked to be the only familiar site. As he walked, he noticed his body did not move as easily as he remembered. Glancing at his hands, he did not recognize them or his arms, or his legs. His entire body appeared different, as did the strange clothes. He saw his reflection in a window of the building behind him. A person he had never seen stared back; a man with pale almost gray skin. It couldn't be him. He lifted his arms and moved his head as the reflection did the same. He touched his face with his fingertips of both hands. His skin did not feel right and it looked too pale. It felt cold and dry with little elasticity. The people around him walked passed with no concern to his situation. They wore similar bizarre clothing made of bright colors. Both men and women wore pants and shirts. Not a single person had a tunic or a toga. Only a few women wore dresses and even then, the fabric did little to cover their legs.

He turned to a young man, whose dark hair pointed up in a spiked kind of way, and asked, "Pardon me, good sir, could you tell me what city we are in? I feel my conversation with Zeus has left my mind bewildered."

The young man gave Prometheus an odd look as he walked past without saying a word. He tried to ask the next woman who walked by, but before he could finish his question; she picked up the pace of her walk, and gave him an angry stare while she sped past him. Fear built up inside the Greek man. He made a general announcement to all on the sidewalk with him. "I only ask a kind favor from you good people. I have somehow arrived in your city and do not know where I am. Could one of you please offer some simples guidance, so I might find my way home? I live in Athens. Perhaps, you are on your way to the market there and I can join you on your journey."

An older man placed his hand on Prometheus's shoulder and spoke to him in words which sounded like complete gibberish, moans and hissing. As Prometheus tried to respond, the expression of concern on the old man's face, turned to fear, as he retracted his hand and walked away. Paying closer attention to the conversations around him, he realized that they all spoke in this strange language. It did not sound like actual words, but more like grunts and groans. Surely, he would find someone who spoke his tongue. So he decided to walk around the area and listen to the conversations, but all the people spoke using the same incomprehensible words.

On the other side of the grass and trees, he saw a large group of people marching in a kind of parade. They walked slowly, dragging their feet with stiff upper body movements. Their clothes looked torn and dirty and most were covered with blood. Prometheus concluded they must have returned from a battle. Most of the people in this macabre promenade appeared happy, and they carried vessels filled with ale, so they must have won the war. Perhaps, these victorious soldiers would help him get home.

His strange body continued to feel stiff as he moved. He felt as if he walked the same as the people in the celebration. When he finally reached the crowd, he noticed their wounds and blood appeared to be nothing more than stage makeup. They wore costumes making them look as if they were the dead who have come back to life. He concluded it must be a celebration of a long ago victory over an enemy. Music radiated through the area, but he could not see the musicians anywhere. The vocals of the songs were the same type of strange language spoken by those around him. With his hand extended, he asked for help again. Even though, this group spoke in the same grunts and moans, they did not seem frightened of him as the people across the park. One person in the celebration placed a cup full of beer in his extended hand.

Confused, Prometheus sniffed the drink, which he recognized. He could not smell the aroma that he expected. In fact, he realized, he could not smell much of anything around him. The trees and flowers in full bloom offered no fragrance. Trapped in a strange body, where he did not know how to take control of the senses, only added to his overall befuddlement. He took a sip of the beer and could feel the liquid on his throat, but it gave no flavor or sense of temperature. Hoping he could get some kind of sensation, he quickly drank the entire cup. Doing so, seemed to make the young people in costumes happy and someone handed him another beverage. "No. I appreciate your kindness to include me in your strange celebration of the dead." Prometheus downed the second beer. "But I need your help to return to my home. I do not live in this grand metropolis which you inhabit. Would someone offer such a kindness?"

He turned and watched the costumed people in celebration walk past him. They continued to speak in the unknown language, but appeared to be pleased with his stressful situation. Through the sounds of the moans and groans and the loud music, he heard a lone voice speak to him. "Hey Butt Head, that beer isn't going to do much for you, you're dead."

Prometheus turned to find the source of the voice. On the edge of the sidewalk, stood a tall black haired slender man in a dark suit and red tie. His white shirt had a patch of blood around a hole pierced through the pocket. Across his outfit, his clothes had areas of dirt and scuff marks. "Yeah, I'm talking to you," the man said.

Prometheus took a few steps toward the man in the suit. "Finally, someone who speaks Attic Greek."

"I don't speak Greek. I speak American."

"I have not heard of such a word, nor have I heard it spoken. The only languages I speak are Attic Greek and Latin. If I understand your words, you must be speaking in one of those two-"

The man in the suit interrupted, "Awww great, you're another one of those ancient guys."

"I do not understand your words in their entirety. Let me start with a proper introduction." Prometheus extended his hand and stepped closer to the man. "My name is Prometheus. I hail from Athens."

As Prometheus grabbed the man's forearm and patted his shoulder, the man replied, "Yeah, I'm Vic and I hail from Chicago."

"Is the city where we stand right now, Chicago?"

"No, we're in Denver. Ironically, the folks here are right in the middle of their Zombie Festival. This is the big mall crawl where they get dead drunk… Get it, dead drunk."

The Athenian shook his head in confusion. "I do not understand this celebration. Are you in a position to assist me in my efforts to get back to Athens?"

"Look, Mr. Proper Pants-"

"Prometheus."

"Whatever, you're not going to Athens, you're not going back to your time, and you're not going to finish you're conversation with Socrates or visit Atlantis again. You are a few thousand years in the future and you have a lot to learn before you can get started on your mission."

"Mission?"

"Yeah, we've all been given a mission. Just follow me and keep your pie hole shut."

"Pie hole?"

"Yeah, that thing you're yapping with."

"Yapping?"

"Stop talking. Keep your mouth closed and start listening. I have to take you back to the safe house. There's a guy there from your time, who will explain things in a way, you can understand."

* * *

Sitting in the center of his lab, scientist, Dr. Daniel Cronsworth, turned from his computer screen and wrote down a few notes in his journal. Occasionally the man in his late forties finger-combed his thick dark hair that had streaks of gray showing through. Hutch, his young undergrad lab assistant, with his own mop of brown hair, walked in the room and placed a file on the table next to the spectrophotometer. "Hey boss, your presence has been requested in the conference room."

Without turning from his lab journal, Daniel continued to write notes as he replied, "And who wants to see me in the conference room. If it's for Monica's birthday party, you can start without me. Will you check the autoclave? It stopped making the beeping sound when it finishes and I don't want to leave the instruments in there all weekend."

Hutch walked toward the door as he gave his answer. "Monica's birthday party was last week. The autoclave is still cooling down and will be doing so for another hour and there's a gigantic military dude waiting for you."

"He can wait until I'm finished with my notes."

The lab assistant stopped at the door, turned back toward his boss and said, "He arrived in a helicopter that landed in the parking lot. There are guys standing guard at the front door. I wouldn't make him wait, but heck, you have fancy microscopes and Petri dishes, all they have are big guns."

Daniel dropped his pen and quickly took off his reading glasses. With a light jog, he caught up to Hutch and exited the lab.

He entered the conference room and saw a six foot seven, light red haired general with a slight beer gut waiting for him. "Dr. Cronsworth," the military man said and stuck out his hand, "I'm General Christopher Brown." The two men shook hands. "I'm sorry for the sudden interruption to your work, but we have a situation that needs your immediate attention. Normally, when something strange like this happens, I call the Collins Institute, but they said you might be better equipped for this situation."

Still confused as why the General was here, Daniel had all kinds of questions spinning through his head. Moments ago, he was engrossed in his gene splicing project and now he was talking to a man who travels with armed guards. "Collins Institute? Why would they recommend me? Wait, what do you mean strange situation?"

The tall general motioned his hand to the chairs so they could take the weight off their feet. Sitting across from each other at the long mahogany conference table, Brown explained. "I didn't believe it when the details came across my desk, but it appears to be verified. I saw security video, talked to several morticians and coroners, it appears to be true."

Daniel glanced at the two soldiers stationed by the door and back at the general. "I still don't understand. What appears to be true?"

Brown rubbed his hand along the side of his face while he thought about his answer. "We have thirty two reports from various parts of the country. Some from morgues, some funeral homes, one vehicle accident scene, people or I should say bodies, which have been declared dead, returned to life for no apparent reason. You would think it's a simple case of misdiagnosis, but thirty-two? Those are odds Vegas wouldn't touch."

A young soldier walked in the room and set an electronic tablet on the table, pushing it toward Daniel. As Dr. Cronsworth glanced at the electronic documents, the General continued. "We've been doing what we can to keep a lid on these stories. Hell, nobody wants to start reporting dead bodies coming back to life. They would look like idiots. If it continues, someone will eventually run it on the evening news. At that point, I'm going to get calls asking me what the military is doing about it." Two more soldiers walked in with two large olive drab military storage crates and set them down on the floor next to Daniel. "When that call comes in, I want to be able to say we have already neutralized the situation."

Daniel skimmed through several more pages on the tablet. "All of these cases happened within twenty minutes of each other on the same day."

"Yeah, and they're scattered all across the map," the General replied. "I hope this is just a hiccup in the natural order of things and year from now it will all be forgotten."

Glancing up from the tablet, Daniel pointed to the boxes. "What's in the crates?"

"Four of these incidents happened right here in Denver. One happened during the autopsy of a man who was hit by the light rail train. The coroner had already taken out several organs when the guy stood up and walked away. I confiscated the body parts, plus his clothes and everything that touched the deceased." Brown motioned his head toward the door, signaling the soldiers to exit. "Obviously, I'm not a scientist, but I'm guessing you're going to find this is some kind of new strain of African sleeping sickness. Maybe all these people had some bad Fugu for lunch. I never did understand the need to go into a sushi restaurant and pay thirty bucks to eat the most poisonous thing on the menu."

Still reading the pages on the tablet, Daniel responded, "It says here, the coroner removed this man's kidney and pancreas before he walked out the door. I can't see how African sleeping sickness or eating some bad puffer fish could overcome missing organs."

The General leaned back in his chair. "I had an uncle who donated one of his kidneys and later had his gallbladder removed. He lived to be 87."

"But this body walked out of the room while his abdomen was still cut open. I'm sure your uncle was stitched back up before he left the hospital. "

"Look Doc, I've seen boys on the battlefield get all kinds of holes blown through them and they still did all kinds of things. When I was a Lieutenant, I watched one of my buddies get ripped open by a mortar. He ran across a hundred yards of tarmac holding his intestines with one hand and carrying an ammo can in the other. While waiting to get medevac'd out of there, he ate a turkey sandwich and drank a beer."

"Did he live?"

Brown stood up and turned toward the door. "He married my ex-wife's sister and made General two years before me." As he walked out of the room, he said, "Get me some reasonable sounding answers and let's put this whole damn thing behind us."

Chapter 2

Inside the dark abandoned warehouse, a little over seventy undead stood or sat, while they listened to the tall man speak from the center of the group. His clothes suggested the body he inhabited used to be part of a heavy metal band wearing leather and studded wrist cuffs, heavy black boots, and a denim jacket with the sleeves cut off. He spoke in a loud voice as if he had addressed large crowds many times. His long hair had colored streaks, which wove in and out, creating a tiger stripe-like pattern. The man slowly turned so he could address all bodies in the room.

Vic led Prometheus into the area where they stood at the edge of the crowd. The man from Chicago whispered to the Athenian, "That's Gunnar Benwa. He's one of the ancient guys like you. I don't know my history all that well, so I don't know which one of you is older. Before he was transferred to that body, he was some kind of Viking." Pointing to another man near a wooden crate, he continued, "Benwa and that guy dressed like a gang banger are both from the history books. The banger's name is Titus and he's like a Roman or something. Both of these guys used to be somebody in their former lives and they've kind of become our new leaders in all this chaos."

Prometheus scanned the upper rafters of the deteriorating warehouse. Blackbirds nested in several of the support beams and old wires hung loose across dilapidated ventilation ducts. Dirt and grunge covered all the surfaces. Bright blue sky peaked through several of the grime-covered broken windows offering the only light in the building. "Dear friend, I still do not understand many of your words." He brought his attention back to Vic. "My ears have not heard of the people you call Vikings and Romans and gang bangers. These countries and regions from which they hail did not appear on the maps I have read. This is one more unanswered question, I have to add to the already numerous inquiries, which only go back to the time you and I met on that unusual street. From what I understand so far, our souls have been transported into these bodies and I now stand thousands of years in my future. This is the extent of my understanding of where we are at this time."

"You got it, chief." Vic pulled the lower half of his sport coat back and placed his hands in his pants pockets. "I used to be just some shmuck from the South Side. I was overweight with a bad ticker and diabetes. Now look at me. I'm styling in this new body of some guy who had money and must have belonged to a gym. Other than the fact we're dead, I feel like I'm living large."

Prometheus shook his head with confusion. "This language that we are speaking. I do not understand many of the terms. Perhaps you, my new friend, good Vic, you could explain why we have all been brought here and placed in these bodies."

"Yeah, actually Benwa and Titus have been here the longest and seem to have the best insight on what's going on around here." He pointed to the two men who were in a heated debate. "And, somewhere in this group, there's this ancient Princess chick who gathered a bunch of us to fill us in on what's happening."

"You speak of royalty with little regard to their status." Prometheus turned to watch the two men arguing. "This is the queerest dream that I have ever experienced."

Standing in the center of the crowd, the Viking said to the Roman, "With the fear the living have in us, it is more important to organize battle groups for our own protection. It will not take long for them to rally and eliminate what they consider a threat to their way of life and their spirit itself. We are their perceived threat. I would think of all the people here, a Roman would understand the need for a legion."

Titus, with a wide red bandana wrapped around his head like a headband, long loose shirt, baggy jeans and a small teardrop tattooed underneath his right eye, spoke in a calm well-educated voice. "Speak not as to Roman aggression upon the people. I recall an attack by the Visigoth on a small and unprotected port city. As we have memories of similar events, my good friend, you may have been one of the barbarians who excelled in the art of pillaging. But, we are not to renew battles, which this day and time have long forgotten. We have a mission to save our descendants, which is why I propose we gain organization within our structure of gifts. Layered government, so to speak, will be most vital for us to accomplish this daunting task. The formation of a legion might only be beneficial for certain needs. It will only distract us from the purpose of why we have been placed here."

"It is just like a Roman to ignore the threat at the door only to rebuild his grand empire." Benwa turned to those closest to him. "If we are dead but continue to live, it is this thread of life still beating in these foreign bodies that I am to protect."

Prometheus said to Vic, "Finally, a discussion more comfortable to my ears and to my knowledge." He spoke up directly to Benwa and Titus. "I fear the tension you have for each other might be blinding you to the obvious alliance you already possess."

Both the Viking and Roman turned to the new voice. Benwa said, "I see we have a fresh member to our merry band. What name do we call you and from what land and time do you hail?"

"My name is Prometheus." He took a few steps from Vic and moved closer to the crowd. "I hail from the land I knew as Athens. I can only describe my origin time as the onset of the war against the Peloponnesian League led by Sparta."

Titus moved away from the crates and into a spot of sunlight cast down from a hole in an upper level window. "Ah, a Greek man from time of the great thinkers. Tell us good Prometheus, what kind of fortune is blinded from our vision?"

"You are both correct. Any large group of citizens would need a structure of organization. If such a society were to be threatened by opposing force, the need of such military would also be advantageous. Without the knowledge, many of you hold as to why we are here, I see no problem with both a military and governmental structure. Dear and good Benwa, you seem to be from a city similar to Sparta, where soldiers dominate the population. Perhaps, you could organize those willing to take arms. And good sir, Titus, you appear to understand the structure of a Senate. You may well be a good choice to orchestrate such a governing body."

Benwa turned toward Titus and nodded his head in agreement. "A Visigoth and a Roman leading a clan of the undead, it is no more absurd than the fact that we are here in a future world inside bodies, which not our own. What say you, Roman?"

Titus walked up to Benwa and placed his hand on the Vikings shoulder. "I can cast aside my animosity to your people, if you can do the same."

Benwa slapped his hand down on the Roman's shoulder and let out a deep laugh. "My wife would cut my throat as I slept if she knew I would serve next to a Roman. Based on how much it would anger her, I will serve with you."

Prometheus asked, "Could anyone please explain why we are here? I do not understand this gift to our descendants, but realize it is of utmost importance. As we were all sent here by Zeus, I'm sure we can agree it would be ill advised to anger him."

"Zeus?" Benwa replied in surprise. "I walked in Valhalla and drank ale with Odin himself."

Vic replied, "Valhalla? I stood at the Pearly Gates and spoke directly to St. Peter."

Random voices sprang up from the crowd. "I came here from Zion."
"Abraham gave me very detailed instructions."
"Buddha told me of my purpose."
Titus raised his hand and interjected. "As I stood at the feet of Jupiter, it appears we have all been sent by different Gods. It does not seem of consequence who sent us, but why." He pointed to the Athenian. "Good Sir Prometheus has questions. The same questions all of us had when we arrived in the strange world. I say while we still have light of day remaining, we gather all newcomers and instruct them to our purpose of existence in this era." He pointed with an open hand to the edge of the crowd. "As she did an excellent task of explaining such details to me and others, I request once again upon our Sumerian royalty, the fine Princess Rachel."

From the edge of the crowd, a young Harajuku Girl stepped from the shadows into the light. The five-foot tall Japanese girl with bright pink hair, pale skin, light blue lipstick, and short black dress with a red tutu around her waist, stood with aristocratic aplomb. She had a dried streak of blood which ran from under her scalp down past her ear which gave an indication of how this body died. She carried her posture as a princess would when she addressed a room. With her hands clasped in front of her, she said, "I will gladly speak with our new arrivals."

Prometheus joined several of his fellow undead inside what remained of the warehouse manager's office. Rachel stood on top of an old plastic crate in front of the whiteboard hanging crooked on the wall. As she turned to write the letters, "DNA" on the board, he noticed her backpack shaped like a small black and white bear clinging to her shoulders. Facing the group, she said, "We have all been sent here for this magic string of life called deoxyribonucleic acid or DNA for a name much friendlier to our tongues and ears."

Prometheus spoke up. "Before you explain this DNA, would you first instruct me as to how we arrived here? Was it some form of necromancy?"

A large middle-aged man in an ill fitting dirty t-shirt replied. "Dude, the powers that be turned us into zombies. Deal with it."

Completely confused, Prometheus turned back to Rachel who said, "We all had many questions when we first arrived. It is better you remain patient and your answers will eventually arrive." She glanced around the room and went back to her speech. "This DNA is what gives us life and determines our height, the color of our eyes, if we are men or women," she touched a strand of her hair, "and apparently if one would be born with bright pink hair. This string is what we must collect in order to give our endowment to our living descendents. Our gifts are all different, but apparently, much desired by those still living. My endue is the cure for something called arthritis. I do not know what it is, only these people with their flying machines and lights with no flames, do not know how to relieve themselves of this affliction."

A very elderly man in a nice suite said, "I was attending college only last week. Apparently, chugging a bottle of whiskey can kill you. I guess I lost that bet. Anyway, DNA is in our skin and muscle tissue, and blood and our organs. How do we turn the DNA into whatever cure we have?"

Princess Rachel turned toward him keeping the poise of her royal title. "Many of us have already begun the process. The bodies we have been given will transform the strings of life the same way it transformed the food we ate into blood and skin and the energy to move. It will be stored in our spirit."

Prometheus asked, "How are we to get this string of life into our stomachs?"

"We must take a bite out of one of the living. Their flesh is not to sustain our existence, but it is to process into what will give our descendants longer lives."

The crowd let out a common sigh of disgust hearing they would need to eat the living as the college student in the elderly body said, "Hey, we're dead. The thought of being a zombie freaks me out more than what I have to do as a one of them. Whatever I need to do to get through this crazy ride, let's get on with it."

The Princess continued. "We seem to exist without the need for food or water. Many of our desires remain. Companionship, music, laughter, earthly desires, all continue because they are a part of our essence which has been transferred into these bodies. I have heard some refer to it as our soul."

A man wearing a fire retardant racecar drivers suit riddled with burn marks raised his hand and asked, "You said we all need to process different amounts of this DNA. How do we know when we have processed enough? I do not wish to eat any more human flesh than necessary."

Rachel explained, "As told to me by An and Enlil, our eyes will turn to bright green, when only one additional strand is needed. When we have processed our required amount of this string of life, our eyes will glow bluer than the sky."

The college student replied, "What's the big deal? All we need to do is explain it to the living and I'm sure we'll get all kinds of freaks who'll volunteer. Hell, I've got some buddies who'll do it on a dare if they know there will be beer for them at the end."

Rachel smiled politely. "I do not understand all of your words but the process will not be as easy as you have imagined. We will go out in search of supplies and strings of life. You will experience what we have already witnessed. However, currently this great city appears to be in the midst of a celebration of the walking dead. They dress up as us, drink ale and make merry. We may be able to conceal ourselves within their ranks."

* * *

Daniel sat in his lab with the contents of the military crate spread over a stainless steel autopsy table. Dirty torn clothes with several small plastic ice chests labeled, "Human Organs" covered the surface. Each item had a numbered yellow identification tag attached with a thin wire. He lifted up a flannel shirt with a pair of tongs and examined the bloodstains. From the doorway, he heard, "Are you thinking about going grunge?"

He turned to see his wife, Wendy, walk into the room and set her purse down on a table. Pulling off his latex gloves, he turned to greet her with concern running through his mind. As he put his arms out to hug her, he asked, "What did Dr. Gorstein say?"

Wendy, with shoulder length straight brown hair, and medium build, wrapped her arms around him, kissed his cheek and said, "He thinks we should be able to eliminate all the cancer with a combination of chemotherapy and radiation."

Daniel let go and said, "He didn't want to do the surgery?"

"He said the chemo and pinpoint radiation will take care of it better than surgery. Even if we did the surgery, I'd still have to do the chemo." She smiled. "So I lose my hair for awhile and drop a few pounds. I'll wear wigs and buy some new clothes."

"Are you going to be okay with this?"

"Considering the alternative is to do nothing and die before I turn fifty, I think this sounds great." She put her hands on his hips. "Besides, I can get a whole variety of wigs. You can go out with a blonde one night and a redhead another. I'm sure you'll get a kick out that. Plus, I might be able to squeeze into some of those tight dresses I used to wear back when we were dating. We can try to have some fun with it."

He gave her a little peck on the lips. "I'll have fun when I know the cancer is in remission and we're going to grow old together."

Wendy walked over to the table and glanced at all the spread out clothes. "Let's start the growing old together tomorrow. Right now I'm hungry." She circled her finger over the table. "Why don't you pack up your toys and take me to dinner?"

"I can't." Daniel stepped up to the table. "I was given this new project today. I'm going to be here all night."

"Tell the nerdist who gave you this project that it'll be a few hours late. Ignore it and let's eat."

"I really want to take you to dinner and celebrate the start of the end of your cancer, but I can't tonight. The nerdist who gave this assignment to me happens to be a gigantic army general. When he comes back to hear the results, he'll be surrounded by men with guns. I think my heath will be best served if I get this done as soon as possible. We'll go to dinner Friday night and stay out late. Maybe we'll even go to the Gaslight."

"Wow, a karaoke bar. You scientists really know how to party. It sounds like you're planning on staying out past your bedtime."

Daniel snuggled up to her and said, "I might even wear jeans."

As he leaned in to kiss her, he heard a voice from across the lab. "Excuse me. I don't mean to interrupt your hypothesis session, but I'm looking for Dr. Cronsworth."

Both Daniel and Wendy separated. He turned toward the door as she hand straightened her dress. Standing at the entrance to the room, he saw an attractive woman in her late forties holding a stack of blue file folders. Her glasses, pushed up on top of her head, pulled her sandy blond hair away from her face revealing her light blue eyes. He stuttered in response, "I'm Dan Doctor, I mean, I'm Dr. Cronsworth... Dr. Dan Cronsworth... Daniel... Dr. Daniel.... Cronsworth."

Holding the stack of folders against her chest with one hand, she extended the other while walking across the room. "I'm Dr. Towers with the CDC. General Brown assigned me to work with you on this new strain of virus." The two scientists shook hands. "It's a pleasure to meet you, Dr. Cronsworth."

"Please, call me Daniel...Danny... Dan... Da-"

Wendy placed her hand over his mouth to stop his rambling. "Call him Dan." She reached out her hand. "I'm Wendy, the wife of Dr. Dan Danny Daniel."

Dr. Towers shook hands with Wendy. "It's nice to meet you both. Please, call me Lisa. I am not into all the formal protocols or the pleasantries. I prefer to focus on the work." She set the stacks of folders down on the table and revealed a shirt straining to contain her larger than average chest.

Wendy picked up her purse and slung it over her shoulder. Glancing at her husband and turning toward the door, she said, "I'll leave you and the pretty doctor to have fun with Petri dishes all night. I'm going to get some Chinese take-out and plant myself in front of an old movie on cable."

Daniel stepped away from the table and said, "I promise you, we are only here to work on isolating this virus, nothing is going to happen."

His wife turned back to him with a smile on her face. "Oh sweetie, I'm not the least bit concerned. I know nothing will happen."

"You're not going to tell me to behave? You're not even going to pretend to be the slightest bit worried or jealous?"

As she turned away from him she replied, "No, it's you we're talking about."

"What's that supposed to mean."

Walking out the door, Wendy let out a laugh and said, "She's way out of your league."

Chapter 3

As the sun set behind the Rocky Mountains, Prometheus walked along with a group of twenty other undead across the park toward the mall where the Zombie Crawl celebration was in full swing. Hundreds of humans dressed as zombies, drinking beer, and listening to the loud music, which bounced off of the tall buildings. He stared at the streetlights and neon beer signs in the bar windows, as he could not imagine such a light or how it could be produced. Never had he seen the darkness lit up so well without the use of many large fires and torches. He thought, *how could they contain this light in all these glass tubes?*

A young Goth woman ran up to him and spoke with a British accent. "Excuse me kind sir, I am in need of assistance as I do not belong in this strange land. Can you please offer me some guidance? I have nothing to offer in exchange but I promise my father will see you are greatly rewarded upon my return to Billington Manor."

Prometheus continued walking with the group as the Goth woman matched their pace. He explained to her, "I am also new to this world, apologies as I may not have the answers your ears desire. If you join us in our quest, you will gain some of the knowledge you seek. Others, who have experience in this strange land longer than I, can assist in many of your questions."

"Finally, I meet a person who speaks the King's proper English. I do not understand this gibberish spoken by these strange people who have the most peculiar ways." She glanced at her arms with the needle marks and long brown streaks, and tried to brush them away. "I do not mean to appear daft but my soul seems to have been placed inside the body of another woman. A body which is difficult to move yet it feels strong. It is as if I am the subject of an extreme bag of nails."

Prometheus explained, "As we have all been placed inside bodies which we do not own, I can only offer obscurities as I cannot answer all of your questions. As for speaking the King's English, I feel I am speaking my native tongue of Attica. However, I also seek many answers just as you desire and have learned to be patient and observe what happens around me. When we return to our building of solitude, you will gather with others to learn more about this world and our purpose here." He turned to look at the young woman. "My name is Prometheus and I hail from Athens."

"T'is a pleasure to meet you Mr. Prometheus. I am Candice Billington of the Cardiff Billingtons."

As they approached a street corner, the loud screech of tires followed by a thud startled them. Turning toward the sound, he saw one of his fellow living dead lying underneath the bumper of a car. As the accident victim crawled out from under the vehicle and brushed off the dirt, the driver exited and screamed at him in his un-discernible language making very animated and large hand gestures to accent his speech. While this one-way argument continued, more tire shrieks and a bang. Several members of the zombie horde had walked in front of oncoming traffic forcing a car to veer into a street light pole knocking it down. The exposed power lines sent colored sparks bouncing across the concrete sidewalk, onto the grass. With interest in the bright sparks, one of the ancient souls picked up a live wire. The powerful current sent the dead man into convulsions. His hand clenched tight around the line as his body lurched on the ground. Another zombie grabbed his hand in an attempt to assist. The connection sent electricity into the second man causing him shake uncontrollably. More of the ancient souls walked toward the men with the intention of helping the burn victims. The college student in the elderly body raised his hands and said, "Dudes, stop! You're going to get electrocuted."

With curious expressions, the other zombies halted. An undead man with a beer gut and an ill-fitting dirty t-shirt asked. "What kind of witchcraft has taken control of these men? They have fallen under the spell of a powerful sorcerer."

The crowd of humans, dressed as zombies, gathered around the two men still connected to the live wire and let out screams as the two living dead burst into flames. The college student glanced at the humans and back at his fellow dead. "Wow, you ancient guys don't know what electricity is or how cars and traffic work do you? I think we need to get you more training before you can come out in public again."

Two of the human men took off their shirts and tried to beat out the fire on the charred bodies still connected to the live electrical line while others dumped their beers on the flames. Other living people threw their plastic cups at the zombies and yelled angry untranslatable words at them. Vic stepped up to the group of undead and explained, "We need to get away from this scene.

The police are here and this is going to get out of control real fast. Let's get back to the warehouse as quickly as our dead legs will take us."

Prometheus saw the flames die out on the two charred bodies, as the humans covered them with blankets. More vehicles arrived with multicolored bright flashing lights. He turned to walk with his horde when a man in a dark uniform and silver badge on his chest, grabbed his arm, stopped him, and spoke in a loud voice. The human's words remained insensible, but something unexpected happened. An urge he never felt before took charge of the newly arrived zombie. A feeling he couldn't control just as the instinct to run from a lion would take command of your body, this drove his actions. He grabbed the officer's hand and gouged a bite out of the man's forearm.

The human with the silver badge fell to the ground holding his bleeding wound. There was no need to translate the strange language, as this man screamed out in pain. Vic grabbed Prometheus and said, "Hey Socrates, we need to get you out here. This whole scene just went viral." He pointed to a human holding a small video camera pointed at them.

Prometheus, with fresh blood around his mouth dripping down on his chest, had no idea what the video device did. The feeling of flesh inside his host body felt wondrous. The stiffness in his joints, disappeared. He had the strength of a mule and the vision of an eagle. "I have to get more of this meat." He said with desire in his face.

Vic pulled him away from the crowd. "Dude, taking a bite out of that guy's arm made you stoned. I can see it in your eyes." Vic viewed the growing crowd and saw two men, next to a police officer point to Prometheus. "Really, we need to get out of here. I'm guessing they still had jails in ancient times. Trust me we don't want to go there."

Back at the warehouse, candles placed throughout the building provided a yellow glow. The horde gathered and spoke in small groups as to what happened, at the mall. Gunnar Benwa approached Titus and Prometheus. "It does not sound like you return with news of a successful campaign."

"I fear the task assigned to us may not be as simple as originally thought." Titus glanced at Prometheus and back to the Viking. "Our descendants have a natural fear of us. Perhaps due to our large numbers, they see us as a threat."

Pointing to the dried blood around the mouth of Prometheus, Gunnar said, "It may be more than our numbers they fear. As in our time, the living does not enjoy being the main course of another's meal."

"This is not all there is to the complication. Those of us not familiar with this world can easily fall subject to the dangers that are not so apparent to our eyes." Prometheus tried to rub the dried blood off of his chin. "Two members of our merry band burst into flames for reasons unknown to those of us not of this time."

"I say our first order of business should be to only set out in small groups as to not bring attention to ourselves." Gunnar ran his finger through the flame of a nearby candle sitting on top of a metal table. "Second, those of us not known to this world need to find a way to become familiar with all the strange contraptions and the ways of the living."

"I can help with this."

All three dead men turned toward the source of the voice to see a woman in her mid twenties, shoulder length brown hair, wearing a waitress uniform. A burn ring around her throat told the story of how young lady died by strangulation. "Up until last week, I was a history teacher at the University." She glanced down at her body and smoothed the front of her uniform with her hands. "You know, for decades, I always thought how great it would be to be twenty again." She turned and looked at the three ancient men. "It's not so good."

Prometheus said, "You mentioned you could help those of us who are not from this time. What assistance can you offer?"

"Like I said, history is my forte. I can give all of you who are pre-automobile and pre-electricity a crash course on what's happened in the world, since you walked as one of the living."

Titus reached out a hand with his palm up and slightly bowed to the young lady. "I am Titus Arilius a Roman of good standing and I am at your service."

The history teacher replied, "It's a pleasure to meet you, Titus. My name is Jennifer." She turned to Gunnar Benwa and said, "…and you are?"

The Viking wrapped his arms around her and lifted her off the ground in a great big bear hug, as a smile spread across her face. "Enough of this civilized garbage." He set her back down and she pulled her hair off her face and caught her breath. "They call me Gunnar and it's about time we started to get some more Norse ways into our new family."

The college student in the elderly man's body moved closer and engaged in a loud conversation with a nicely dressed black man wearing an expensive pinstripe suit. "It's me, Drew. I've been put in this old dude's body, but you have to know it's me."

The black man said. "I do not know this body or anyone named Drew and stop calling me Greg. My name is Haru Tochigi. I must find my way back to my village. It is under attack and they need me to help defend it."

"You have to be my friend, Greg. That is his body and you have the same suit on that he was wearing the last time I saw him. We were drinking…. Oh, wait; we were both downing a bottle of whiskey. I guess we had the same fate."

The black man took a martial arts defensive stance as if about to attack. "I insist you take me back to my village and return me to the body of which I am accustomed." Looking at his hands, a confused expression crossed his face. "I have never seen skin so dark. Why is this body this color? No one in any of the villages, even as far away as the mountains surrounded by mist, have skin like this." He relaxed his stance and grabbed his groin to make some adjustments. "How did your friend Greg ever fight in battle? With this man part as big as a tree between my legs, I cannot move freely without it getting in the way."

Gunnar slapped his hand down on the man's shoulder and let out a deep laugh. "My new friend, Greg. If your ability to drink ale is as great as your willingness to fight, you will make a fine Viking."

* * *

Military personnel and the suit-wearing foundation executives, who fund the lab, occupied all the seats in the large conference room, Daniel listened to the presentation and wondered if he had ever seen this room actually filled to maximum capacity. General Brown pointed the remote at the projector screen. "Local news crews have been airing random videos of people suffering from this sleeping sickness."

On the screen, the video showed a zombie stagger across a busy street in downtown Chicago. He walked in front of a city bus, which crushed him underneath the tires. Blood and pieces of internal organs splattered across the windshield. Some of the suits cringed at the sight. "Unfortunately or luckily, depending on how you see it, the people suffering from this disease have lost their rational mental state." The video switched to another undead in Dallas stepping in front of an oncoming train. As his body came in contact with the engine, it vaporized into a red mist. "They have no sense of danger, no basic instincts to keep them from walking in front of trucks or grabbing live electrical lines. I'm not worried about a few small news channels." The screen changed to the video of the zombies from the mall crawl that caught on fire.

"There are videos showing up on the Internet getting much more exposure than some local TV station. This event occurred last week, right here in Denver at the Zombie Festival. At first, they thought it was some drunken participants staggering into danger. When the dental records came back to identify those people, it turned out they both died in a car accident two weeks earlier. Their bodies were never reported missing, because the Adams County Coroner didn't want to sound crazy trying to explain how two dead bodies sat up and walked out of her office. It's not just happening here. Reports are flowing in from coroners and morticians all across the country."

The General turned the projector off and opened his briefcase, which was sitting on top of the table. He pulled out a silver flask with a small dent in the side and an army star on the front. After opening the cap, he took a swig. He handed the whiskey to the executive sitting next to him. The suit cautiously took the container and glanced around the room, giving the impression that he didn't know what to do next. With a bit of fear expressed on his face, he took a sip. Immediately, he coughed, choked and almost vomited. The General grabbed the flask back from his hand and said, "Smooth, ain't it." He almost placed the cap back on the flask, but then decided to leave it off. "The way I see it, if we can't find an anti-virus, they will eliminate themselves by walking into traffic or being attracted to fire like moths. However, until that time, you nerds need to find the cure. It won't take long before teenagers start treating these folks like a live video game, trying to run them down, scoring more points than their buddies."

The Captain sitting across the table said, "Actually General, reports have come out of Texas of kids doing exactly that."

"Shut up, Bill." The General turned back to Daniel and Lisa. You two are going to stay here 24/7 until you have good news for me. If I have to, I'll place armed guards at the door to keep you from leaving." He took one more sip from his flask before placing it back in his briefcase and snapping the latches shut. "Now, I have to go out there and give all those media clowns a load of official B.S."

* * *

A large group of media and protesters gathered in the parking lot behind a line of armed soldiers. As General Brown stared at the ground and moved fast to avoid answering questions, the crowd moved across the lot with him. A young journalist with a microphone at the front of the crowd, and, standing next to his cameraman, called out, "General! Is it true the Zombie Sickness is a failed attempt at population control by the military?"

Brown stopped in front of the man. "The what sickness?"

"The Zombie Sickness."

"Who the hell is calling it the Zombie Sickness?"

The journalist gave a proud smile. "Actually, I'm the one who came up with the name. I'm hoping it starts to catch-"

The General cut him off and continued his walk to his car. "They really need to make it legal to shoot the media. It would be such a great service to the country." One of his aides opened the backdoor to his waiting black sedan. Just as he put his briefcase on the seat, he heard a familiar voice from the crowd.

"Are you really going to ignore me, Chris?"

With a sense of dread, he turned and saw a woman in her late thirties, long sandy colored dreadlocks, leather sandals and a t-shirt which read, "ZOOM."

"Hellion, damn it! I really hoped to get through this without you turning it into one of your movements du jour."

"It's nice to see you too." Hellion squeezed through the crowd to reach the front. One of the armed soldiers put his hand up to keep her from going any further. "This is bigger than you and me. It's the next step up the ladder of human evolution."

"This has nothing to do with evolution and in what bizarre hippie world of yours, do you think there's ever been any you and me?" He glanced at her shirt. "What the hell is ZOOM?"

"It stands for Zombies and Others On the Move."

The General moved back toward his car. "Go back to the Arctic and try and save those… what were you trying to save there?"

"Caribou."

"They're not even endangered! There's more caribou, than people in the Arctic. Why do I waste my time talking to you?" He looked at one of his aides and pointed to the protester. "Shoot her and I'll promote you to Major."

Hellion smiled and reached back into the crowd. "Don't be so army with me, Chris. Look who I brought."

She pulled her friend to the front of the crowd. The General's eyes widened, his shoulders dropped, and his mouth opened slightly agape, which turned into a non-characteristic huge smile. He scanned up and down the woman with the darkish red hair and natural classic beauty. "How've you been, Pink? I didn't think it was possible, but you get even better looking each time I see you."

Pink replied, "Wow, you used my actual name, instead of making up some cardboard cutout biblical moniker. I'm flattered."

Hellion cut in, "Sorry to break up the love fest, but the military really needs to leave these people alone. You are messing with the greatest event in human history since we stood upright. We need to let nature takes its course."

The General covered her face with his large hand and pushed her back, while still gazing at Pink. "Why do you insist on hanging out with her? She's going to get you into trouble, real trouble. The types of trouble, where I can't come rescue you."

"This time, I agree with her." Pink replied, with a slight flirtatious glance and smile. "These people have been given a second chance at life by God or nature or whatever living force, you want to assign. A big machine has been set in motion and we should step aside to let it do its job."

Brown stepped towards his car. "The flaw in your theory is that these people are not dead. It's a more potent strain of the African Sleeping Sickness." He placed one foot in the doorway of the sedan. "I would be open to hearing your whole theory over dinner, if you promise to leave Hellion on a leash."

Before Pink could answer, the waiting journalists pushed and crowded their way in front of her and called out questions, which all blurred together. The General closed the door and tried to get one more glimpse of the only protester who could turn his knees into jelly as his driver pulled away.

Chapter 4

Prometheus stood in the warehouse at the front of the empty wall, where Jennifer had drawn a large timeline of events spanning from ancient Greece to the modern day. To see thousands of years into the future made him feel overwhelmed and fulfilled at the same time. Other living dead walked through the building extinguishing the candles. Behind him, random beams of light from the just rising sun streamed down from the broken windows, illuminating the scattered small groups of zombies, who discussed what they learned in the history class, taught by Jennifer. Their voices echoed around the open space, reminding the Athenian of spending a day at the forum. A raven flying from rafter to rafter echoed in the background as Titus approached. He stared at the timeline, along with the Greek man. "Having my eyes see this far into the future, provides some aid to overcome the fact that I am dead." He pointed to a section of the line labeled, "Fall of the Roman Empire." "We lasted one thousand years. Given the time span of all other great societies," he paused in thought, "what is the vernacular the good Jennifer spoke… oh yes; I hope I use this in the correct form. The Roman Empire rocked."

Prometheus responded, "It is interesting the class of slave no longer exists. I am glad to hear the teaching of the Greek philosophers has lasted to this day and the stories of Homer have been preserved in these written books."

Constance approached and joined in the conversation. "I remember Father reading to my brothers and me about the adventures of Odysseus." She focused on the Greek. "I am so astonished to find the lost city of Atlantis not only existed, but also to meet a man who actually visited the metropolis."

"When I paid them a visit it was not a lost city. As impressive as it appeared to my eyes, it stood as a simple village, compared to the magnificent city where we now stand." Prometheus glanced at another section of the timeline. "I hope to someday see a performance of a play written by the good William Shakespeare."

Gunnar walked up and pointed to a spot on the timeline. "I would have liked to meet this Genghis Khan. I feel the two of us working together could have greatly angered the Romans." He held up and rotated his hands analyzing the rock star leather and metal studded wrist cuffs. "I wish, I could have also met the previous owner of this body. He appears to have been a brave warrior."

Prometheus continued to stare at the wall and speak to his fellow undead. "So many events that I could never have imagined during my life. Two great wars, machines that can fly and the honorable Neil Armstrong setting foot on the moon. Our descendants have accomplished greatness and achieved heightened times of sorrow. My eyes are filled with joy in the knowledge of what our people have done with their time on this planet, which I am surprised to learn is in fact, round."

A man wearing a t-shirt and jeans with streaks of dried blood down the back of his neck stepped up on a small crate, held up a magazine and spoke out to those close enough to hear his voice. "This magazine came out four weeks ago. I know this, because I recognize the picture on the cover and remember buying it at the grocery store while I was still alive. I know it's written in English, my native tongue, but I can't read any of the writing. It looks like some kind of scribble to me. We're in the city of Denver, where they also speak English, but I can't understand anything the citizens are saying. They sound like they speak gibberish. We need to find a way to communicate with the living, so they know we are here to help them." He pointed to various zombies. "This man speaks ancient Greek. This man speaks Norse. We all speak different languages, but can understand each other perfectly. There has to be a way for us to transform this universal translation ability to the living."

Titus replied, "You have made a wise suggestion, my friend. What is your name, kind sir, and from where do you hail?"

The man on the crate, with the medium build and light brown hair, which hung just above his shoulders, stepped down and answered, "I'm John and I lived in Vegas."

Prometheus spoke up. "I agree with the good John of Vegas. Each of us should write a message on the streets and walls. We can scribe in the language of our birth. With the large population in this city, surely one of the fine citizens will recognize these messages. Apparently, the ability to read and write is quite common in this day."

* * *

Wendy paced across the short length of the examination room, anxious to hear the results of her latest test. The florescent lights above hummed and slightly flickered, as they cast a dull yellow light. The sudden appearance of her doctor through the door startled her out of her trance-like state. She turned to him as he read through the lab results. "What's the news doc? She asked."

The doctor closed the file and turned up to her with a lamentable expression. His face forewarned her of the approaching news. "I'm afraid there has not been any positive change to the tumors."

The news hit her hard and sent a heavy feeling into her stomach. She focused on not getting sick all over the floor in front of the doctor. Putting on a false smile and façade, she replied, "No positive change. Does this mean there has been some negative change?"

The doctor crossed his arms pressing the file against his chest. "Your white blood cell count has increased." He paused to clear his throat. "The cancer is showing no reaction to the treatment. We need to increase the chemo and change the type of radiation treatment. Instead of the pinpoint laser, we need to use a broader spectrum."

"When do we make the change?"

"The sooner the better. I say we start tomorrow. We already had you scheduled for your next chemo treatment anyway. I'll set up the radiation therapy in two days, so we can give the next set of drugs a chance to do their job."

The smile faded from her face and the sag of her shoulders showed the disappointment sinking into her body. "Do their job, therapy; you make it sound so happy when we are killing my immune system, so that radiation can devastate parts of my body."

"If surgery were an option, I'd open you up right now, but this is our only chance to eliminate the tumors."

Wendy nodded her head and gave a partially more relaxed smile. "I know, and thanks for putting up with my complaining. I know you're doing all you can to help me."

Waiting in the hospital lobby for Daniel to pick her up, she watched news reports of the outbreak on the wall mounted television. The news anchor reported, "The outbreak, now named the re-animation virus, is reaching alarming numbers across the world." The story switched to video clips of zombies walking down city streets of various countries. "The number of people, who have been declared dead, only to appear to come back to life, has reached an estimated one hundred fifty thousand world-wide. The World Health Organization has issued this statement." The video changed to a man standing at a podium reading a statement at a press conference surrounded by reporters, microphones and cameras. He pushed his glasses far down on his nose and squinted at the printed announcement.

"It has not yet been determined that the re-animation virus is in fact a virus. It may possibly be a new strain of bacteria, but a new form of virus has not been ruled out. Until we can conclude the exact cause, we cannot declare this outbreak to be a pandemic. What we can say is that, this disease is contagious, but only if one comes in contact with an infected body. People contaminated with the sickness have a propensity to bite those who are not infected. As a precaution and for the safety of the population, we advise cities and towns around the world to section off and quarantine areas where there is a high concentration of those suffering from the re-animation sickness. When we arrive at a remedy for this affliction, our contracted laboratories will work day and night to help bring this crisis to an end. "

Two nurses, who stood in the lobby watching the report, referred to a local incident. "Did you hear one of these re-animation contaminations happened right here in our morgue last Monday night?"

"No."

"Yeah, Dr. Cole had just started an autopsy of a DOA brought into the emergency room, when the body sat up and walked out of the morgue."

Wendy listened to the two women talk and processed what all of this would mean to her husband. Daniel had been assigned to find the cause and cure. As the outbreak builds, so would the pressure for him to find the remedy. He needed to stay focused on his work and not have any distractions at this time. If he knew her cancer had become worse, he might lose his concentration and possibly make mistakes. At that moment, Daniel came through the front door and smiled, as he walked across the marble floor towards her.

"Hi sweetie. What did the doctor say?"

With another forced smile, she replied, "He said everything is looking good. I might have more of a reaction to the treatment than originally thought, but I will be just fine. In fact, he wants me to come back tomorrow."

"Tomorrow?" Daniel's smile diminished. "Why so soon? I thought he was going to postpone this week's second treatment. If the chemo is working, he should give it time to see more results before the next treatment. Maybe I should talk with him."

Wendy patted her husband on the chest to calm him down. "He wants to try a new drug that has seen some positive results for someone in the stage I'm in right now. It's all about getting rid of the cancer as quickly as possible. If it works, we should be sunning ourselves in Mexico this summer, worrying about getting skin cancer."

The smile returned to his face as he held her hand to escort her towards the front door. "Okay, but can you get your sister to drive you? I have some intense deadlines I have to meet with this outbreak. If I don't start showing results soon, the military is going to keep me in my lab day and night."

* * *

The early morning sun cast long shadows along the back alley of the downtown business district. Sounds of trucks backing into loading docks and the building of traffic for the morning rush hour filled the streets. Three Flickers hopped through a small puddle near a dumpster as Prometheus finished writing his chalk message on the red brick wall. He took a few steps back gazing at the large paragraph and felt proud of his well-crafted calligraphy. The usual stale and sour smells wafting through the back street smelled pleasant to the undead. John, who wrote his message with a black marker on a dumpster, walked up next to the Greek man and said, "Looks good. I can't read ancient Greek. What did you say?"

As if he addressed a crowd in the forum, Prometheus read the message. "Attention, good citizens of this fine and such grand city. We who inhabit these bodies are your ancestors and friends who mean you no harm or ill will. The gods have sent us here on a quest to give you gifts, which will allow you to continue your evolution into a greater society. I, the author of this scribe, have for you the cure for an affliction known as cancer. Many other cures for diseases along with gifts of new abilities await you. If you join us, we can work together to eliminate many of the unwellnesses and troubles from which you suffer. For the gods would not have sent us if it were not for a more noble purpose and is therefore compulsory for your actions to be conjunctive with ours. I signed it, the most humble Prometheus of Athens." He turned to John and asked, "What message did you scribe on that sturdy garbage receptacle?"

John pointed to his message on the dumpster and said, "People, you need to chill. All of us zombies carry antibodies to cure all the big diseases of our time. We just want to help you."

With a perplexed expression, Prometheus replied, "My ears do not comprehend such a statement, but I must assume it is a condensed version of what I wrote."

John shrugged his shoulders. "Yeah, sure."

On the opposite side of the dumpster, Greg continued to paint his message in Japanese calligraphy. John noticed a pile of old clothes someone had set next to the wall. He picked through the apparel and said, "This is some good stuff and in pretty good shape. We should take it back to the warehouse so we can all have a change of clothes." He pulled out a blue satin dress and held it up to his body. "Sweet! I can't wait to try this one on."

Greg stopped painting his message and gave John a quizzical stare. "Were you a woman when you were alive and the gods have placed you in a man's body?"

"No." John said with a bit of surprise in his voice.

Vic walked into the alley and saw John holding the dress against him.

"Let me guess, you're a Nancy boy."

Again, with surprise in his voice, John replied, "No, not even close. I'm straighter than any of you could imagine."

"Then why do you like wearing dresses?"

"Because, I really, really love women. I love everything about them, including their clothes."

Prometheus asked, "Are you an actor? In my time period, it is common for actors to own dresses. We did not allow women to appear on stage, so men had to perform all the female rolls."

Vic interjected, "I think I'm going to call you GQ."

"Because of the handsome good looks that came with this body?"

"No, because your gender is questionable."

A loud voice from one of the living, yelling untranslatable words, came from the end of the alley. The four undead turned to the source of the sound and saw two police officers cautiously walk toward them with their guns drawn. Prometheus said, "This will work to our advantage. We can show these men, who enforce the peace, our messages of goodwill and demonstrate we are only here for their aid."

John picked up the pile of clothes and slowly walked backwards. "Those are weapons in their hands. They're not here to have a conversation; they see us as a threat."

Greg dropped his brush, threw his suit jacket down, grabbed an old wooden broom handle from the ground and held it up like a Samurai sword. "They have no swords. I will make them understand we are a powerful village and they must listen to our demands."

As the officers closed the distance to the zombies, they opened fire on Greg. The bullets passed through and shook his body, but did not harm him. Angered, he charged the police with his stick. Shots continued to hit their target until the chambers emptied, but did nothing to stop the oncoming assault. Using the broom handle as a sword, Greg attacked with the skill and moves, he knew as a samurai, beating the living men at will. One officer pulled out his nightstick and tried to fight back using it like a sword. His skills were no match for the veteran warrior. Greg knocked the nightstick out of his hand and hit one officer across the head, rendering him unconscious, as his partner pulled out a taser and tried to shock his attacker. The electricity caused Greg to jump back, but he continued his attack, swinging the stick with precision. With a blow to the head, the officer fell backward, but he reached out to break his fall and grabbed Greg's arm. Almost instantly, Greg bit into the living man's hand. The officer screamed out in pain as the zombie dropped his stick and took another bite out further down the man's arm.

Vic ran up to Greg, pulled him off the man and said, "Hey man, we better get out of here. There's going to be more cops here soon, and you're not going to be able to hold them all back with a broom handle."

Greg took another bite out of the screaming officer, who pounded the zombie in the shoulder with his free arm. Greg looked up at Vic with blood streaming down both sides of his mouth and said, "I cannot control my actions. This body wants nothing more than to taste his flesh. The feeling it gives is not only being alive again, but also even being better. I feel stronger, with more energy and more awareness of my surroundings."

Vic pulled him away from the officer. "You're whacked out on goofballs, my friend. Taking bites out of people has this effect on us. It might feel good, but we need to get out of here fast."

The four zombies hurried out the opposite end of the alley and disappeared into the back streets.

* * *

Lieutenant John Colton, one of the youngest officers in the Sheriff's Office, walked in the conference room and stood at attention in front of the long table, filled with his fellow officers and military brass. His short dark hair and muscular build gave an indication of his dedication to the job. He felt his charming looks also helped his rapid promotion. Sheriff Watson said, "Relax John, have a seat. We're going to be here a while."

Colton pulled out the chair and sat next to his boss. Across the table, General Brown began his slide show presentation. The first photo showed the alley where Prometheus, John and Greg wrote their messages. Instead of readable words, the writing appeared as cryptic scribbles. "Here, in our town the re-animated have begun writing symbols on walls, dumpsters," the slide changed to another message written in chalk on a sidewalk, "windows and trees. Our cryptologists can't decipher the code if there even is a meaning to this scribble. What they have determined, based on the placement of the markings, the number of sightings in those areas, and the fact some of your local men were attacked when they were caught tagging the walls, these are some kind of territorial markings."

Sheriff Watson, with his gray hair and weathered face, which displayed decades of wisdom, spoke up, "Marking their territory would indicate some intelligence and organization within their structure. We can no longer continue to combat this as if it were a pack of stray dogs getting into trashcans."

"You got that right, which is why we're asking you to form this new unit. We're rounding up these people or ex-people all over the world and holding them on our bases, out of the public eye. The President doesn't want the military conducting these roundups and captures on our soil. He thinks it will look like the situation is getting out of control. There also happens to be this group of hippies who want us to respect the civil rights of the non-living and they are drawing a lot attention to the problem. If we bring soldiers into the streets, this group is going to bog down the whole operation in the courts.

This is why you need to start combating this problem within your ranks. You're the first responders and therefore you get to respond first." Brown opened his brief case on the table. "It shouldn't be too difficult. In most of the areas around the globe, my men treated it like herding cattle. You surround them, move them into trucks, and then haul them away. Only a few areas showed resistance, but it was easily squashed. If they resist, they respond well to tasers or you can set them on fire; tear gas moves them along like any other crowd. You can always smash them under your car. This isn't make-believe, they can't put themselves back together like in the movies. If the body is destroyed, the problem is solved. But, like I said, most of them act like cattle and will walk wherever you point them."

Sherriff Watson turned to Colton and said, "This is why we brought you in. You grew up here. You played on these streets. You know all the nooks and crannies where theses re-animated people can hide. We want you to head this new unit. Once we have the cure for this disease and the population is immunized, you can go back to regular police work."

Without hesitation to the new orders, Colton asked, "How many men will I have and what is our objective?"

"You'll handpick eight other officers and your objective is to round up these poor souls and hand them over to General Brown's men. If the re-animated offer any resistance, you're authorized to put them down, and to neutralize any danger."

Brown took his flask out of his briefcase and took a sip. Sheriff Watson turned to him with a judgmental eye and said, "Isn't it a bit too early for whiskey, General?"

"Early for whiskey?" Brown extended his hand, offering the flask to the Sheriff. "I've been up for three days, which makes it really, really late at night for me. If it's too early for anything, it's too early to be talking about having to round up zombies."

Watson reached across the table and grabbed the flask from the General. He tilted it back and took a long sip. He noticed the astonished expressions on the faces of his men and the military around the table and replied, "This is going to be a long one, gentlemen. It might be awhile before I see the outside of this building again. You bet, I'm having a shot."

Chapter 5

Candles placed throughout the warehouse, lit the interior with a soft yellow flicker, as the last of the sunlight faded from the windows. Ravens flew across the rafters several stories above the ground. Prometheus stood near a window and collected water from a broken pipe as it dripped onto his hands. He tried to wash the dried blood, which had been on his face and throat for days. After he scrubbed his pale skin with the palms of his hands, he checked his mouth in a small piece of broken mirror. It still did not set in; this strange person with the odd hairstyle was him. In the reflection, he saw the Viking inside the musicians body walk up behind him. Gunnar spoke up, "An undead that still has a sense of vanity. Perhaps all hope is not lost for us."

Prometheus turned around and asked, "What gift do the gods pass through you to the descendants?

"I will give them the ability to see in all light spectrums. I didn't know there was more than one kind of light. As to why one would need to see in these different lights, this is beyond my understanding." Gunnar noticed a new body stagger into the building. He motioned his head toward the stranger. "It looks like we have a new arrival to our merry band of men."

Prometheus glanced in the direction of the door and saw the body of the police officer he bit at the mall. His eyes opened wide and with a feeling of remorse. He walked across the open space and greeted the undead arrival. "Welcome to our place of sanctuary." He placed his right hand in the center of his chest. "Apologies, as I fear I am the one who caused your new life as an undead. You see, it was I who bit your arm during the city festival and might have caused your demise."

The man in the police officer's body gave Prometheus a confused expression, pointed to the surrounding building and said, "Augh, moore tam buk."

"I'm afraid my ears do not always translate the modern version of your speech." He glanced around at some of his fellow zombies in the room and spoke up. "Perhaps, someone more familiar with this day's vernacular could offer assistance."

Wearing the blue dress he found in the alley, John walked up and scanned the new person. He explained, "You have to remember, this is only the body you bit. It's inhabited by a different person, probably from a different time." He stuck out his hand and said, "Hi, I'm John."

The officer appeared quizzical at the offer of a handshake. He leaned over and sniffed John's hand then returned to his puzzled state. John pressed his hand into the center of his chest, just above the neckline of the dress and said, "My name is John."

The officer touched his own chest and said, "Hod." He pointed to different parts of the warehouse and continued speaking. "Baum do gran, do mat gorum storr canuum."

"We may need additional ears to hear his words in order to understand his intent." Prometheus said.

"I have a feeling that we hear his words exactly as he intends." John slightly shook his head, as if he had solved a new clue to the puzzle. "Quite possibly, the person inside this body is from the ice age or earlier. He's a caveman named Hod."

Hearing his name, he pointed to his chest and said, "Hod."

John gently took hold of the caveman's hand, brought it to his own shoulder and said, "John."

Hod replied, "Ohn."

Placing his hand on the Athenian's shoulder he said, "Prometheus."

Hod pressed his lips together, moved them around and attempted several times to say the name of the Greek man, but gave up and placed his hand back on John's shoulder and said, "Ohn."

Titus stood in the center of the room and announced, "The good Gunnar Benwa would like to take a small group out under the cloak of darkness to help us gather supplies. He needs some volunteers to assist him."

From the position near the windows, Gunnar continued, "For some reason, the messages we wrote on their streets have had the opposite effect of our intentions. The descendants have moved away from the areas with our writing, instead of embracing the message, as though they are afraid of what we had to say. However, we can use this to our advantage and go to those areas and scavenge for supplies with little concern of attack."

Prometheus stepped away from door and said, "I will accompany you into the city."

A man wearing a motocross jersey, pants and motorcycle boots with his neck slightly out of alignment with his shoulders, spoke up. "In my land, if we had a formal message to give, we used the language of pictures, instead of the symbols the men from Greece wrote."

Titus asked, "And good sir, what shall we call you and from where do you hail?"

The dirt bike racer rolled his head toward his shoulder, which let out a loud crack. "I am called Nemi of Egypt. The upper kingdom is where I have my home and make my trade bringing bales of cotton up the river of life."

Constance joined the conversation. "I believe, Mr. Nemi might have a point. If the living cannot understand our writing, perhaps a simple language of symbols and pictures could transfer our intentions more efficiently."

Gunnar appeared to think about what the others suggested and pointed to Jennifer. "History teacher, what do you think?"

"I think Constance may be onto something. Simple pleasant pictures might show the living we are not here to harm them."

Princess Rachel spoke up, "I am adept at telling stories through pictures. It might be of some benefit for me to accompany this group out into the streets."

"There we have it." Titus announced. "Gunnar shall lead this group back out on the streets of this fine city to gather needed supplies and convey our message to the descendants in another form."

* * *

General Brown stood in front of the unit of police officers in the alley of a downtown street. "Congratulations, you're now all property of Homeland Security, enjoy the ride. I'm sure you've seen the videos all over the Internet. These round ups go pretty much by the book. No resistance, no trouble, they simply gather to get away from the smoke and like cattle, they'll move into the truck. For some reason, they like to come out at night and scavenge through the abandoned buildings. This makes them an easy target."

One of the officers raised his hand and asked a question. "Is it true they are taken to an island in the Pacific, where are allowed to live freely."

Brown gave a smile and shook his head thinking how gullible the public had become. "We've set up close to thirty thousand fake profiles on all kinds of social media sites. We're the ones spreading those rumors of this ideal quarantine to keep the disease from spreading. There's no island, no secret utopia. These re-ans are housed on military bases all over the world. Trust me; they're never going to leave. Most of them can't survive the medical and scientific tests we put them through."

* * *

A cough echoed through the wood paneled courtroom. Judge Patterson sat up and leaned forward resting his elbows on the bench. "I'm sorry counselor, what did you call your organization?"

Chris Schring, the rather tall and slender attorney with wire rim glasses, stepped to the side of the table and replied, "ZOOM, your honor. It stands for Zombies and Others On the Move. We are an egalitarian movement dedicated to the rights of zombies."

The silver haired judge sat back in his chair and shook his head. "You have stood before me in the past with all kinds of fringe clients and outlandish arguments, but this one is by far, your best. By best, I mean the top of the nutcase list. You really want to represent these disease ridden bodies who don't know they are dead?"

"Your honor, these people have been automatically cast to the lowest levels of society, based entirely on the fact that they have been given a second chance at life and nothing else." Chris reached in his briefcase, pulled out a document, and held it up. "There are hundreds of thousands of re-animated citizens, currently being held prisoner on military bases all across this country and other parts of the world. They have not been charged with any crime or given the opportunity to speak with an attorney."

"These things you are trying to defend are biting people and infecting them with a virus, which turns the victim into a zombie. As for speaking with an attorney, I don't know if you've noticed, but they can't speak. They just make moaning sounds and do a lot of pointing." Patterson replied.

"This is exactly our point." Chris moved around to the front of the table. "These people are in need of medical attention. There's no doubt they will have mental health issues. Keeping them in prison is a violation of their civil rights."

"The dead don't have civil rights."

"They are the non-dead, your honor."

"Dead, non-dead, zombies, re-animated, it doesn't matter. Civil rights are for citizens who still have blood pumping through their veins." The judge picked up his gavel and brought it down on the block. "Your motion is denied."

As Chris stepped back around the counsel table, he saw Hellion and Pink approach the bar from the gallery side. He placed his documents back in his briefcase. "Sorry guys. I didn't think Judge Patterson would bite on this one, pardon the pun. We still have other options, which we can explore. There's a class action, individual representation-"

Hellion interrupted, "That's okay." She glanced at Pink. "We didn't think this would work and we have already set our next plan in motion."

Closing his briefcase, he turned to the two women. "Is this plan going to require me to bail you out of jail again? This isn't going to be another Seattle, is it? I have news for you. I like coffee and I don't care about the donkey that carried it down the mountain, as long as it means my java is hot and waiting for me when I wake up."

Hellion pushed one of her dreadlocks back behind her ear. "A Beast Of Burden is another term for slavery and you know any day when the sun rises, there's always a chance, you'll have to bail me out of jail."

* * *

The streetlights lit up the empty city block. Scattered trash, boarded up windows, doors, and missing tires on the few parked cars, indicated the area had been vacated by the living for some time. Concrete barriers blocked the end of the street, marking the line between the living and the undead. Prometheus walked out of the abandoned store with a sack full of batteries, matches and flashlights. He watched Gunnar use a piece of chalk to draw a boat with a dragonhead bow on the sidewalk. Holding up the bag, he said, "I'm not sure what these items are or for what purpose they serve, but the good Vic of Chicago told me to gather as many as I could carry."

The Viking stood from drawing his picture and glanced into the bag. "I'm sure they will be of good use once the moderns explain it to us." He scanned the block where several other zombies scavenged the trashcans and any stores they could access. "Where is Hod? I have not seen him since we left the warehouse."

Prometheus pointed down the street. "He arrives from yonder."

At the end of the block, Hod walked around the corner, holding a broom handle that he had converted into a spear, complete with a hand chipped flint tip. Over his shoulder, he carried two dead rabbits strung together at their feet. He wore the police officer's utility belt over his other shoulder like a bandoleer, with the nightstick hanging at his waist. Watching the primitive man approach, Drew, with a handful of newspapers, stepped up to Prometheus. "You can dress them up, but can't take the hunter out of your caveman."

The ancient Greek offered only a confused expression as a response. Hod noticed the drawing of the boat on the ground. He handed the rabbits and his spear to Gunnar and took the chalk out his hand. Down on one knee, he drew primitive cave drawings of what appeared to be a large buffalo type animal and stick figures of men hunting it. Hod stood from his drawing and told the story of the hunt, but Prometheus and the others could not translate his language. The primitive man in the officer's body, proceeded to act out the story. He pointed to the buffalo drawing and placed his hands at the side of his head, protruding his fingers like horns. Bending over and simulating a charge into Drew's stomach, he then grabbed his own and pretended to die.

Prometheus made the observation, "It appears our friend Hod met his death while hunting this horned creature.

Hod knelt down and drew three more stick figures, two large and three small people. He pointed to the tallest person and said, "Hod."

Drew replied, "He had a family with three kids."

Loud explosions and bright flashes came from the opposite end of the block. Prometheus turned and saw several police officers climb over the concrete barrier. They had face shields, gas masks, body armor and batons. Teargas canisters landed in the street and sidewalks, streaming smoke into the air. Undead, who had been scavenging the abandon stores, ran away from the advancing enforcement. Two officers tackled a fleeing zombie and beat him over the head with their batons until his skull broke open and his brains spilled onto the asphalt. Gunnar picked up a large rock and said, "Finally, the descendants speak a language I can understand."

He ran towards the advancing police unit with a loud scream. The officers drew their handguns and opened fire. Bullets pelted the Viking's body from his hips to his shoulders, but it did nothing to slow his assault. When he reached the first line of police, he smashed his rock on top of their helmets with no effect. An officer grabbed his arm holding the rock. Gunnar quickly bit the man's hand. As the human screamed out in pain, the Viking bit a large chunk out of the man's cheek. Two more officers pulled him off their colleague and tried to pin him to the ground. Greg quickly thrust a three-foot long piece of rebar through the throat of one officer.

Gunnar sprang to his feet. Bullets flew through the air like rain, but did nothing to the undead. An officer shot his taster into the Viking. The electrical jolt sent his body into convulsions. He fell lurching on the ground, as Hod's spear thrust into the officer's body. Hod grabbed Gunnar's shoulders and pulled him away from the attackers.

Prometheus felt helpless, just as he did when the Spartans attacked Athens. Only these weren't powerless civilians this time. He watched Greg use his skills as a samurai to maim and kill the attacking force, wielding the rebar as a sword.

Hod jumped from cars and trees onto the living men, demonstrating this was not his first battle. He bit the ears off each victim. Drew and Jennifer stood further back, throwing rocks. Accustomed to her royal position, Rachel stood on a plastic crate and ordered those around her to attack, as though she sent her army into battle.

The police slowed the assault, took cover behind vehicles and trees, and they called out in their strange language. Gunnar waved his arm forward and yelled in his Norse accent, "Come on men! Let's teach these scoundrels what happens when they start a fight with our clan."

* * *

Dressed in riot gear, John Colton quietly addressed his men, who were all huddled close together. "There's a group of re-ans on the other side of the quarantine barrier around the corner. We're going to do this by the book, just like we practiced on the range. The flash-bangs will confuse them and the gas will corral them together. We should have them in the truck in no time."

As he glanced around the corner, one of his rookie officers said, "This is so surreal."

He turned back toward the skinny man with thick glasses and a slight overbite and asked, "What's your name, officer?"

"Schimmple, Morton Schimmple."

"Well, Schimmple, why is this surreal?"

"Just a week ago, I thought this re-animated outbreak was only a myth, some kind of Internet hoax. I thought the news blew the whole thing out of proportion and we'd forget about it once the playoffs started. But here I am about to go on my first goose roundup."

Checking around the corner again, Colton waved his hand forward and said, "Now!"

Three officers stood and threw the flash-bangs into the street. Two more officers threw several teargas canisters into the quarantined block. Pulling their gasmasks over their faces, the policemen scrambled over the concrete barrier. Colton remained behind the lines to coordinate the assault. He watched as the closest zombies ran from his men. Two of his men tackled a living dead as he came out of a store. He struggled and tried to bite them. As one officer held the zombie down, the other pulled out his baton and beat the undead over the head. "Oh holy crap!" The officer screamed out. "His brains are pouring out of his skull."

Colton called out to his men. "Watch out! That one has a big rock."

A zombie with long hair, chain necklaces and leather wrist cuffs, charged the officers while holding a piece of broken sidewalk in his hand. He had gray rotted skin and patches where dried muscle showed through. The police drew their guns and fired. With bullets hitting their target, the crazed heavy metal band re-animated body continued running at them. When he reached the front line, he tried to smash the rock into the helmets of the men. One officer grabbed the deceased's arm and tried to shake the rock loose. The zombie turned and bit the man's hand. As he pulled a large piece of flesh back, blood splattered over the zombie's face.

More officers opened fire and more of the undead retracted their retreat, turned and attacked. A black zombie in a business suit and tie, swung a piece of rebar like a sword. He showed the dexterity and skill of a martial arts master. Firing bullets had no effect as the well-dressed dead man dropped each officer he approached.

Colton stepped over the concrete barrier, lifted his gas mask and called out to his men. "Bring the line together. You're too spread out. They're breaking through the openings and flanking us." He watched, as his men hid behind cars and trees, firing wildly down the street. "No, come back to the center of the street and form your tight line."

Through the cloud of smoke covering the street, just beyond the barrier, more zombies appeared. They grabbed his men and began biting any exposed skin. Through his radio, Colton heard General Brown ask, "Colton. What's going on over there? Why haven't you called for the truck?"

John grabbed his radio and replied, "General, this went south real fast. It's not the goose roundup we expected. These re-ans are fighting back. My men are out of ammo and they've overrun our front line. We need to withdraw from the quarantined zone."

Over the speaker came, "Out of ammo! Ignoring every science fiction movie ever made, you thought bullets would stop zombies? Get your men out of there now!"

As Colton called out the order for his men to fall back behind the concrete road barrier, another wave of undead swarmed over his men. Outnumbered and out of bullets, the police force tried to flee, but the zombies overwhelmed them. With several re-animated holding each officer to the ground, they took bite after bite out of the living. John continued to call out to his officers to retreat, but he could no longer see any movement through the smoke. Slowly, the screams of his men died out, until only the moans and hisses of the zombies remained.

A shadow grew large in the smoke, as something ran directly at him. Colton pulled out his taser and aimed at the approaching body. From the smoke, Morton Schimmple, his only remaining officer, appeared and jumped over the barrier. John relaxed his grip and asked, "Where are the others?"

In a panic, Morton responded, "They're dead! Those things are eating them. We need to get out of here now."

As his officer tried to run away, John grabbed his shoulder and said, "Wait, here comes someone."

A silhouette moved out of the smoke, close to the barrier. John saw one of his officers walking slowly toward him. The man had blood covering his face with several areas of skin and muscle bitten and torn away. "Johnson, is that you? Let's get you to the paramedics."

As the officer walked into the light, Colton saw the white milky eyes and blank expression on his face. Morton turned and ran as he called out, "He's one of them!"

Colton raised his taser and said, "You're going to be okay, Johnson."

The approaching officer answered in a language of moans. Two more officers walked out of the smoke speaking in the same un-translatable words. Colton holstered his taser and ran off down the street.

Chapter 6

A squirrel ran across the floor with part of a cracker in its mouth. Outside the building, ravens cawed and the gentle breeze whistled through the tree branches. Voices of the small groups of zombies echoed and bounced around the warehouse. In the center of the large vacant industrial space, Hod tried to start a fire on a pile of broken wooden pallets sparking a piece of flint against a shard of steel. Prometheus stood near a window letting the sun's rays bask on his face. He could not sense the golden warmth, but he let his mind imagine what it should feel like if he were still alive. With his eyes closed, he saw himself back in Greece standing on a cliff overlooking the dark blue sea. The wind blew through his toga as the salt air filtered through his nose. He could hear the seagulls squawking and the waves crashing on the rocks below. For the first time, a sense of calm flowed through the body he inhabited, but it all came to a sudden stop.

"Hey, dude, the Roman and the Viking want you to join their little pow-wow."

Prometheus opened his eyes and saw Drew standing next to him pointing to a group gathered next to a large hydraulic press. Nemi, the Egyptian in the motorcyclist's body, waved him over.

As he joined the group, Titus caught him up on the conversation. "To organize our growing society, I have scribed a structure of government to help us achieve the task given to us by the gods. It is the system we used in Rome with governors and senators representing the greater number of voices. I have spoken with many of the moderns and this structure has endured through the centuries and with various forms it is still in use today."

"It sounds similar to the style of government that we used in Athens. It worked well then, it should operate with the same efficiency now," Prometheus responded.

"Truer words have not been spoken," Titus replied. "With the events of last night, I along with many others have ceded to the fact we will need a military force for our protection." He pointed to a duffle bag filled with 9mm handguns, Remington shotguns, and several boxes of ammunition. "The good John of Vegas and Vic of Chicago gathered these for us early this morning from an abandoned merchant who sold such devices. We are told they are modern weapons we can use in our defense against the living who intend us harm."

Prometheus picked up a Glock and pointed it directly in his right eye to see inside the barrel. "How do such weapons operate? I see no sharp edges to cause damage to an enemy soldier."

Vic reached over and gently pulled the gun down from the Greek's face. "Careful there, Socrates. You just put the business end up to your mug. If you had pulled back on this thing here, called a trigger, your head would be gone."

Examining the weapon with it pointed into the warehouse, he pulled the trigger. The recoil caused the gun to jump out of his hand and land on the ground. The bullet hit a startled zombie across the room, causing nothing more than confusion, as to what just hit him in the chest.

Pointing to the angry undead person, Vic said, "See, if you did that to the living, they would be one of us right now."

With an open hand, palm up, Titus pointed to the Viking. "This leads us to the formation of a military. We have discussed the issue of a leader and consensus dictates that we choose the good Gunnar Benwa."

Scanning the duffle bag, Gunnar said, "I don't understand these strange weapons, but the moderns insist they are effective. For me, give me a sword and mace, and I will fall any living, daring enough to challenge us."

"The descendants outnumber us greatly. Will we truly have a chance to defend ourselves?" Prometheus asked.

"I wondered the same." Titus responded. "Would we be a sufficient force to combat the descendants, or merely fodder for their next gladiator games? This brought to mind the mistake made by praetor Gaius Claudius Glaberus when he thought the rebellion would be an assault on disorganized slaves. Unknown to him, they had been trained in the military arts by the gladiators Crixus and Spartacus. Judging by the lack of knowledge the moderns have of our time, I feel the living are about to re-live this same error in judgment."

Standing at the edge of the group, Jennifer spoke up. "It's settled then, we are to promote Gunnar to the rank of General, so he can lead our new army."

Titus turned to the Viking and said, "All hail General Gunnar Benwa." Several zombies joined in the chant.

Jennifer tapped Prometheus on the shoulder and said, "We should be making a video of this to document our rise to save humanity."

Confused, he replied, "Video? What is this you speak of?"

"Remember when I taught you about movies and television? It's the way we record the actors and events to be played back for others to see."

"Can we use one of these videos to act out our message to the descendants?"

Jennifer thought for a moment. "Yeah, I guess we could. I didn't see any electronic stores in the abandoned parts of town. We would need to send some of our folks into the population. Once they see us, it might not go so well."

Drew injected, "Yeah, the only electronics store within walking distance would be over on the mall, past the museum. There's a good size crowd there night and day."

Walking over to the group, Constance offered her help. "I often assisted in many performances in our city playhouse. I do not mean to sound boastful, but I received high praise for my application of stage makeup and costumes. I can dress us up in a way that we won't be discovered for who we are."

"I say we take the charming Constance up on her offer for assistance." Titus replied as he addressed the group.

* * *

With his whiskey flask in hand, General Brown stood at the end of the conference table and addressed the room full of military officers. At the opposite end of the table, a monitor teleconferenced Daniel and Lisa from their lab. "How long until you have the cure?" He said to the scientists. Daniel moved closer to the camera, causing his face to have a fisheye lens effect. He cleared his throat and with a nervous tone said, "Dr. Tower and I have made great strides in finding a cure. We have isolated what appears to cause the re-animation effect."

"So you found the virus."

"No, General. We can't classify it as a virus at this time. Truthfully, we don't know what this is."

"You don't need to know what it is, just figure out how to kill it." The General turned to the other men in the room. "Until they come up with a cure, we need to step up our efforts. I have reports coming in from several countries the re-ans are fighting back only not in the soccer riot fashion. They are organized and using military tactics. Albeit, rather ancient strategies, they are still effective methods for this type of street fight."

One of the officers at the table asked, "Are the re-ans capable of communicating with other groups in different countries?"

"As far as we can tell, they can't even communicate with each other when they are only feet apart. These rebellious outbreaks are isolated incidents, but they are similar in execution. This is why we can no longer rely on our first responders to take care of the situation. The President has given me the go ahead to bring in reservists and eliminate the threat."

Another officer asked, "But bullets and conventional weapons have no effect on them. What will we use?"

"Everything we have. They burn extremely easy. Once you squish them under a tank tread, it's just a matter of cleaning up." He pointed to the folders on the table in front of all the men. "You have your objectives in front of you. When you get back to your home state, use whatever tools you have at your disposal. Try not to break any building or infrastructure, because we would have to go back in and re-build it. This whole operation has already thrown us way over budget." Brown took a swig from his flask and glanced at his cell phone. He saw a text from Pink, which said, "How about you take me to dinner?" He became so captivated with the message that he did not notice Daniel had spent a few minutes explaining the progress they had made on the anti-virus. He came out of his trance and focused back on the meeting.

On the video screen, Daniel continued, "…so it acts more like a parasite than a virus taking control of the nervous system, much the same way as the parasitic fungus Ophiocordyceps unilateralis takes control over the brain and nervous system of an ant. Only, this is a much larger scale with more complexity to the operation of the host body."

Hearing the words "parasitic fungus," caused Brown to take another sip from his whiskey. "Why does this fungus want to take control of an ant?"

Daniel moved to the side as Lisa moved into view of the camera to answer the question. "Hi General, it's me, Dr. Tower."

"Yes, Doctor, I know who you are."

"Okay, the fungus has the same purpose as all living entities. It simply wants to reproduce. When it takes control of the ant's brain, it forces the ant to climb to a high point, so it can spread its spores. We can only assume the virus, fungus or parasite controlling these re-animated bodies is using them for the same purpose. It will eventually cause the body to go somewhere or do something needed for the reproduction cycle of the entoparasite."

Having an expression of dissatisfaction, Brown responded, "So, can we just spray them with bug killer and then be done with this whole thing?"

Daniel moved his way back into the screen. "Actually, that gives me an idea, General. I'll go over some theories with Dr. Tower and get back to you tomorrow. We may be only weeks away from a cure."

* * *

Prometheus, along with a group of his fellow zombies, walked down the sidewalk in the bright sunshine. An unusual amount of ravens gathered in the trees and watched the journey through the city. Outside of the quarantined zone, the undead tried to blend in with the living by wearing the costumes and makeup applied by Constance. The makeup looked overdone like a vaudevillian actor, which did manage to give some living color to their graying skin. The costume portion of the disguise consisted of nothing more than a large handlebar mustache given to each member of the group, except for John. He wore his blue dress, a wig and applied his own makeup, which made him blend in with the living better than all the others.

As they walked, Jennifer asked Prometheus, "So what did you do for a living back in your time?"

"I don't understand your words. For me to live, I needed to breath, eat and drink. I would have to assume the moderns did the same."

With a slight smile, Jennifer replied, "Yes, my terminology might be a bit confusing to you. What I meant was how did you earn your money?"

"Oh, from where did I arrive at my wealth?" Prometheus reflected for a moment. "My family owned an olive orchard. We found a very lucrative market in Egypt. The Egyptians had quite a taste for both the raw olives and the pressed oil."

John entered the conversation. "I spent a month in Greece a few years ago. From the amount of olive groves in the area, there is a good chance your orchard still exists. With all the wars through the centuries, I doubt your descendents still own it, but it might still exist."

"When we are done with our mission here, I hope to see my home and stroll through the orchard once again."

In a window, a poster with a picture of a samurai sword and an ancient battle-ax, caught the eye of Benwa and the group stopped with him. He pointed to the weapons and said, "Where can we get some of those?"

Greg stepped up next to him and his eyes opened wide. "That sword looks very much like mine, which has been in my family for almost a hundred years. I must hold it in my hands again."

A few feet behind them, while staring at the poster, Drew said, "I remember that. It's an ancient weapons exhibit at the museum. I think it's only a few blocks away from here."

Benwa asked, "What is this museum?"

Drew shrugged his shoulders. "It's where we keep all of our old stuff."

Greg replied, "Then we shall attack this museum and take these weapons. We will have the element of surprise on our side. They will not be able to gather their forces before we can overtake them."

Scratching the side of his head, Drew said, "Yeah, the museum is not exactly known for going into battle with anyone. I doubt they have any forces," his face lit up and he threw his fist in the air," so what the hell, let's storm the place!"

As Drew, the Viking, and the Samurai cheered with others, several of the living walking down the sidewalk realized the crowd with the mustaches was in fact zombies and they ran off screaming. This created a chain reaction and more panic from the surrounding humans on the street. Prometheus pointed to Benwa and said, "You take a group to the place where they store the old weapons and I will lead the rest to the merchant who has a video camera." He turned to Jennifer, who also wore a large mustache, and asked, "Where is the location of this market?"

She pointed to the next block and said, "Its right up here. Let's hurry."

The zombies scurried as quickly as their dead bodies would allow. They limped and staggered down the street, as the humans continued to run away in fear. Prometheus turned to one of his fellow mustache-clad zombies and said, "Perhaps these disguises are not as effective as the good Candice had expected."

With all the panic, humans ran into the streets, causing cars to veer away and crash into light poles, benches and other cars. Car alarms went off and blended in with the screams, and windows breaking.

Several blocks away in the distance, he heard an alarm bell sound followed by the faint sound of sirens. He announced, "Benwa and Greg must be in a grand and heroic battle with the army of the museum."

Inside the electronics store, Prometheus scanned all the odd-looking equipment, while the customers panicked and ran out the front door. Several displayed video cameras projected the zombies on the television screens. In all the chaos, he turned to Jennifer and asked, "Where is this tool which will deliver our message and help our cause?"

Jennifer pointed to a small pocket size video camera on a display directly in front of them. "Right there." She grabbed the white rectangular camera and the package of batteries next to it."

As she picked up the device, a screaming woman ran into her. The human appeared frozen in fear, standing inches from the dead history teacher and shrieking in her face. Jennifer pulled her mustache off, placed it under the human's nose and shouted back, "Boo!" After the frightened woman ran away, she turned to Prometheus and said, "We should get out of here before-" She was cutoff as the security guard grabbed her arm and yelled in his strange language. Without hesitation, she pulled his hand toward her and bit into his forearm. The man jerked his arm back and ran off holding his bleeding wound.

With blood pouring from her mouth, Jennifer turned to Prometheus and said, "I don't know what came over me. I just bit him without thinking about it. But, it felt so good. I feel great, full of energy and strength."

As he pulled her towards the door, he replied, "I too have felt the controlling effects of eating the flesh. It can take over your actions just as a bottle of wine. We must get out of here before it consumes you and the rest of us."

Out in the street, humans ran out of stores in an attempt to flee the undead. Prometheus and his group tried to escape the panic, but traveled down the center of the street. The cars swerved to avoid the zombies. Some ran into the living dead and some crashed into each other creating a blockade. As they maneuvered their way through the wreckage, several smoke canisters fell down on the asphalt, adding a white fog to the chaos. Police officers dressed in riot gear, appeared at both ends of the block. The group of zombies gathered in a circle in the center of the street as the police slowly moved closer. Pulling his mustache off, Prometheus said, "It looks as though our fancy masks are no longer working."

Jennifer tried to climb over two of the wrecked cars in the street to join her clan. As she slid across a hood, four officers grabbed her and pulled her back from the group. "Prometheus!" she screamed, as they threw her to the ground. Three of the zombies ran to her rescue, but met resistance. Several officers fired their tasers and sent the undead into convulsions. Through the smoke, which now covered the entire block, two more officers that were human, appeared with fireman's axes. While the zombies continued to lurch on the ground, the axes came down and decapitated them.

Prometheus glanced over at Jennifer and saw her wrapped in large leather straps and a face muzzle strapped to her head as she struggled and fought to get free. Two officers dragged her away, as another attended the bleeding bite wound on his colleague's shoulder.

Surrounded with a line of shield and ax wielding humans closing the gap, the zombies moved closer together. As the several humans pulled out their bright yellow tasers and pointed them at the undead, Benwa charged through the smoke with a battle-ax in one hand and a sword in the other. He quickly thrust his sword into an officer and buried his ax into the chest of another. Greg shot through the crowd, swinging a samurai sword, giving lethal blows to every officer, he could see. A human drew his handgun and shot Benwa in the chest. The Viking pulled a similar gun from his waistband, pointed it at the officer and shot him in the chest. As the man fell to the ground, Gunnar looked at the weapon with a puzzled look of awe.

As the remaining police ran off and disappeared in the smoke, Prometheus walked over to the last place where he saw Jennifer. On the ground next to the tire of the wrecked car, he found the blood covered camera and batteries. He picked up the electronics and turned back to the center of the block where his fellow zombies feasted on the dead officers. They pulled organs out of bodies, shoving them into their mouths, covering their faces with blood. Tussles broke out over severed limbs, as several zombies would bite into each body part like piranhas stripping a carcass. The urge to consume flesh grew too strong and Prometheus quickly joined in the feast.

Chapter 7

Candles and oil lamps lit the warehouse with a gold flicker. A raven landed on a steel I-beam above the crowd. Below the bird, surrounded by the horde, which now numbered in the hundreds, Titus announced, "It is clear, the living have sectioned off the portions of this city where we gather. I say they have already made a gift of this land to form our own territory. We may be a sovereign nation in their eyes. Why else would they attack us when we venture into their land?"

Prometheus responded, "No we must continue our mission and give these gifts to the living. The gods have chosen us among all who have inhabited the earth. Great is this honor for us even to carry these endowments. The descendants only attack us out of fear."

John, still wearing the blue dress that he found in the alley, interjected, "Before we continue this debate and decide our next direction, I want to thank Gunnar Benwa for showing up like the Calvary and saving our butts."

"Yes, a cheer must go out to our brave warriors and their grand victory." Titus replied.

The crowd called out in unison and threw their hands in the air, "Hurrah, hurrah, hurrah."

Turning back to their debate, Titus said to Prometheus, "How many times have they attacked us unprovoked? With each assault, they kill more and more of our kind. I am no longer in favor of helping my descendants. If they are this aggressive and so quick to go to war, I will no longer claim them as family. I say we find land where we can exist without threat of attack and finish out our second lives."

Many in the crowd voiced their opinions. Some were in agreement with Titus and some sided with Prometheus. As the debate grew, more ravens gathered in the rafters like an audience watching a play. Titus said, "I say instead of fighting, we simply divide into two villages. This will allow each side of the argument to exist as they wish." He scanned the crowd and raised his hand. "Who stands with me and wants to form the village that resists the humans?"

One third of the zombies raised their hands. Prometheus responded, "There it is. If this is your belief, you shall go and find another sanctuary to live. Heed this warning; you will take with you the gifts intended for the living. I do alert you to be aware of the anger of the gods. Their wrath may not have any compassion."

Titus gathered those who wanted to join him and asked Gunner, "Viking, who do you and your warriors support?"

Benwa calmly replied, "We have vowed to protect all of our kind. Our duty will be to protect all of you, no matter where you live, or what you believe. I still consider all of us undead to be of the same clan."

"You are a man of honor, my friend." Prometheus said.

Titus placed his hand on Benwa's shoulder. "For a Viking, you would make a good Roman."

Gunnar walked over to Greg who studied the samurai sword he stole from the museum. "The watermarks tell me of the family who owned this sword. It is a person I knew and helped build a shelter for their horses. He must be repaying me now by giving me his sword."

"It is a fine sword." Gunnar said. "When our people live in two villages, we must divide in order to protect both clans. You are as fine a warrior as I have ever seen. Will you take some men and defend Titus and his new village?"

Greg fed the sword through his belt, gave a half bow and stared at the Viking's feet. "I consider it an honor to be given such a responsibility."

From the far door, a woman's voice called out, "I guess this is where I'm supposed be."

Prometheus turned and saw a nicely dressed blonde businesswoman in a white shirt, dark gray blazer and matching short tight skirt. She wore high heels but walked across the warehouse with the gate of an athlete. "Either I've found the secret zombie lair or I've stumbled into a gigantic dork convention," she said as she moved closer to the group.

Prometheus stepped forward to welcome the newcomer. "Greetings to the fair lady who joins our clan. What is your name and from where do you hail?"

The attractive woman stopped at the edge of the group with her hands on her hips, turned her head, spit, and addressed the Athenian. "Greetings? From where do I hail? Who are you, Henry Higgins?"

John stepped forward. "We are all from different parts of history and the present. It's like we have two factions here, the ancients and the moderns, which explains his strange vernacular. I'm guessing you're of times that are more recent. How about you start with your name, where you're from and how you died."

The businesswoman relaxed her stance and replied, "Call me KC. I'm from Golden at the base of the foothills. As for my last memory while alive, I was working in my lab. The contamination alarm went off and the doors automatically sealed. It doesn't take a scientist to determine that I didn't make it out." She scanned her body, ran her hands down her hips and felt the material of her skirt. "Judging by the pharmacy this chick had in her purse, I'm guessing we both met our demise by modern chemicals."

Prometheus said, "Well KC, the gods have bequest to all of us a power to hand over to the living. What is the gift you are to give?"

KC noticed the duffle bag on the ground with the handguns. "Hey, I've always wanted one of these." She bent down, picked up a 9mm, pulled the slide back to chamber a round and placed it in her skirt waistband in the center of her back. "The gods? Gifts to the living? I don't know anything about that. Some gray haired guy, he didn't give me his name, but I'm guessing by his looks and outfit that he was Father Time, gave me a message to give to all of you."

John asked, "You don't carry the cure for a disease or a new ability?"

"No, just a message." She scanned his blue outfit. "Nice dress, by the way."

Prometheus asked, "Then please tell us, KC of Golden, what is the message given to you by the Father of Time?"

She walked into the center of the group and surveyed the other zombies. "Here's what I'm supposed to tell you." She took a deep breath and spoke rather fast. "The soft colored song will carry the words of the chosen one. These words will be held silent for 100 years until the one who holds the spark of the flame gives them to the children of the descendants." She let out her breath. "There, I said it. Can I go now?"

Prometheus asked, "What does this mean? What is a soft colored song? Why do the words remain silent for 100 years?"

KC noticed the ravens perched in the rafters, and then brought her attention back to the group. "Look, when I woke up this morning, I thought my day would end with me downing some beers, slamming some shots and hooking up with some young hard body. Me, deciphering a prophecy, while standing in the middle of a scene from a B-movie was not on the agenda. I don't even know how I became a re-an. I never went near any of the quarantined zones. There's no way, I could have been infected."

Titus stepped forward. She noticed the Roman inside the body of the gang member and said, "Hey, Holmes."

With a confused expression, he replied, "My name is not Holmes. I am

Titus of Herculaneum. If you died only today, you have knowledge of what the living are trying to do. Have they sectioned off this area of the city to give us are own land?"

"No. They quarantined this area to keep the virus from spreading. Until they come up with a cure, the plan is to stay away from you." She held her hands out and examined them. "I mean us."

Several of the undead called out questions at once. KC held her hand up and said, "Quiet! I didn't pay much attention to the re-an uprising. I didn't watch the news or read about it. I only have gotten little tidbits from my friends who texted me."

John asked, "How could you not pay attention to the dead coming back to life?"

"I worked long hours in an A4 lab, several stories underground. To unwind after work, I'd hit the bars. The last thing I wanted was to tax my brain with a dose of reality. So no, I didn't pay attention to the uprising here or anywhere else in the world."

"This is taking place in other countries?" Prometheus asked.

"Yeah, it's everywhere." She let out a big sigh. "Now that I've given you the message and done my job, what happens next? Do I get to leave and go to my next life? I hope I come back as a dolphin, because that would be cool. No worries or responsibilities. I just swim around and eat little fish."

Princess Rachel, using the body of the Harajuku girl, took her by the hand and said, "Come with me, my friend. I will teach you of our ways."

* * *

On the military base, General Brown stood in front of the double set of steel gates that were topped with razor wire, which held back the massive horde of captured zombies. The dead prisoners pressed against the opposite side of the fence spewing their hideous moans and hissing. Their dead skin hung loose on the bodies, as they continued to decay. Dried blood covered the mouths of most, several had clothing saturated in dried blood, which had turned brown from the oxidation. The large numbers gave them very little room to move in the confined makeshift prison.

Ravens perched on top of the light posts, watching the movement below, while a light fog hung in the air, adding to the eeriness of the situation. Brown spoke into his satellite phone, "Yes, Mr. President, simply containing them is no longer an option. Storage space has become limited and we've had isolated incidents of uprisings. There are containment camps on every military base on every continent. I mean every base, Army, Navy, Air Force. Hell, there was even an outbreak at McMurdo in Antarctica. We have coordinated efforts underway with the British and Germans to solve the storage problem... No sir, relocating them into the ocean turned out not to be a good plan. They walked ashore two days later. Increasing the number of quarantined areas is only a temporary solution. … yes, Mr. President, I'll see to it."

He handed the phone to the soldier next to him, stared into the compound holding the zombies and took out his flask. "How many are in there?"

The young soldier checked the clipboard hanging next to the guard shack. "Eighteen thousand, sir."

After taking a swig of whiskey, the General replied, "Damn, there's more of them here than there are of us. Counting what our allies are holding, they outnumber the entire world military forces. It's a good thing that they don't know that."

A Humvee pulled up next to the gate and a Colonel stepped out, giving the General a salute. "Have you heard from the President?"

Brown returned a half effort salute and said, "Yeah, it looks like we have the green light. We are to burn, electrocute or both to get rid of all the re-ans. The White House will have a series of press releases about the health hazard that they pose to the living. Then they will say whatever else they need to sell it to the public. Notify all centers they are to begin the elimination as soon as the supply trucks arrive."

The Colonel replied, "Yes sir."

A Military Police van drove up next to the Humvee and two MP's exited. One of the soldiers approached the officers, saluted and said, "General, sir, we caught these two women leaving a secured building without any clearance documents. They will not give us any information, other than they want to speak with you."

Afraid of whom it might be, Brown walked over to the van as the other soldier slid the door open. Inside, chained to the bench, sat Hellion and Pink both dressed in black, with dark knit hats. The MP held up a flash drive and handed it to the General. "This is all they had on them. We tried to see what the drive contained, but it made our computer crash."

"Damn it!" Brown grabbed the flash drive. "Take those restraints off them."

With the chains off, the two women stepped out of the van and stood in front of the tall General. With his hands on her shoulders, Brown looked Pink directly in the eye and said, "This is the last time I'm going to do this for you." He turned to the Colonel standing behind him. "Mitch, put her in your vehicle and get her out of here."

"Sure thing." The Colonel took Pink by the hand and led her over to his Humvee.

The General glared at Hellion and asked, "What kind of trouble are you causing now?"

"You can't keep these people locked up like this." Hellion responded. "They haven't done anything wrong. They have rights, just like you and me. These are our friends and our family. They deserve just as much respect as any other living being. We need to let them live their lives without interference."

"These aren't people and they aren't living beings." He pointed to the fence where the zombies collected and watched the conflict. "They're dead. The only thing they want to do is eat us and turn us into more of them." Brown turned back to her. "Now tell me what're doing here!"

"I'm here to free these souls."

With more anger building in his voice, the General yelled, "Okay, you want to free them? You want to help these bastards? Here's what I'm going to do. I'm going to put you in there and then you can socialize with them for the rest of your short life. Make all the friends you want. Reason with them. Explain how you're here to help them. And while they are biting into your major muscle groups and pulling your organs out for desert, I'm sure you'll find comfort in the fact you stood up for their rights."

He turned the soldier next to him. "Open up the first set of gates." Grabbing Hellion by the arm, he pulled her over to the entrance. She resisted, but could not break free from the grip of his massive hands wrapped around her thin arms. "Throwing you in there is going to save me years of therapy. I should have done something like this a long time ago."

As he held her in place, waiting for the first set of gates to open, all the power failed and the base went dark. The electronic locks released with a loud click and both sets of gates eased open. With the zombies pushing through the first set of gates, Brown pushed Hellion into the van with the MP's. "You have no idea what you have done." He turned to the soldier near the guard booth. "Get on the horn and find out why our generators are not kicking in."

Before the young soldier could reach the inside of the guard shack, the horde pushed through the outer gate and several swarmed around bringing him to the ground. Brown dove into the van, slammed the door shut, and told the MP's, "Get us the hell outta here."

Zombies poured out of the gate into the base and encircled the vehicle. The MP tried to start the vehicle, but it wouldn't turn over. After several tries, the engine fired up. With the undead rocking the van, the driver asked, "What do we do, sir?"

"Just run over the bastards."

With the crunch and splat of bodies being crushed under the tires, the van pulled away from the gates.

Speeding down the road, the General saw the living dead storming out of the various buildings where they had been contained. Soldiers tried to stop them with gunfire, but their bullets had no effect. The zombies overtook the men, massing over their bodies and feasting on their flesh like wild dogs. "Get Fort Logan on the radio. Tell them we need back up."

The MP in the passenger seat, held up the microphone to the radio and clicked it several times. "The radio is dead, sir."

The van smashed through the closed entrance gate and out onto the road. Through the back window, he saw a large explosion from the center of the base. The orange fireball climbed into the dark sky, as the pressure wave hit the back of the van, causing it to fishtail briefly.

With a snarl, the General turned to Hellion. "I know you cut the power, but how did you knock out the radios?"

Sitting on the floor of the van, leaning against the back door, she answered, "You are so caught up in all your big guns and powerful weapons and super technology, it never occurred to you this was also your weakest link. You have everything so automated and networked together, even your backup systems and satellites have to send data down the same sets of fiber. All this superior strength needs sophisticated electronics to make it work. It was so simple. Get past your multi-layers of firewall and place one massive virus into your machine, a localized magnetic pulse and then look what happens, "she motioned to the back window. "The world's military is reduced to throwing sticks and rocks. And, it's not just you," she checked her watch. "Right now, this same scene is happening at military bases in every country that illegally held these Second Lifers."

"You have no idea what you have done." The General drooped over and lowered his head while he stared at the floor of the van.

With a slight smirk, Hellion replied, "I've brought peace to the world."

Brown snapped upright, quickly grabbed the sidearm from the MP driving the van, spun around and pointed it at the center of her face. With a definite deep angry tone, he said, "You've brought destruction to the world."

The van swerved and flipped onto its side, which sent the occupants tumbling through the air and caroming off the interior. When the vehicle slid to a stop, confusion bounced around Brown's head. Dust and smoke settled to the ground outside the open rear doors. *What just happened? Where's my weapon? Where's Hellion?* Realizing he was upside-down, he pulled himself up in time to see Hellion scramble out the back of the vehicle. He picked up the handgun next to him and chased after her.

On the street, zombies staggered along the road, sidewalks and yards. As he pointed his handgun at his prisoner, two of the undead attacked him from the side. He swung his huge arm and swept them away as though they were little dogs jumping on the couch. Refocusing down the road, he took aim again, but his prisoner had vanished into the darkness. Lowering his weapon, another living dead charged directly at him. Without much thought, Brown threw a right cross which landed square in the center of his attacker's face, knocking him flat on the ground. Gunshots erupted from the front of the van where the two MP's crawled out of the vehicle and fired at the zombies closing in on them. Within seconds, the living dead surrounded them and feasted on their bodies.

Brown pulled the attackers off his men only to find he was too late.

Chapter 8

The early morning sun sparkled with light gold shimmers off the water as a raven landed on the branch of a nearby tree. Barely audible above the water rushing over the rocks, sounds of distant city traffic lingered. A gentle breeze ruffled through the tips of the tall grass, where Prometheus stood on the bank of the river, watching it flow past. His thoughts bounced between, *Am I being punished or rewarded having my soul placed in a foreign body in this strange time, or is it a blessed gift to see the future and help our descendants?*

Gunnar Benwa approached the Athenian and said, "Greetings, brother."

Prometheus turned to him and replied, "Greetings, brother. It is nice to see the sun rise on such a peaceful morning after the wicked events of last night."

With a slight look of surprise in his eyes, the Viking responded, "Your eyes."

"What about them?"

"They have turned green, not a green which is normal, but a bright green like a jewel with light shining through it. It appears the debauchery of last night has brought you close to the end of your journey."

"I do feel stronger and more energetic, more so than when I was alive." Prometheus held his hands out and examined them. He saw more color in his flesh and no signs of deterioration. "Hopefully, when I reach the point where I am able to relinquish this gift to our descendents, I will also acquire the knowledge of how to pass it to them."

Gunnar sat down on a rock, with a slight bit of depression apparent in his body posture, as he watched the water flow. "I hope my gift arrives soon, so I might go to Valhalla to be with my father and leave this mad world. Although, I did not give much thought as to how the future of our world would look, I could have never imagined it to be like this." He motioned his hand to the distant abandoned apartment buildings with graffiti and broken windows. "Why would so many people want to live together stacked on top of each other, and in buildings with no character, function, or art of design? It is only one of many things, which do not make sense in this future world of our descendents. During conversations with the moderns, I have learned people of this time no longer have the knowledge or skill to build a boat or forge their own iron. These large chariots with no horses fill the air with such a foul smelling smoke."

"Still," Prometheus smiled, "the smell of their chariots is not as displeasing as streets filled with horse manure. They may have lost the ability to craft a fine boat, but I would so desire to take passage inside one of their iron birds which sail the sky."

Vic and Constance approached the two men as three more ravens landed on the ground behind them. The man from Chicago pointed to the British woman. "Hey, Socrates, the Queen here said you have the green eyes." Prometheus turned to him. "Damn! Those are some awesome peepers you have."

Constance spoke up. "You appear to be the first of our group to reach this point. As a great explorer once said, 'You have ventured off the map.' I say we focus our efforts toward you attaining the remaining strings of life required to turn your eyes blue. Perhaps, we will all learn what is needed of us to pass along our gifts and leave this place." She pointed to the dilapidated building across the field. "Living inside the body of a dead person in this grotesque world is a hell that not even Dante' could have imagined." She cast her eyes down. "Excuse my language please."

Gunnar said, "The sensible lady with the fine manners makes a good argument. The next time we come across a living, we should save the feasting for our brother, so he may finally take his journey to Valhalla."

"When he does reach the point where his eyes turn blue," Constance took a step closer, "how do we let the living know that he holds this cure for the plague they call the cancer?"

Vic answered, "Maybe, if we ask Miss Wall Street some more questions about the prophecy, we can find some kind of coded message that will give us the answer. At least that's how it always happens in the movies."

As the four undead walked back to the deserted warehouse, Constance asked, "So, Mr. Vic, how did you spend your days during the time you were alive?"

"During the week, I worked in a Dispatch Center for the Metro Line. On weekends, I would hang with my guys playing the ponies, downing some brews, and making a play on some skirts. I'd usually stumble home between one and three, get up the next morning, and then I'd do it all over again."

With a wrinkled nose, Candice replied, "I do not understand anything you just said, but it sounds much worse than our good friend the Viking who spent his days pillaging." She turned her focus toward Prometheus. "And what about you my friend from Greece? What did you do during your days on this planet?"

The Athenian pondered thoughts of his home. "My family owned an olive orchard, which brought us great wealth for many generations before me. As my brothers and father conducted the majority of the work, I sought to use my time in other matters. During my many afternoons engaged in debate at the forum, I formed business arrangements with many investors to build a temple honoring Zeus."

Vic asked, "Why would a temple built for Zeus, be considered a business venture?"

"During the days that you call ancient Greece, a temple could make a large income for the owners. The offerings the citizens contributed accumulated rather quickly. The owners, to cover the expenses, collected these offerings. Even after the tax amount had been withdrawn, it was still more than most people would make in a lifetime."

Outside the building, they approached K.C. who shared a thermos filled with coffee with several other zombies. As she took a drink, she said, "Damn, my friend. I wish coffee had this same effect while I was alive. Work would have been so much more tolerable."

Vic said to her, "Yo, K.C. we have some questions about the prophecy."

She handed the thermos to another undead. "Look, I've been telling you dorks, I have no idea what any of it means. My job was to recite it. I did that. Now I'm just waiting for one of these gods, all of your keep talking about, to come and take me to Nirvana, so I can donk a blunt and get wicked stupid with Bob Marley."

Constance asked Vic, "Can you explain to me what she just said?"

He replied, "Nobody knows what she just said."

Prometheus interjected, "We have so many questions and the prophecy is the only guidance given to us."

"Then write the words down, memorize them, sing them out loud, tattoo them on your decaying bodies. It will not change the fact that, I don't know what the hell it means."

"Such vulgar words you speak for a lady," Candice replied.

"Listen Princess Pudding, if my vocabulary disturbs you, you can stuff it up your tea and crumpets. I didn't ask to be here, I don't want to be here and I don't plan on playing nice with others while I'm dead."

Gunnar called out, "In all of Einherjar," he pointed across the field next to the warehouse, "does someone want to tell me what they are doing."

Prometheus turned to see a small group of the living, all dressed in long white flowing gowns, walking toward them. The strange sounds they made almost came across as some kind of singing. They carried a young woman on their shoulders, and calmly with caution approached the horde. Twenty feet away, they stopped, gently placed the woman down on the parking lot asphalt, and finished their strange melody. The lady on the ground kept her eyes closed as if in a peaceful sleep while the singing transformed into what sounded like a chant and they danced around the woman.

Nemi, the Egyptian, asked, "Will someone please tell me what these people are doing?"

K.C. responded, "Oh how cute, the nut jobs think they can make all of this go away with a human sacrifice. I take it all back. Being dead just got fun."

She held both of her arms straight out in front of her, tilted her head to the side, and walked toward the living with stiff legs. The humans quickly backed away from the woman on the ground, keeping their eyes on the zombie female as she approached. When K.C. reached the sleeping lady, she bent down until their faces were inches apart. The sleeping lady quickly opened her eyes as K.C. blurted out, "Boo!"

The human sacrifice sprang up and ran toward her group of the living. K.C., along with several others, ran after them yelling, "You kids get off my lawn!" "Scat, you varmints." "Come back and be our dinner. I mean stay for dinner."

* * *

Inside the small examination room, the fluorescent lights gave off a slight buzz along with the greenish light. Wendy Cronsworth tried to pace back and forth, but was only able to take three steps, before turning around began to make her dizzy. The door swung open, breaking her out of her light trance, and the doctor burst in staring down at the chart in his hands. Almost bumping into her, he glanced up and stopped just in time. Anxious to hear the verdict of her tests, Wendy blurted out, "How's it look, doc? All better?"

The doctor turned to the second page and said, "There's no way to sugarcoat this. The cancer has spread and it continues to grow. It's showing no reaction to any of the combinations of treatment that we've thrown at it so far."

Even though her continued weaken condition supported the test results, hearing the words hit her like a lead weight. She leaned back against the table and tried to hold back the tears forming in her eyes. "I guess, I shouldn't be surprised. It's just that I had hoped for a miracle or at least a small glimmer of improvement."

Closing the file with her chart, the doctor replied, "We're not done yet. You are not even close to point where you can give up. I've had patients in worse condition than you who made full recoveries."

"Thanks, doc, but my husband is a research scientist who has studied diseases his entire career. I know the odds and they are not exactly in my favor."

"Yes, I'm familiar with your husband's work. If I'm not mistaken, he's currently working on the re-an virus. I hear he's close to a cure."

Hearing the doctor talk about her husband's fame helped Wendy cheer up. "Yeah, he's been working hard on the cure. He practically lives in his lab, these days. I just want to be here to see him save the world."

"I'm sure you'll be standing next to him in Stockholm when he accepts his Noble Peace Prize."

"What makes you so confident?" She replied, with a bit of optimism in her voice.

Her doctor set her chart down, crossed his arms and leaned against the scrub sink. "We're going to turn up the heat, so to speak. We're stepping up the radiation and the chemo. As my son would say, We're turning it up to eleven. I don't really know what he means, other than we are going to do a full blitz and completely overwhelm your tumors. Starting Monday, you need to go to my clinic on 28th."

Hearing the location gave Wendy a bit of a startle. "Isn't that right on the edge of the quarantined zone?"

"Yes it is, but it's the edge of the green district. I can give you a pass, which will let you cut across the Broadway Bridge and save you an additional mile walking around the perimeter of the quarantined section. It's not as dangerous as it sounds. The area is only barricaded as a buffer from the segment where there has been a lot re-an activity."

"Are you sure it's okay to cross the bridge?"

Her doctor gave a reassuring smile. "Not only do I have several patients, who cross Broadway, it's also how I get to the clinic. Parking rates in that area have gone astronomical, plus it's actually faster for me to walk across the bridge, rather than drive all the way around the barricades."

Wendy felt a slight bit of relaxation on hearing that her doctor takes the same route through the green zone. "Well, I would like that trip to Sweden. I guess the walk to the clinic will only help towards my recovery."

"Now that's the attitude I want to hear."

* * *

John Colton stood in the center of the parking lot on the concrete block at the base of a streetlight. The small crowd of civilians armed with hunting rifles, handguns and axes surrounded him. The light at the top of the pole let out a buzz, flickered and slowly lit up as the grayness of dusk settled around them. He spoke loudly, so his voice would carry over the crowd.

"We no longer have the luxury of being simple civilians. In order to save our families, our city and our way of life, we need to form our own civilian militia. What's left of our military is overwhelmed with the burden of fighting off this ever-growing population of re-ans."

A slender man with sandy colored short hair approached the group. His dirty and torn oxford shirt and tan pants showed signs of a battle. He called out, "Is this were I need to be if I want to help fight those demons?"

Colton glanced over the heads of the other men at the new arrival. "Yes it is, brother. What is your name?"

"Jeremy Larski."

"Do you have any police or military experience?"

"No, I've spent the last fifteen years being parked behind a desk as a data analyst. I've never held a gun or any kind of weapon in my hand, before today, but I'm ready to fight."

John jumped down from the concrete block and walked through the crowd to the recruit. He placed his hand on Jeremy's shoulder and asked, "What brought you out here today, my brother?"

Larsky's face turned red, as he appeared to hold back a tear. "Those devils killed my family. We came home from the store and they appeared out of the bushes. I tried to get everyone inside, but they surrounded my wife and kids before I could get the door open." Two ravens landed on the asphalt behind Jeremy as he continued. "They took one bite out of my wife's arm and wandered away down the street. We tried to clean the wound with alcohol and hydrogen peroxide, but you could see the death spread fast. She asked me to cut her arm off before it spread to her body. No matter how loud the voice in my head told me it was the right thing to do, I couldn't bring myself to get the ax. I sat with her, through the night in my arms, until the sun came up, and it was then that she finally lost the battle. I went downstairs to get a blanket to cover her up, but when I came back, she had already transformed into a re-an, and had bitten both of our kids. Nobody should have to go through what just happened to me. I'm here to fight with you until this curse is gone."

Several of the other men walked over and placed their hands on Jeremy's shoulder to welcome him to the group. Colton said, "We all have similar stories. We have all lost someone. I promise you that we will fight until we rid the world of these monsters."

One of the men in crowd pointed to the far end of the parking lot and said, "Here come some soldiers. It looks like a whole unit."

John turned to see close to forty men in camouflage uniforms walking toward the group. Their clothes looked ragged, dirty and torn. They walked aimlessly, without the discipline of a soldier. As they moved closer, he could see their hazy white eyes, graying skin and dried blood around their mouths.

Open wounds allowed the muscle and organs to show.

"They're re-ans!"

Another man in the crowd called out, "Behind us!"

Colton turned to see another group of zombies, entering the parking lot from the opposite end, surrounding his civilian militia. Several of the men opened fire with their hunting rifles. Only, their bullets had no effect on the approaching dead. The men armed with axes charged in all directions to take on the horde by hand. They swung their blades, landing in the bodies of the zombies, only to be overwhelmed by several more. The men armed with rifles used the butt-end as clubs to bash in the heads of the undead, breaking open their skulls and splattering brain matter over the crowd.

The re-an soldiers swarmed the men, biting them in the shoulders, arms and necks. The civilians continued to fight back as a mist of blood filled the air and the asphalt turned crimson. Colton realized it was a losing battle and called for his men to retreat. His militia had to fight their way out of the crowd to the edge of the parking lot. Re-grouped in the street, he scanned the men who had been bitten. The looks on their faces told the story. Jeremy spoke up. "What do we do? Do we shoot them and put them out of their misery?"

Colton stared at his injured men. "Shooting them will not stop them from turning into re-ans. There's nothing we can do for them now."

He motioned his head for all of his uninjured men to follow him away from the site. As they ran off, John forced himself not to look back at the men he had to leave behind.

Chapter 9

Ravens flocked in the cottonwood trees, which lined the banks of the river far outside the boundaries of the city as Prometheus walked along the path with Nemi, Greg, K.C. and Hod. As the sun sat low in the sky above the silhouette of the Rocky Mountains, the twinkle of the distant urban lights appeared like the first stars of the night. The makeshift shantytown constructed from discarded scrap found in the area, stood out in contrast to the peaceful surroundings. Small huts built from multicolored car doors, fenders, sheets of scrap metal and plywood filled the open spaced between the trees. Several fires burned inside metal barrels trickling smoke into the clear sky, giving the appearance of a post apocalyptic village.

Titus walked up and greeted the visitors at the edge of the clearing to keep them from entering. He stood with his arms crossed and stared at the Athenian. "Greetings, brother, what brings you to our new town?"

Prometheus stopped a few feet from the Roman and replied, "Evening, brother. We have ventured all the way out here to your new residence to offer tidings. You are still welcome back at the warehouse."

"You really do not grasp our meaning or why we have come here. We have given into the realization that this is all a punishment, not a gift." Titus circled his hand toward the distant metropolis. "There is no noble reason to continue feeble attempts to communicate with the livings. They do not want what we have to offer. The most rational decision would be for you to join us."

"But, what about the gifts we are to pass from the gods to the descendants? This cause is not our own, but one given to us as an honor. We are duty bound to carry out this mission," Prometheus responded.

"There is no honor in stealing a dead body and eating the flesh of the living. This is not the act of any loving gods." Titus motioned his head toward the shantytown behind him. "We have committed to make a new home away from the humans to keep from unwarranted conflict. Out here, where they do not live, the only reason for them to make this venture would be to initiate a fight. I promise you, we will not hesitate to go to war and as we are already dead, the advantage is ours. Their attempts to eliminate us will only make our numbers grow."

"But you are an honorable Roman. You must-"

Titus cut him off. "I am no Roman! I am a Thracia, who the Romans captured and forced into the class of slave. When I arrived here, my first thought was to give the allusion of a Roman in good standing to set myself high in the social order of the empire. When I learned Rome had fallen centuries ago, it gave no consequence. Roman citizenship still brought with it a cubit of respect. The false esteem along with this charge handed down from the heavens is no longer of any bearing. We are now only interested in our existence, until we are allowed to leave this retched world."

Prometheus turned toward the city and noticed Hod wading through the river with a spear in his hand and looking for fish. "For those of us still committed to what the gods have given charge, I fear we may never complete this task if all of the gifts are not handed down. You and the people you lead in this new village hold many of these endowments."

As the debate grew more heated between the two ancient men, Nemi stepped between them. "Not all questions have been answered and there is still much for all of us to learn. Perhaps we can agree to remain as two separate villages with a common truce until we have learned all we need to complete this journey."

Titus placed his hand on Nemi's shoulder. "You speak with words of reason, my Egyptian brother." He turned toward Prometheus. "We are more than two settlements. New arrivals have come from the east. They speak of many villages like our own spreading across this land. There are those who share your opinion and those who see this strange existence as we do. Hopefully, one day, we will have the answers as to how we should exist in this world."

The flock of ravens in the trees suddenly flew off and caught the attention of the undead on the ground. Watching the birds fly off in the darkening sky, Titus said, "It might be the fight that we hoped to avoid will be upon us sooner than expected."

The crack of a stick from behind a distant bush brought a tinge of fear into the Athenian's already dead body. More rustling from another group of trees gave the impression that the zombie village had been surrounded. Titus motioned with his hand for the visitors to move closer into the shantytown. Prometheus scanned the area for Hod, but could not see him. The undead came out from their huts and formed a circle. From the east, came the strange yell in the untranslatable sound made by the living. Out of the bushes, ran several of the descendants, armed with axes and wooden poles with sharpened tips forming primitive spears and pikes.

Several of the zombies charged the humans and the battle began. The living appeared out of their hiding places from all points surrounding the town. They stabbed and hacked at the zombies with their weapons as the deceased surrounded individual attackers, biting and tearing large chunks of flesh from the men. Greg sliced off limbs and decapitated his attackers with the precision of his Samurai soul. Blood from the living and dead splattered through the air and mixed with the ground forming crimson mud. Not knowing what to do, Prometheus watched the carnage. *Should I pick up a weapon? I have no fighting skills.*

He saw a human charge at him with an axe held high. With his legs and body frozen in fear, he could only watch as the axe came down toward his head. A spear sailed down from the sky and pierced through the body of the axe wielding man. Prometheus searched for the source of the spear, when he saw Hod jump down from the nearby tree. The caveman picked up the axe and went into action, running through the battle, hacking at every one of the living he could see. As more and more of the living fell, the battle slowly trickled out. With only a few of the living remaining to fight, the greater numbers of undead quickly overran them.

Prometheus scanned the battlefield. In the flicker of the fires, he saw each of the bodies on the ground had several living dead on top of it. They bit, scratched, and pulled flesh off like vultures on a carcass. They ate their victims as if they took part in a celebratory feast holding up organs and body parts like trophies and shoving them in their mouths. Hod ran up to him with a smile and three fingerprint smears of blood smeared across his face. He raised his bloody hand and ran his fingers across the Greek's face to make the same three lines. For the first time, Prometheus wondered if the living really deserved saving.

Nemi approached with Greg and said, "The living captured K.C."

Prometheus responded, "Did they kill her?"

Greg replied, "No, I saw them take her away. They wrapped her in a tarp and dragged her into the bushes over there."

"Why did they want to take her?"

"I've talked to some of the new arrivals from the present. It appears the livings are capturing some of us for experimentation. Even though we are dead, there are rumors the experiments are painful and quite brutal. Unable to die, the torture will only continue indefinitely."

"Where are they taking them?"

Greg motioned to an undead in a t-shirt and jeans. "Tell him what you told me."

The t-shirt zombie said, "I was a cop just a week ago. We were taking our captives to the basement of the courthouse where these government scientists conducted their experiments. They had set up a temporary lab."

Greg asked, "Why the courthouse?"

"All the hospitals are too close to the quarantine areas. The courthouse was far enough into the green zone and even the public wouldn't suspect there to be re-ans in the basement. It was like hiding them in plain sight."

Nemi looked at both Greg and Prometheus. "We will have to assist Gunnar and his troops in rescuing K.C. She holds the prophecy and will play a valuable role if we are to complete our mission."

* * *

Dr. Towers stared at the red blood cells moving across her monitor. After months of running the same tests, she finally saw the pattern emerge. She flipped through the pages of a file next to her keyboard and ran her finger down a data table until she found the numbers in question. Behind her, Daniel walked out of the large walk-in freezer and stacked several Petri dishes in his hand onto a table.

"Sample 1628 is showing the same pattern as samples 1439, 1011, and 956."

Daniel placed the dishes on the shelf of the glass cooler as he pondered what she said. "Are you talking about the transfer between red blood cells when exposed to radiation?"

"Yes, it is not acting like a virus at all."

Daniel walked over to Lisa and glanced over her shoulder at the screen. She pointed to one of the cells. "Look here. When the infected cell is irradiated, the contagion is not only not affected, it transfers to the closest non-irradiated cell."

"You mean-"

She interjected, "That's right. I don't think we're dealing with a virus at all. This looks and acts more like a parasite as we earlier suspected."

Daniel walked over to a pile of files on a nearby table. He searched through them until he found one close to the bottom of the stack. As he scanned the pages inside and said, "This would explain, why two months ago we started to show results with serum 461, but failed with the next three."

"That's right. We were trying to kill a virus which only transfers to the next cell by mitosis. If we vaccinate all the cells against the parasite, when it transfers to what appears to be a healthy host cell, the serum will stop it before reproduction occurs."

Daniel smiled and walked back over to Lisa. While staring at the screen, he placed his hand on her shoulder, and said, "This is the breakthrough we've been looking for."

She placed her hand on top of his to hold it in place. "With this data, we should have a beta version of a re-an vaccine as early as four or five weeks from now."

The sound of breaking glass from a distant room startled both scientists, causing them to turn toward the disturbance. With a loud bang, the door to the lab burst off its hinges and fell to the floor. Several people dressed in black clothes, black hats and sunglasses poured through the opening. They swung baseball bats wildly through the room, smashing equipment and knocking over files.

Daniel stepped in front of Lisa and called out, "Stop!"

Hellion, with her dreadlocks pouring out from under her black knit cap walked up to him pressing the end of her baseball bat into his chest. "We are here to protect the Second Lifers. You're going to stop your torturous experiments and let them live."

As her crew continued to destroy the lab and all their work, Daniel pressed his palms into his forehead. "You have no idea what you're doing. We were weeks away from a cure."

Hellion replied, "You can't cure a life."

Pink walked up to her and said, "We gotta go. The police are on their way. You've already worked your way to the FBI's top ten. I don't think you need to move to number one."

As Hellion backed away from the two scientists, she pointed her bat at them and said, "If you continue your research, we'll continue to destroy it. We are here to protect the Second Lifers and will continue until they are allowed to live free with the rest of society."

She along with her crew quickly disappeared through the door leaving the lab in ruins, as the strobe of police lights flashed through the windows.

* * *

Still wearing her orange jumpsuit from the jail, Hellion sat behind the table next to Pink and watched Judge Patterson look through the file and then he handed it back to the bailiff. An open window near the front of the room, allowed the only airflow into the old building. "I'll allow this to be admitted," the judge said.

Chris Schring, their attorney, pointed to his defendants and said, "Your honor, these women are not international terrorists. They're simply activists who are exercising their freedom of speech. The event of two nights ago at the Collins Institute Lab was a protest which got out of hand. The prosecution's motion to deny bail is unwarranted."

Judge Patterson took off his glasses, set them down, folded his fingers together and glanced at the raven, which landed on the ledge of the open window. "Counselor, your clients are not being charged with trespassing by chaining themselves to a tree. They have some misconstrued sense to defend these creatures that are intent on killing us. The destruction of the Lab is the least of their worries. The magnetic spike they allegedly planted within the military's network along with this laundry list of charges brought up by the FBI, Homeland Security, the ATF and the U.S. Marshals, means that I will be hearing their case until long after I retire. They seem to have a vast web of friends to help them with all these unscrupulous plans. I'm not taking the chance of letting them out of my sight where this network will help keep them hidden. And, don't try to use the "these creatures have rights" defense. I fully support the military's intent on wiping them off the face of the planet. They are an abomination and scourge to civilization."

Chris replied, "But your honor-"

Screams, commotion and gunfire from the hallway interrupted his rebuttal. Hellion along with the rest of the courtroom quickly turned toward the doors as they burst open. Several zombies armed with primitive weapons, swords, axes and clubs, poured into the room. The observers tried to fight them off, but a black zombie with a samurai sword quickly sliced off hands and thrust his way through the crowd. Several more of the undead, including a man in a blue dress, swung axes and bats, taking down all the living that stood in their way. They continued to call out in their strange moans, as they pointed to different people in the room.

Two of the undead pounced on the judge and brought him to the ground next to his bench. They bit into his face and shoulder pulling out strips of bloody flesh with their teeth. He tried to fight back, but his wounds proved to be too severe and Patterson died as his blood ran across the marble floor.

Hellion and Pink ducked under the table as their attorney swung his briefcase at the zombie in the blue dress. An undead in a motorcycle rider's jumpsuit grabbed Pink and pulled her out from under the table. Chris punched the zombie in the face, knocking him down. The samurai sword wielding re-an thrust his blade into Chris's abdomen. As the attorney glanced down at the blood running out of his wound, he looked at his clients and motioned his head toward the open courtroom window. While he fell to the ground, Hellion grabbed Pink's hand and pulled her toward the window through the mob of fighting. A zombie pinned the bailiff against the wall next to them. As the court officer tried to push the re-an off him, the undead bit into the man's neck, spraying blood over the two women. Hellion grabbed Pink and pushed her out the window. The zombie grabbed one of her dreadlocks, jerked her head back and kept her from leaving. The bailiff pulled out his gun, placed the barrel against her lock of hair and shot the re-an's hand off. Diving through the window, Hellion quickly glanced back and saw the bailiff overrun by two more zombies, now feasting on his organs.

* * *

Gunnar led the charge down the courthouse hallway followed by his squad of living dead soldiers. The humans let out screams and ran in the opposite direction. The Viking slowed and raised his battle-axe high to signal the other dead. He pointed to a set of double doors, and said, "Brother Greg, take your men through those doors to see if she's inside."

As Greg and his men burst through the doors, Gunnar continued to lead the charge down the hall. Drew grabbed the leader on the shoulder, and pointed to a stairway. "This is the way to the basement."

Gunnar stopped, stared at two of his soldiers, and said, "You stay here with your group and protect our backs as we go down into this cellar."

Running down the marble stairs to the basement, he could hear the crash of metal trays and glass. In the dark hallway, he pointed to the room where he thought he heard the noise. His soldiers smashed through the door and they poured inside.

The room had been set up as a makeshift lab with metal cadaver tables, grossing stations and necropsy equipment. Scattered trays and broken glass on the floor, told the story of the quick and hasty exit by the workers. Strapped down on one of the tables at the far end of the room, Gunnar saw the naked body of K.C. He and the others ran through the maze of tables and equipment to free her, as she remained unmoving. They unfastened the straps while the Viking called to her, "My sister, we are here to gain your freedom."

K.C. remained motionless with her eyes closed. With all the straps pulled off, he grabbed her shoulder and slightly shook her. "It is considered poor manners to sleep through your rescue. Wake up K.C., so we may take you back to our stronghold."

With his thumb, Drew opened her right eyelid. The white clouded pupil told all of her rescuers the story. Placing his hand on her chest to feel for a heartbeat, Drew replied. "It can't be." He held two fingers against her neck. "I think she's dead."

One of the zombies in the back of the group said, "We're all dead."

"I know we're all dead and none of us have a pulse, so it's hard to confirm when we are no longer one of the living dead. It does appear that the person we knew as K.C. no longer inhabits this body."

Gunnar placed his hand over her eyes. "The Valkyries have brought a new warrior to Valhalla." He lifted his hand and addressed the rest of his soldiers. "Tonight, we will celebrate our sister's triumphs."

Drew interrupted, "There's more to this than a fallen soldier and don't debate with me that we are already dead. But, it appears the living have figured out a way to kill us. If they did this to K.C., it won't be long until they can do it to the rest of us."

After a moment of silence, Gunnar placed his hand on Drew's shoulder. "We will address this issue at a later time. Our task at hand is to wrap up our sister's body so we can take her with us and give her a proper Viking send off."

Chapter 10

Wearing leather gardening gloves, Daniel carefully picked up pieces of broken glass and tossed them into the large trashcan in the center of his lab. The mess and destruction caused by the activists left all of his work in shambles, scattered across the room. Two of his assistants pushed the tall refrigerator back upright, as Dr. Tower tried to gather the paper documents scattered throughout the rubble. While gently pulling half a sheet of paper from underneath an overturned set of shelves, she said, "I really hope all of our data is still backed up on the server. It looks like we're not going to get it all back from our hardcopy notes. We should've kept them in the walk-in freezer. That thing is like a bank vault. I'm betting it will still be here long after we are all gone."

Grabbing a push broom from against the wall, Daniel responded, "If we do have to start over from scratch, at least we know which direction to go. Once we have the lab back up and running, we should have the first serum in two or three weeks. Besides, Dr. Kolhoff and his team in Miami are just as close to isolating the parasite. By this time next year, the re-an outbreak will be a distant memory."

Lisa sorted through papers spread across a table. "I hope so. All the major labs have been so focused on this outbreak, we let the Omega Virus sneak up on us. There's indication it might be more destructive than the re-an if we don't get it under control."

"One theory circulating around, states the Omega Virus," Daniel swept some glass shards into a pile, "is a variant of the Reanimation Virus that, instead of placing the host into a zombie-like state, it overwhelms the vital organs."

Dr. Tower glanced up from her papers. "But, there have been cases, where a person who showed symptoms of the Omega Virus has been declared dead, only to have the re-an virus bring the body back to life. This would indicate there are two different strains. With our findings, the re-an may not be a virus at all, which means these are two different outbreaks."

"This is true. The Omega appears to create more re-an cases. It's a perfect storm of A4 outbreaks."

Lisa set the stack of papers in her hand down on the table and walked over to Daniel. He leaned the broom against the wall and wrapped his arms around her waist as she did the same to him. Holding each other close, she asked, "Have you had the talk with your wife yet?"

Daniel let out a breath and said, "She's dying of cancer. I can't tell her something like this right at the end of her life."

"How's her chemo going?"

"It's not going well. The tumors are continuing to grow. I'm afraid it will not be long before it spreads to her lymphatic system and then her entire body."

Lisa released her hug and placed her right hand on his chest. "I'm so sorry this is happening to her and to you. I wish this thing between us," she motioned her hand between her and Daniel, "didn't happen right now. I feel so bad. I really like Wendy and never meant for this to happen. The last thing I want would be to hurt her."

"I know. With our emotions running so high combined with all the stress of the outbreak, and her cancer, it was bound to happen with us spending so much time in close proximity. We've practically been living together in this lab."

As Daniel leaned in and gave Lisa a soft kiss on the lips, his lab assistant, Hutch, called out, "Hey Dr. Kissy-Face, some of these samples didn't break." He pointed to some Petri dishes on the ground. "Do you want me to toss them or put them back in the cooler?"

Dr. Cronsworth stepped back from Lisa, cleared his throat and glanced at the specimens on the floor. "Let's keep 'em. I'll examine them later to see if they have become contaminated."

Dr. Tower's face turned red with embarrassment as she turned to walk back to her table with all the documents.

* * *

John Colton's police uniform appeared tattered and worn as he crawled through the dark field surrounded by his civilian militia. He came to a stop behind a large golden currant bush and pulled his machete from its sheath strapped to his back. In the distance, he saw two re-ans standing in front of the abandoned warehouse. Turning to the man next to him, he pointed to his right with his blade and said in a low whisper, "Go tell Frank and his men, we're going in when I give the signal."

His fellow soldier crawled away through the tall grass and quickly vanished into the darkness. Colton continued to watch the re-ans in front of the building. They moaned to each other as if they carried on a conversation.

Through the windows, the shadows and silhouettes of other dead souls ambled across the floor. He leaned forward for a better view and his knee broke a dry twig on the ground. The snapping drew the attention of one re-an at the door. John froze so he would not make another sound. At the door, the two undead went back to their moans and groaning.

As one of the zombies walked into the building, the former police officer stood, waved his machete in the air and yelled, "Let's go!"

The militia of seventy men sprang up from all over the field and charged into the dim light emanating out of the building. As they poured inside the warehouse, the civilian soldiers met a wave of well-armed zombies. Pulled from a scene of a nightmarish ancient battle, the two armies collided with a clash of metal weapons. Colton and his militia called out actions to each other, "On your left! Watch out behind you!" While the re-ans appeared to communicate in their strange uncomprehended moans. The living dead poured out of the shadows from behind crates and far corners, giving the impression that their numbers were unending. The former police officer wondered; *where did they learn to fight so well? How did they make better swords than ours?*

One of the militia ran up to Colton with his face and hands covered with blood. The man's face had the look of fear frozen on it. "They're everywhere! There has to be over a thousand of them!"

Four of the undead pounced on the man, taking bites out of his face and neck, tearing away pieces of his flesh with their teeth. Blood sprayed into the air, indicating his heart continued to beat and he remained alive while being eaten. Before John could help the man, two more living dead, attacked him with hardened swords made from pounded scrap metal. He swung his machete wildly, clashing metal on metal, keeping their weapons away from him while backing away from his attackers. Another one of his soldiers, armed with an axe, hacked at the neck of one undead until the poor soul's head came off. The two men, chopped at the other attacker until his body parts lay scattered across the ground.

Colton surveyed the battle and realized how grossly they were outnumbered. He saw three of his men hack and stab a bright green-eyed zombie, only to be killed by a sword wielding dead Harajuku Girl with a Panda bear backpack. To save the few men he still had, he waved his arm towards the door and called out, "LoDo Militia, retreat!"

His remaining bloody and wounded soldiers ran with him toward the exit. He left with only half the amount of men he brought to the battle. Outside, the living dead continued to chase them into the darkness. As they crossed the Platte River, Colton stopped on the opposite bank, helped his men out of the water, and saw the dark silhouettes of their attackers turn and stagger back to their stronghold.

* * *

Candles and torches placed at all levels filled the warehouse and cast a yellow light through the building. The once small group of undead had now grown to hundreds. As they spread out across all parts of the large abandoned building, their numbers filled all the spaces, while they wandered about with nothing to fill their time. The inability to sleep forced them to find any type of activity to occupy the long stretches between searching for supplies and fending off attacks. Most resorted to pacing in small areas to place themselves into a trance so they would not be aware of how many minutes had passed.

Gunnar approached Prometheus and gently placed his hand on the Athenian's shoulder. "Walk with me, my brother. I have the need to talk to someone from the land of great thinkers."

The two men walked through the side door of the warehouse into the night, and saw the lights of the city form a glowing bubble in the dark sky. Between them and the lights lay a mile of dark empty buildings abandoned by living. As they stopped at the edge of the light, Prometheus asked his friend, "What do you need to talk about my friend?"

Gunnar glanced at the distant glow. "It's the war building between us and our fellow dead brothers. I am bothered by the feud."

"There are so many troubling facts about this existence. What troubles you about the Clan of Titus?"

"In all of the different lands I have fought, I have never seen brothers fighting brothers. I was asked to protect this clan, and for the first time in my memory, I have failed at such a task. My father and clan elders would be greatly disappointed in me."

"You have not failed, my friend." Prometheus stared out at the city lights. "Our numbers have only grown stronger and your soldiers have proven their worth many times over. The knowledge and skills you have brought us will help complete our mission."

"But I cannot protect our clan when it is divided. Titus and his people are still part of our brotherhood. A disagreement does not change this fact."

"Perhaps Titus no longer asks for your protection. You should relieve yourself of this burden, and focus your efforts on those, who still depend on your shelter."

"As you said, there are many troubling facts about this world." Gunnar glanced down at his strange clothing. "My life as one of the living consisted of conquering villages, drinking ale, and rousting with women. In this world, with iron wagons and ships which sail the sky, there are no more villages to plunder."

"But, there are still battles to wage. The villages are bigger, but the fight is still the same."

Gunnar took in a deep breath and let it out as he stared up at the stars. "I have led my entire life as a brave warrior, just so I would be rewarded with entrance into Valhalla."

Prometheus placed his hand on his friend's shoulder. "And one day, you will receive such an honor."

The Viking turned to his dead brother. "You are from the city of thinkers. Tell me where my logic contains flaws. As one of the living, my job was to be fearless and brave. A glorious death in battle would mean eternal life in Valhalla with my ancestors. I would get to see my father again and show him how his son had grown into a strong warrior. All of this would happen after my death. I died in a battle against a tribe of Gauls. I fended off three of them at once so our women and children could seek shelter."

"You are not only brave, but you are also courageous and regal."

The Viking joined in staring at the city lights. "Thank you for your words of kindness, but my bravery is not what troubles me."

"Then, my friend, what is the cause of your concern?"

"As you have heard, I lived the life of a brave warrior and died heroically in battle. Because I am dead," he motioned his hand out toward the lights of the city, "this must be Valhalla."

Prometheus did not respond right away. He tried to find the error in his friend's argument, but could not see any. "Perhaps, this is one last test of bravery before you enter your eternal life with your ancestors."

Gunnar stared off in the distance as he walked away from the Athenian. His voice faded off as the distance between the two men increased. "If this is a final test, I must decide if I have the determination to continue the fight."

As he watched the Viking step out into the darkness he called out, "Where are you going my friend?"

As he waited for the answer, Prometheus noticed another living dead wandering into the dim light from the field. He turned his attention toward the newcomer. "Greetings friend, are you new to this world?"

Slowly emerging in the yellow flicker from the candle flames, he saw a bloody and bewildered soldier appear. His dirty uniform had tears, scuffs and patches of dried blood. The military man with the short dark hair staggered up to Prometheus and asked with bewilderment across his face, "Am I a re-an?" He glanced at his clothes. "I mean, I feel like I'm still alive, but this is not my body."

"It's okay, my friend. We have all gone through this adjustment period. Let's start with your name and from where do you hail?"

The confused soldier scanned the front of the warehouse. "I'm Norman Patterson, I'm a judge." He held his hands out and looked at the bloodstains. "Or, I guess I used to be a judge."

"Are you from this time period or earlier?"

"I'm from this time. It seems like it was only moments ago, a bunch of vile re-ans stormed my courtroom and killed me. One minute, I was behind my bench, and the next I was talking to the big man himself."

"You are now one of us, my friend. Perhaps your view of our life will change. Have you been given a gift to pass on to the living?"

"Yes, I carry the cure for all rhinoviruses, which would include the common cold." He turned from the warehouse back to Prometheus. "How does that work?"

The crack of a stick from out in the dark field caught the attention of the Greek man. He called out to the darkness, "Gunnar, is that you?"

With no reply, he turned his attention back to Judge Patterson. "Inside, you will find Princess Rachel; she will educate you on your new world."

As the newcomer walked into the building, Prometheus heard more rustling in the bushes, just beyond the light. "Gunnar, are you out there?" The sound of muffled human voices told him that they were about to come under attack.

He ran into the building and shouted, "The livings are here! They are spread out in the field and I fear they mean to attack."

Greg ran toward Prometheus with his sword drawn and others grabbed manual weapons scattered around the building and followed. The samurai in the business suit, waved his arm and yelled, "Prometheus, take cover!"

Prometheus ran toward a nearby large crate, as he saw a small army of the living pour through the door. The two armies collided in the center of the warehouse with the clash of their metal weapons. The Athenian curled up behind the cover and watched the battle take place before his eyes. The living used mostly axes and spears with some poorly made swords. One man who appeared to be their leader waved a machete. Only a few of them had modern guns, which they fired with no effect. As the two forces merged into battle, the fight reminded him of when the Spartans attacked Athens.

The living used their weapons to slice body parts off the living dead. Those who had a leg chopped off, continued to crawl across the ground, toward any of the livings who had fallen. The humans would attack with two or three against each zombie. When they could pin a re-an to the ground with spears, another would use an axe to cut off arms legs and finally the zombie's head.

Most all of the dead souls fought like soldiers. They had no choice with the battle that was taking place inside their safe haven. The ancients, who had more experience with swords, proved their superior fighting skills, by dropping the humans with one or two quick strokes of their blades. Greg used his Samurai sword to slice through the living with ease. As the humans fell to the ground, several undead would converge on them, like a pack of wolves and feast on their still living bodies. Biting and tearing away flesh as the victims screamed out in their strange language. Minutes after the start of the battle, the humans found themselves greatly outnumbered.

Three of the living soldiers found Prometheus behind the crate and pulled him by his feet out into the open. One of them thrust his pike into the Athenians abdomen, while another came down with an axe on his knee, severing the lower part of his leg from his body, spraying blood over the area. The third human swung a hatchet toward the re-an's head. Prometheus tried to roll away, but he was still pinned to the ground by the pike in his midsection. All he could do was turn his head, as the blade cut through the side of his neck. While the human retracted his arm for another swing, the long blade of a sword pierced through the human's ribs. As the man fell to the ground, Prometheus saw Princess Rachel, who was still wearing the Panda shaped backpack, swing her sword at the living person holding the pike, decapitating him with one smooth slice. In a recoil motion, she beheaded the axe wielding man.

The Princess knelt down and placed her hand on the forehead of the Athenian and stared into his bright green eyes. With his head only partially attached to his body, she told him, "My good friend, it looks as though your journey in this strange world will soon come to an end and you will not get to see this world through blue eyes. I hope that whichever god sent you on this mission will show mercy in your next life."

Prometheus could feel his energy drain, just as he did when the Spartan soldier killed him centuries ago in Athens. He reached into the inner pocket of his suit jacket and pulled out the small white video camera. Placing it in Princess Rachel's hand, he wrapped her fingers around it. "Protect this artifact. The good teacher Jennifer fought bravely to keep it from the descendants. She said it will be most valuable in spreading our message to the living. I feel I will be leaving this world, so I trust you will protect this I know you value our charge given to us by the gods."

As the battle continued to rage behind her, the Princess calmly replied, "I promise you, my friend, I will guard this as though it were the palace jewels."

Staring into her face and her multicolored hair, Prometheus slowly closed his eyes and his world faded to black.

Chapter 11

Lying on the ground, Prometheus opened his eyes to a flickering orange light. The sounds of gunfire and distant explosions filtered into his ears. The silhouette of a bug-like metal flying machine flew past, close to the tops of the buildings, making an awful pounding sound. As his vision slowly came into focus, he saw a bright chrome cutlass protruding from his ribs, while he wore the same clothes as the modern day soldiers. Standing above him, a man in a black leather motorcycle jacket, leather chaps, a black cowboy hat and heavy boots, pulled the sword back and slid it into a sheath strapped on his belt. Broken windows and burn scars covered the surrounding downtown buildings with the only light emanating from scattered small fires. A few skirmishes took place on the street between the livings and re-ans, behind the leather-clad man with the long sandy colored hair and one earring dangling from his left ear. A bullet hole in his chest with a blood soaked t-shirt gave indication as to how the body died. The biker bent over, with their faces a foot apart, and glared into the Athenians eyes. "Ya dirty bilge rat! I just killed ya." He placed his fingers in Prometheus's mouth, opened it, and then scanned his teeth. "Do ya be living or ya be a necromancer?"

With the fingers still in his mouth, Prometheus garbled the words, "I believe, I am still one of the living dead."

The leather-clad man pulled his fingers out and stood up. He reached his hand down to help Prometheus stand up. Back on his feet, the man from Greece scanned his new body. He wore a soldier's battle uniform with a large bloodstain where the biker stabbed him.

"Ye be one of da lucky ones," the biker said.

Still scanning his clothes, Prometheus ran his hand across the top of his head and felt the short buzz cut. "Your words offer confusion, my friend. What do you mean, I am a lucky one?"

A truck smashed into the building across the street. Several zombies stormed the vehicle as flames emanated from the engine compartment. Undead pulled the driver out and began to feast on his still living body, while he screamed in agony. They used large knives and swords to cut open his abdomen, pull out his organs and then pass them around to the other undead. The man remained alive long enough to see his organs cut and pulled from his body.

The biker replied, "Yar have a new body. Tis a rare commodity these days. The descendants have been burning thar dead, leaving only the older decayed bodies fer us ta inhabit. Ya have da makins of a fine crewmember."

The Athenian looked at the man and asked, "What is your name, friend, and from where do you hail?"

The biker appeared a bit puzzled. "I be the one who should ask ye those questions. I be Captain Galen Bartholomew and I hail from da sea. I once called England my home until Queen Anne revoked me charter as a privateer. On that day, I proudly took da moniker of pirate."

"My name is Prometheus and I hail from-"

While passing behind Captain Bartholomew, Princess Rachel heard the name and cut him off with excitement. The Harajuku girl with the pink and blue hair had traded the Panda backpack for an oversized military universal camouflage jacket with a large battle sword strapped across her back. She ran over, wrapped her arms around the Athenian, and said, "The good Prometheus, I have missed you so much." She released her hug and turned to the Captain. "This is the Prometheus you have heard us talking about." Turning back to her friend, she said, "I have been hoping you would return. A few of the originals have left and come back in new bodies, but I really hoped I would one day get to talk to you again." The Princess moved close and studied his eyes. "It appears you will not have to collect the strings of life from the beginning, because your eyes are still bright green. You attained a rare position in our society. Very few have been granted the green eyes and to this day, none has remained in our presence long enough to reach the blue. I have been here all this time, feasted many times to gather the strings of life and yet I do not have the status of the bright colored eyes that you hold."

Another military helicopter flew above the skyscrapers and rained explosive bullets down on a group of zombies across the street. From behind the wreckage of two burnt out cars, a rocket powered grenade streaked into the sky, impacting with a fireball. The explosion brought the helicopter tumbling out of the sky, bouncing off the buildings, and smashing on the ground. The Captain and Princess Rachel didn't flinch, as the concussion hit them, indicating they had grown immune to such battle damage. More re-ans pulled the crew out of the chopper and feasted on their warm bodies.

Bartholomew paid no attention to the downed aircraft and said, "The legendary Prometheus, the one who built the Village of Dead Souls."

The Greek man gave a puzzled expression and asked, "The Village of Dead Souls?"

Princess Rachel replied, "As our numbers grew, we used the government model you drafted for us back in the early days. It helped us create structure when we outgrew the warehouse and moved into the city. The livings have not occupied the city center for a very long time and they gave in to allowing us to reside here." She motioned her hand toward the top of what remained of the skyscrapers. Re-ans occupy all these tall buildings. We named our new town, The Village of Dead Souls."

Still confused at what he heard, Prometheus responded, "You said the early days? How long have I been away? It feels like I was in the warehouse battle only moments ago. I can still hear the clashing of the swords and see the faces of the humans who killed me. Your face is the last that I saw before I opened my eyes to this leather clad pirate."

She hesitated and answered, "It has been six years since we have spoken together. So many events have occurred since those days in the warehouse. The livings no longer consider us an uprising. They now refer to us as a War of the Dead or the War against the Dead."

As more explosions resonated through the streets, the pirate Captain said, "We should move back to the stronghold or risk losing our friend again."

He placed his hand on the Greek man's back, and led him down the street away from the fighting. Princess Rachel walked next to him and summarized what had happened since Prometheus died in the warehouse. "The morning after the battle where you died, we noticed the brave Gunnar Benwa was also missing from our ranks. We sadly determined that he had been captured by the livings during their raid, since we did not find his body." She stepped over some building rubble on the sidewalk. "In the coming years, the descendants began to die in large numbers, but not from our blades. They blamed those deaths on a demon they called the Omega Plague. It is a sickness brought on by a cough and nose bleeds. When a descendant catches the Omega, they only have a few days of life before their soul leaves their body. As their numbers decreased, ours multiplied rapidly."

The Princess pointed to the pirate. "The good Captain joined our clan and attained the position of our new leader because you and Gunnar were no longer here. With his experience of leading a crew into sea battles, he has proven to be a valiant chief of the clan."

Captain Bartholomew explained, "Da living thought da uprising would go away, but it turned into an actual war. As human numbers dwindled, they started burning dar bodies ta keep dem from turning into more necros. Many of our souls are inside the bodies of those who had been buried beneath da ground for a long time. Thar bodies be not as seaworthy as da moderns. We use dem more for canon fodder ta support da strong soldiers."

They turned a corner and Prometheus saw several living dead staggering through the streets. As the Captain described, they inhabited gray decayed bodies. Torn and partially disintegrated clothing covered their torsos with exposed ribs, bones, muscle fiber and dried, shriveled internal organ showing through openings of ripped flesh. The scene stunned him, but he kept his composure and said, "I know I am one of the living dead, but this sight still gives me a bit of a fright."

The Captain replied, "Yar be getting used to it."

The Princess reached inside her jacket and pulled out the small white video camera. "I have protected this device all these years, just as you asked. As it was originally entrusted to you, I will place it back in your care."

Prometheus took the camera from her hand and placed it in his shirt pocket, as the three zombies entered a large building past some burnt out cars placed in the front, as a protective barrier. "Gratitude to my sister, the Princess. I hope we soon learn how this will help in our cause."

Inside the building, he saw the large open interior lit up by oil lanterns and small fires contained inside metal barrels. Torn papers, old magazines, and scattered books all written in the strange scribble of the living covered the marble floor. Several of the modern and decayed bodied undead wandered through the various hallways on the multiple platforms. Many carried automatic rifles, shotguns, swords and pistols strapped to their hips.

Princess Rachel explained, "This used to be the library of our descendents. It is a sad truth, we cannot read any of these books, because the stories would truly help pass the time."

Prometheus asked, "What news is there about Titus and the clan he established outside of this city?"

Princess Rachel responded, "The good Titus still has his village of those who do not want to accept their charge from the gods. It is with some sadness that I must tell you the number of his followers has grown."

The Captain interjected, "Titus and his clan keep dar guard ready fer war at all times. However, da living give his camp a large berth. They not be incurring the battles, we face almost daily. Da humans have learned dar bullets have no effect on us, but they be still vulnerable to da hot lead. But, they've learned, we do not fair well with de explosions."

* * *

Surrounded by stacks of sandbags forming a bunker in the parking lot of the city football stadium, General Brown yelled into his radio handset, "No, you can't wait for a napalm strike! We don't have any napalm! We haven't used napalm for fifty years. If we did have napalm, we don't have any planes to deliver the crap. This isn't a movie and the Calvary isn't coming over the hill to save your ass. Stop complaining and move your men up two blocks, so you can cover Colton's south flank!"

He threw the handset on the table with the radio. The small video screen mounted to the lid of a storage crate lit up with the face of another officer who saw the temper tantrum and asked, "Did I catch you at a bad time?"

Without turning toward the video call, Brown replied, "Tell me you have good news about sending me more troops."

The officer on the screen appeared to be located in another bunker, surrounded by tan colored sandbags. "The Provisional Congress is still trying to find an interim President. They don't seem to be concerned about rebuilding the military at this time."

"Whatever happened to the succession of power? Someone has to be next in line to become President."

"We're down to the Secretary of Housing and he quit his position two weeks ago. Everybody in line after him is dead."

Brown turned to the video screen. "What do you need? I doubt you called to let me know how we are so screwed."

The man on the screen responded, "Unfortunately, for you, it gets worse."

"Great."

"It looks like public enemy number one is back in your area."

The General picked up an ammo canister and threw it across the bunker. "Hellion! That's just what I need now. Can I shoot her on sight?"

"As much as that would bring you pleasure, we need her alive. There's too much knowledge bouncing around her brain that we can use. She still has a vast network of followers, who still think the re-ans are just a group of misunderstood people looking for a new start on life."

"Thanks for the pick me up." Brown said sarcastically.

"Oh, there's more."

The large General placed his hands on top of the crate, holding the video screen, and placing his face close to the camera. "And what other wonderful things do you have for me?"

The officer on the screen, pointed straight into his camera and said, "I think I'll let your aide tell you the next part."

A thin man in his early forties, quickly walked into the bunker. He wore denim jeans and a universal camouflage military jacket over his oxford cloth button down shirt. As the lieutenant gave the large General a piece of paper, he said, "We just lost a helicopter. It went down by the convention center."

Brown turned his attention away from the video screen and watched an

M1 Abrams tank slowly drive across the lot toward the stadium. "Did our men make it out?"

"They didn't send up any flares and all we can hear on their radio is a bunch of re-an garble."

Several men ran next to the tank, waving their arms yelling, "Stop!"

The General kept his eyes on the heavy armor. "Johnson's unit is hold up just off of Colfax. Tell them to move in and rescue the crew. Colton and his men are east of his position and should provide some cover."

The lieutenant cleared his throat and nervously said, "Bill's unit has been overrun. We have a report of some re-ans trying to drive their M113 down Broadway."

"Damn it!" Brown lifted his right leg and kicked over an entire side of the sandbag barrier. The crate holding up the video screen fell over and the electronics shattered under a mass of white sparks. "Round up five men and go get that crew! We're running short on pilots and we need them back."

The Lieutenant remained in the bunker, staring at the General. He glanced down and shuffled his feet a bit, and then turned his attention back to the officer.

Brown glanced at the tank headed for the stadium wall and then back at his lieutenant. "What? Why aren't you moving? I gave you an order. I know you're really a civilian, but you do know what an order is, don't you?"

The thin man reached in his back pocket, pulled out another piece of paper and handed it to his commander. As the General unfolded the note, the Lieutenant said, "Admiral Douglas died from the Omega virus yesterday and General Stanton was killed in action with the re-ans this morning in Philadelphia. You are now in charge of the entire military. With martial law in place, and with no sitting President, theoretically, you are now the leader of this nation."

General Brown cringed as he heard the M1 tank crash into the wall of the stadium behind him. "Great, as your Commander and Chief, I'm ordering you to go save our pilots."

Chapter 12

The early morning sun beamed through the broken windows onto the library floor. Ravens perched on light fixtures and the bookshelves through the room, and they appeared to be ready to scavenge their next meal. The once proud building tried to hold onto and display the remaining details of its beauty and unique architecture. Marble light sconces held bird's nests. Detailed ornate crown molding showed streaks of water damage. Soot from trashcan fires marred the brightly colored walls.

As he stood around the large table with the other undead, Prometheus stared at the streaks of light cascading down through the broken stained glass windows and thought of the same scene back in the warehouse. Only this building had more opulence. Bartholomew pushed the brim of his hat up and pointed to a section of the large map spread across the wooden table. "This be the line where descendants have pulled back dar soldiers. We should scout dis new area over here fer supplies. Sometimes, we be finding less fortunate's who stayed behind. Those poor souls be our next feast fer us to be gathering the strings of life. "

Two more living dead approached the meeting. The man wearing a flannel hooded shirt and hardhat pointed to the zombie next to him. "Captain, we have a new arrival who may have valuable information for you."

A dead soul with short red hair and a golf shirt stepped up to the table. Prometheus said to the man, "Greetings, brother, what is your name and from where do you hail?"

The newcomer scanned the room with the empty bookshelves and said, "Tewy, people call me Tewy. Last night, I tried to get back to my house on the south side of town, when I started coughing up blood. I guess the Omega virus hit me fast."

Prometheus replied, "Welcome, brother Tewy."

Bartholomew asked, "What news do you have?"

Tewy stepped up to the table and glanced at the large map. "After Princess Rachel filled me in on our mission here, I came up with an idea of how we might be able to pass our cures and enhancements to those still living."

"Please, brother, tell us more." Prometheus said, as he welcomed the man to the group.

Tewy studied the area of the map on the north side of the downtown area. "The livings still think they can cure us. There's a scientist who is working on this remedy and his laboratory is right here," he tapped his finger on the map, "on the edge of our village. I think his name is Dr. Cronsworth. I read an article about him a month ago."

Bartholomew asked, "How can this man help us if he be trying to stop us with his studies and apothecary ways?"

"He has been studying the re-ans who have been captured. I saw pictures of them in the magazine article. Of all the people there, he should be in the best position to understand that we have cures for all our, I mean their afflictions. His lab is contracted to the CDC and he has the ability to see that our DNA has unusual characteristics."

"We not be able to speak to the descendants." The pirate turned back to the map with an analytical stare. "How we be getting this man to know we be having da cures he be seeking?"

"We break into his lab and leave DNA samples from anyone with blue or green eyes. He surely will show interest in what we leave behind and he might discover what it is we hold for them. He's a scientist. He'll surely think it unusual that we risk the dangers for traveling outside of the quarantined zone, just to leave DNA samples."

Bartholomew stared at the area of the map where the scientist had his lab. "Dar be few soldiers on this side of our village. Perhaps, due to our fighting in da south." He glanced up at Nemi the Egyptian in a motorcycle rider's body. "How many, we be having with da green and blue eyes?"

Nemi replied, "No soul has yet to attain blue eyes. Prometheus and two of our other brothers have green."

"Where are these other two brothers? Bring them to me. We must be sending dem on this next venture."

"We will not be able to send them on this quest. Days ago, they left us, so they could join the Clan Titus. Their vision was not the same as ours."

The pirate captain turned to the Athenian. "You may only be a swab in me crew, but you'll have to travel with us to this apothecary named Cronsworth. We will give him samples of your stings of life."

Princess Rachel entered the room with a woman dressed as a diner waitress. "Captain, we have a new arrival, who you may already know."

Bartholomew turned his attention to the woman in the short green dress with a white apron and collar. A small trickle of dried blood ran down from her left ear, indicating the previous owner may have died from the Omega virus. The waitress with the shoulder length brown hair said to him, "Even in the afterlife, ye still be a yellow bellied scurvy dog. I guess I still get me chance to run you through with me blade." She slapped her hip reaching for her weapon, which did not exist and glanced down at her side. "If I had a sword."

"Naw, it can't be." The pirate captain stepped away from the table, toward the woman, with his mouth agape." Gentlemen, here stands before ye a rare breed of sailor." He stopped in front of her with a smile on his face. "This be da lady pirate, Patricia Quinlan, and I use da term lady, quite loosely." He noticed the top few buttons of her dress undone, revealing her cleavage. "In all our disputes and clashing of metal, I never took in da sight of your curvaceous body. De current day style of clothes be more revealing as to your womanly attributes. If I had known, I would not have been so quick with me sword."

The lady pirate gave a quick scan of her dress and said, "This be not the body me wore in our days at sea. If my bosom had been so full, I would have only used it to distract your treacherous eye to gain advantage with me blade. Besides, rumor passed through the ports your… sword… was always rather quick."

Prometheus turned to the new arrival and interjected, "Your skills may be of better use to the clan, if the two of you join together, and you both forget the feud you had in your prior life. Remember, we are all one family now."

Bartholomew answered, "The Greek man be correct. We all be sailing the same ship." He stepped back to the map table and said to Patricia, "I be giving ye command of a new crew. Even as ye be me enemy on the seas, I be recognizing your skills as a ship's captain. We be taking our soldiers to the apothecary, while ye cover our stern out here on the street." He pointed to a section on the map. "If the descendants attack, ye best be using the gray skins as da first line of defense. They will bring disorder to the ranks of the livings and allow your modern body soldiers to move in on da flanks."

The lady pirate asked, "Do we have cannons and flintlocks?"

The Captain smiled and said, "Oh, wait til ye see what kind of madness the descendants have fer weapons this day. You'll be proud."

Prometheus asked, "My good sister, Patricia, what did the gods give to you to pass on to the living?"

She shrugged her shoulders. "A remedy for something called the Omega virus."

* * *

An explosion in the middle of the street tore apart several of the decayed zombies and scattered the flock of ravens gathered on the streetlights. As the smoke cleared, another wave of gray skins staggered into the front lines of the military spread across the street and sidewalks. They surrounded the human military that fought back, swinging baseball bats and the butts of the weapons at the heads of the grays. At close range, some of the living fired shotguns and blew the heads of the dead off their bodies. Several of the militia charged past the line of decayed undead, but were met by Captain Bartholomew and his more able body soldiers.

The pirate drew his sword in one hand, and a dagger in the other, as he fought through the crowd like boarding an enemy ship. Prometheus stood towards the back of the zombies, watching the Captain take pleasure in the fight, as if it reminded him of his days of storming merchant vessels at sea. One of the human soldiers raised his bat to swing at Bartholomew's head, but he was quick with the sword to man's midsection. Decayed zombies immediately swarmed on the man biting and tearing away his body. Another human soldier leveled his shotgun a foot from the Captain's head, but before he could pull the trigger, Patricia's sword slashed down and cut off the man's hand. The weapon fired as it hit the ground with the hand still holding the gun. The lady pirate quickly turned and fended off a living, armed with a baseball bat, dueling with him as if in a sword battle. Hod, the caveman, jumped from the top of a car onto a soldier and hit him with a handmade stone axe.

Several smoke canisters flew threw the air and bounced on the asphalt, creating a white cloud, which added to the chaos. Dark silhouettes inside the smoke, revealed humans who were being pounced upon by large groups of the living dead, as they bit into the flesh of their victims, tearing off skin and muscle with their teeth. The pirate Captain called out, "Form a circle!"

The undead formed an arc around the front door of the lab, allowing Prometheus to take a group of soldiers into the building. Several living dead picked up a gray skin and used him as a battering ram to smash through the glass door at the entrance. Shredded from the glass shards, they tossed the gray aside.

Inside the dark hallway, Greg led the way with his samurai sword drawn and ready for battle. He no longer wore his suit jacket, and he had cut off the sleeves of his white dress shirt. At the end of the passageway, he slammed his shoulder into a door and burst into the lab. A human man and woman next to a table, hurriedly buttoned their shirts as they stepped backward to the opposite end of the room. As they bumped against the wall, they held each other in their arms, with expressions of panic across their faces, while the room filled with undead who began to smash equipment. Greg stomped over to the two living and held the blade of his sword against their throats. The humans called out in the strange language, but it was easy to understand they begged for mercy.

"Wait!" Prometheus called out. "One of them might be the apothecary we need. It is best if we leave them unharmed. After all, they do not appear to be a threat."

Greg pulled his sword back from their necks, but he remained in front of them, making it clear that he did not want them to move. The man and woman spoke quietly to each other as they stared at Greg.

Prometheus turned to Tewy and asked, "What do we do now?"

Tewy scanned the room until he saw a shelf with supplies. He yelled out to the other zombies, "Stop smashing stuff. We need this guy to be able to do his work." He grabbed an empty Petri dish and held it up in the light. "This looks clean. We just need to get some of your DNA inside it."

"How do I do that?"

Tewy set the dish on the table and grabbed a scalpel. "Give me your hand." He took the Athenian's hand and cut across his palm, but very little fluid flowed out. As a few drops of thick dark brown blood dripped into the dish, he commented, "I guess blood samples from the dead might not be the best." He gazed at Prometheus' mouth and said, "Spit. Try spitting into the dish. Your saliva should work better, than your dried up blood."

The dead Greek man leaned over and spit into the dish mixing his saliva with the drops of blood. Tewy placed the lid on the dish, grabbed a black marker and wrote across the top, "Zombie DNA – It has the cure." He placed it on a shelf in the cooler, as a loud explosion from the street rocked the room. Greg called out, "It is time for us to leave."

* * *

Dr. Daniel Cronsworth ran his fingers through Dr. Tower's hair, as she stood with her back against the wall in the lab. He reached over and turned up the volume on the stereo, filling the room with music. While she unbuttoned his shirt, Lisa asked, "Why did you turn the music up?"

As he unbuttoned her shirt, he answered, "In case any lab assistants are in the next room, I don't want them to hear what we are about to do."

"And what are we about to do?"

Daniel finished the last button, pulled off her shirt and threw it over his shoulder. "We are about to be naughty scientists."

She pulled his shirt off and tossed it across the room. "Is that your hypothesis or your conclusion, Dr. Naughty?"

He leaned in to kiss her and felt a slight tremor in the floor. "Wow, you're actually making my knees shake."

She turned her head and placed her hand in the center of his chest, stopping his forward movement. "No. I felt that too." Lisa moved him back a foot and turned the radio down. With the room void of music, they heard the muffled sounds of a battle taking place on the street outside the lab.

Daniel turned toward the street-side of the room and said, "That can't be a re-an conflict. We're too far into the green zone. They never venture this far out of the quarantined zone. It must be the military conducting drills or something."

Another explosion from the street shook the room and caused the glass vials to shake and rattle. Dr. Towers stepped away from the wall. With a confused expression on her face, she turned back to her colleague and said, "It sounds like they are in front of the lab. Why would they conduct drills here?"

The sound of shattered glass from the entrance way reverberated down the hall outside the lab. Daniel blurted out, "They're inside the building."

The two scientists scrambled across the room to find their clothes. As they hurriedly put them back on, a black re-an wielding a Samurai sword burst through the door and charged them. Daniel and Lisa backed across the room, until they bumped against the wall, still trying to button up their shirts. The re-an with the sword moved within inches of the humans and placed his blade against their throats. The skin on his face, appeared dry and leathery with rotted patches, revealing his gray teeth inside his mouth. The sleeves of his blood-soaked dress shirt had been torn off, exposing the muscle and bones of his arms.

Dr. Cronsworth yelled, "Please, let her go. I'm the one who started this project. She was ordered to join the study. I'm the one you want, take me!"

Lisa responded, "I volunteered for this assignment. I'm just as much committed to this project as you."

"This is not a time to debate semantics. I'm trying to get them to spare your life."

"They don't understand language. How can we reason with them?"

The re-an, holding the sword, pulled the blade back and relaxed his stance, but he remained in front of them. He watched as one of the undead cut the palm of another and let the aged blood drip into a Petri dish. Lisa whispered to him, "This has to be some kind of ritual. Why else would they be doing this?"

Daniel answered, "If this is a ritual, it would indicate more than just a pack mentality. This would show they have developed an entire social structure, which would require complex communication and three dimensional thought."

He watched the re-an scribble on the top of the Petri dish and place it in the cooler. "I'm guessing, he has placed that there as a warning to us. This must be their way of claiming or marking their territory."

The zombie in front of them, who had the sword, turned and left with the other living dead. Daniel and Lisa breathed a sigh of relief as they stepped away from the wall. While finishing the last buttons on her shirt, Lisa said, "If they have claimed this lab as their territory, we may need to leave that blood sample there and relocate to another site. The military has offered us a spot in their compound."

Chapter 13

Ravens perched in the trees, lining the road, while two Turkey Vultures silently soared above in the darkening sky. The usual shades of deep blue had transformed to orange and red from the excessive amounts of smoke, which filled the air. Even the clouds had blackness about them, but not from rain. On the edge of the zombie village led by Titus, Prometheus approached along with Nemi the Egyptian and Hod from the ice age. The scenery gave him a sense of death, no longer full of vibrant colors, all replaced with browns and rusty earth tones. He could not see any visible signs, which gave him this feeling. Demise held a heavy presence hanging in the air. Unlike the days when he lived along the Mediterranean, this experience felt comfortable, as if he belonged in this environment.

The Greek man noticed how the settlement had grown from a small shantytown to a sprawling village, complete with permanent 16th century European style huts made from raw wood and adobe with grass-thatched roofs. He saw a forgery where some of the ancient souls pounded metal into weapons. Two undead, dressed in military uniforms, holding long wooden pikes, approached and stopped the visitors on the edge of the town. Titus stepped forward from between the two guards. He offered a smile, along with a quizzical stare, as he extended his hand. "Greetings, I'm told you are my old friend Prometheus inside a new body. It appears the gods have sent you back to us for a purpose."

"Yes, brother, it is your old friend. I have returned after a long absence from this strange future world of our descendents. It appears the gods do indeed have plans for me. As for what those plans may be, I am still at a loss for ideas."

The two dead men grabbed each other by the forearm, pulled themselves close and hugged in the ancient form of a handshake. Titus said, "It brings me much pleasure to see you again, my old friend."

The ancient Greek man replied, "Gratitude, it is of equal pleasure to see you again. So much has changed. A familiar face is a welcome sight."

The rebel leader smiled and said, "The irony of this afterlife is never ending. You lost your life by the sword of an ancient soldier and now you return to occupy the body of a modern fighting man." He welcomed the three visitors into his village. Other living dead staggered between the buildings, paying no attention to the new arrivals.

As the men walked toward the open village center, Titus explained, "If you have come to continue our old debate, I am afraid you will be greatly disappointed in my answer. The many years you have been gone has only hardened my stance. The descendant's behavior only proves my argument true, with their ways of making war on our tribe, and all other tribes in this land. As the numbers in our village have grown, since we last spoke, it proves I am not alone in this belief."

They came to a stop in front of a large fire, while the sky above grew even darker. Small orange glowing embers floated up from the flames and disappeared into the starless sky. Hod closely examined the chiseled stone point at the end of a soldier's pike. He touched it with his fingertips and even attempted to smell it. Prometheus held his hand out to the flames and tried to imagine what is was like, when he could have felt the heat warm his skin. In the ring of light from the fire, he saw many of the undead villagers stagger and pace aimlessly between the dwellings. He replied to his friend, "Brother, even if you do not believe in our cause, you do not object to our mission. You and your people still consider yourselves one of us. It is of no harm to you, if you were to offer assistance to our clan."

"We feel the descendant's destiny is within their own means. Their actions will determine their fate. We will simply watch. If they showed any compassion towards us, our mood may change, but I feel they are as resolute in their stance, as are we. They must have somehow figured out we are of a military mind, because they have yet to lead an attack on us out here beyond the city of their boundaries." A woman, dressed in a dark blue silk nightgown with dried blood around the corner of her mouth and below her nose, walked up to Titus. He placed his hand on the back of her shoulder and said, "You will be pleased to hear we are not all of a like mind in this village. We have a new arrival, who would like to leave us in order to join your ranks."

The Athenian gave the new comer his standard greeting. "Greetings, fair lady. I am Prometheus. What is your name and from where do you hail?"

The women with shoulder length dark hair replied, "My name is Monica and I hail from Leadville, not too far from here. I," she hesitated for a moment as she glanced at the Rocky Mountains to the west, "worked at the Board of Trade Saloon. My friends called me the Midnight Belle or Midnight for short."

Nemi stepped into the light and asked, "What made you want to join us?"

"I feel the gift given to me which I am to pass along is too important. Given the current plague cast upon the humans, they will need all the help they can muster. I also would like to leave this life of a dead soul as quickly as possible."

"What gift do you offer?"

"I have the ability to see sickness and disease in people."

Prometheus welcomed Midnight to the clan and turned to the soul from ancient Rome. "My friend, I wish-" An undead soldier running into the village and yelling, "Humans," interrupted him!

Prometheus turned to his old friend. "You said the descendants have not led an attack on you out here in this village."

Titus reached out and grabbed a sword from a passing soldier who handed out weapons to the zombies. "For the many years, we have lived in this location. No soldier has come within our view until this moment. Perhaps your visit is what drew them to us." He glanced at his friend with a bit of anger.

A grenade landed on the ground and bounced along the dirt near the large fire. The explosion sent flames and cinders in all directions. The walking dead nearest the blast had their arms and legs blown off, but they continued their fight with their remaining body parts. As Titus leaned forward, ready to charge the invaders, he said, "We have spent years preparing for this day. Our descendants are in for a surprise. Within our ranks, we have many former generals, who fought in ancient battles. It has become obvious our descendants did not spend their years practicing the ways of the sword. As we do not fall so quickly to their bullets, we hold the advantage in what they think of as primitive warfare."

Prometheus saw a massive wave of undead appear from the darkness beyond the firelight. They quickly engaged the front lines of the human soldiers who fought with shotguns and swords. It took only seconds in the battle for the entire village to be consumed. Humans swarmed around individual zombies, while multiple undead pounced on the living. Hod ran through the chaos with a large rock, bashing the heads of soldiers. Immense amounts of vaporized and splattered blood filled the air, creating a red mist, which stuck to the skin of the combatants. The Athenian saw a soldier lunge at him with a sword. He made no motion to get out of the way or defend himself. He no longer cared if he left this world or remained, because he had already died twice. As the bloody blade thrust within inches of his midsection, another sword came down and stopped the attack. Prometheus turned and saw Titus enter into a battle with the human. The two combatants fought until they disappeared into the darkness beyond the ring of light.

Remaining next to what was left of the large fire in the center of the village, the Greek man watched the combat until the remaining living wounded soldiers stumbled away and vanished into the darkness outside the village. Many of the dwellings had caught on fire, flickering light which showed the carnage left from the fight. Both undead and humans lay motionless on the ground, almost carpeting the dirt between the burning huts.

Prometheus saw the upper half of Titus crawl into the light. He ran over and knelt down to next his friend. "Brother, it should have been me in this situation. You sacrificed yourself to save me from a life I no longer own."

Cut in half from just below his chest with his organs trailing through the dirt, Titus rolled onto his back and stared at his friend. "My brother, do not grieve for me, for I will either leave this demon world, or I may return in a new body. Even though I would miss you again, I hope to never return." He closed his eyes as the remains of his body went limp.

Hod walked over, grabbed Prometheus by the arm, and tried to pull him up. Nemi stood behind him and said, "My good friend, we must leave this place now. Our new sister, Midnight, has informed me this village is superstitious as to the will of the gods. As we are the newcomers who arrived shortly before the battle, they may blame us for this attack if we stay. Our best option is to return to our village quickly."

* * *

Hellion knelt down next to the bushes and waved for the crowd of men behind her to do the same. She kept her eyes on the distant flicker of light in the forest emanating from the zombie village. Dressed in all black like the others in the group, Pink crawled up to her in the darkness and whispered, "This still doesn't seem like a good idea. I have got a real bad feeling about this one. It's not too late to turn around and go back to the city."

"These Second Lifers are our best chance to prove they deserve equal treatment. The spoon fed media is making it sound like the military attack the other night was their fault. This colony has lived out here for years without a single incident of ever attacking anyone. These are the peaceful beings and we need them to understand that not all of the humans want to fight. If we make this gesture, they will understand we are here to help them and we can show our close-minded society how we can all live together."

A young man wearing a black knit hat and dark shirt jogged up to the group from the road. Hellion cautiously stood up to talk him. Scanning the ranks of her group, she asked, "What did you find?"

Trying to catch his breath, he said, "They don't have any guards, fences or barriers to their town. We can walk right in."

She stepped out onto the road and motioned for the others to stand. "We're going in, boys. Remember, stick to the plan. Hand out the flowers and try not to show fear. They need to know we are here to help. If you have the opportunity, try giving them a hug."

Hellion led the group of activists down the road to the large Cottonwood trees, which acted as the front entrance to the zombie village. In the forest, a few small fires lit up small patches of darkness, showing glimpses of the primitive dwellings the undead had built. Occasional silhouettes staggered on the edge of the light, only to disappear back into the darkness quickly. Even though she told her people to remain calm, she had a hard time controlling the fear which pulsed through her body. From the darkness, she could hear a low moan, which intensified her trembling. Waving her hand forward, she led her people off the road and into the dark forest.

As she approached the first primitive hut, she could hear staggered footsteps from the blackness around her, crunching the dried leaves and sticks on the ground. The low toned moaning of the undead built up, causing her to clench down on the flowers in her hand. Hellion swallowed hard and with a slight bit of tremor in her voice, she said, "Okay folks, here we go. As the Second Lifers approach, smile and hand them a flower."

A gray-skinned zombie, wearing a decayed brown suit and tie, swaggered into the flickering firelight. The right half of its leathery scarred face had decomposed all the way to the skull. It raised one arm out toward her and moaned as it slowly approached. Footsteps and groans from more living dead increased from the darkness, telling her she had been surrounded. Hellion held out a flower and said, "We bring you a message of peace and love. Our mission is to end this war and allow our people to live together with tranquility."

The gray skin closed the distance between them, reached past her gift, and grabbed her hair. Pulling her head toward its face, the zombie opened its mouth wide, ready to bite off her flesh. Dropping the flowers on the ground, she thrust the palm of her hand into the chest of her attacker. Her hand plunged through the brittle chest cavity into the dried lungs of the undead. Retracting her hand from its body, she tried to shake off the dried crumbles of organ tissue. While the zombie still tried to bite her face, she threw an elbow into its head and dislocated its lower jaw. Pulling herself away from the Gray Skin, she heard the screams of her people, mixed with the loud moans from the undead, resonating from the darkness. Many of the men and women called out for help, but their words quickly turned to cries of agony.

Hellion turned to run, but another Gray Skin grabbed her arm. As she kicked, screamed and fought to get away, several more of the living dead, materialized from the darkness, and latched onto her shoulders and legs.

Frantically convulsing her body to get free, she saw one of her men fall into the ring of light from a nearby fire. He had six zombies on top of him, ripping off pieces of flesh from his still living body. They bit into his shoulders, arms and legs, feasting on his muscles, as his clothes became saturated with blood. His battle tapered off until he no longer had enough life to continue the fight. The undead fed off him like lions on a fresh kill.

The sight of her friend being eaten alive, made her fight with more intensity, but the large number of zombies had her confined as she screamed for help. Her pleas only merged into the darkness with the cries of her people who were in the same dire circumstance. She could no longer pull her arms and legs free as she felt the rough skin and sharp pieces of bone clench down all over her body. Thrown off balance and pushed to the ground, she felt her clothes being torn off and the boney fingers of her attackers scraping at her skin. Her struggle and cries for help ended when she felt teeth bite into her shoulder and tear out a small chunk of her muscle. She knew there would no longer be any hope of surviving.

A zombie, engulfed in flames, fell on top of Hellion and her assailants. The undead pushed their flaming member off and the fire spread to several of them. Free from her aggressors, Hellion remained on the ground, as she stared at the stars above her, no longer trying to escape from the horde.

Pink landed on one knee next to her and pulled her friend's arm. "Come on! We need to get out of here."

While continuing to stare at the night sky, Hellion said, "I'm dead. They've already contaminated me. Even if I get away, I'm still turning into one of them. You need to get away from me before I turn." She rotated her head to see her friend. "You need to run. It's important you live and tell the others what happened. Tell them we were wrong."

One of the men from the group grabbed Pink's arm and said, "Come on! We need to run now!"

Chapter 14

Four Turkey Vultures hobbled on the marble floor of the former city library and scattered the flock of Ravens already scavenging the area. Dispersed throughout the building, gray-skinned zombies mixed with less decayed undead, as they paced on their never ending walk. Patches of sun streaming through the broken windows highlighted the various colors of decomposition in their skin. Their frayed clothing showed fashion styles going back for several decades. It didn't matter, if the body was a gray skin or a newly deceased, the living dead viewed each other as how they appeared during their life.

In the meeting room, Prometheus spoke with Nemi, Greg, Constance and Midnight. Pointing to the new arrival, he said, "The fair Midnight can be of the upmost value to our clan and our overall cause."

Nemi asked, "How can she be so valuable as to warrant the use of assigned body guards? Our appointed leaders do not have such a luxury."

"Her gift to the descendants can be used to our advantage. She can see the disease in the bodies of the living."

"I still don't see how that is of any benefit to us." Greg asked as he shifted his sword on his hip.

Prometheus motioned to Constance, who continued the explanation, "Princess Rachel and I have spoken with many of the newly arrived moderns. They tell us the livings are working on a potion, which will kill us, if we bite into their flesh. If we are to continue feeding to release our gifts, our new sister will be beneficial to our survival, if she can see if into the livings that carry this plague. We will lessen the risk of biting into flesh, which can vanquish our souls from the world without passing our strings of life."

John from Las Vegas ran into the room wearing a dirty and torn wedding dress. With panic in his voice, he announced, "Captain Bartholomew and Captain Quinlan have come under attack on the perimeter. It's a big strike with helicopters and heavy armor. They need all of us to hold the line."

As Greg ran out of the room, he said, "Prometheus, you gather all in this building. I will round up those in the streets. We will rendezvous at the perimeter."

* * *

Smoke canisters covered the block in a cloud of haze. Helicopters fired rockets into the buildings. The resulting fireballs blew large holes in the structures and rained glass and concrete down on the streets below. Rocket powered grenades, fired from various locations on the ground, sent the flying machines into blazing wrecks. Living soldiers wearing gasmasks fought in hand-to-hand combat with the small army of undead. Several light armored vehicles shot streams of flames from their gun barrels across the waves of gray-skinned zombies, turning them into walking firebombs.

Prometheus led a large group from the library towards the battle. They quickly joined in killing the humans by thrusting long pikes into their attacker's chests. As each living soldier fell, the undead swarmed them and fed off their bodies. Making his way through the chaos, Prometheus met up with Captain Bartholomew, who fought off a non-stop stream of human military. He wielded his sword with ease, thrusting and slashing his aggressors, making each move a lethal blow. Patricia fought next to him with the same artistic skill in swinging her long blade. The two pirates made the fight look more like a dance than a deadly defense. The humans appeared clumsy and out of their league when it came to fighting master swordsman. While thrusting her blade into a soldier, Patricia said, "It's like these men have never fought with a sword before. They have no ability to counter some of the most basic attacks. They don't even know how to place their feet when thrusting or deflecting."

Bartholomew replied as he slashed the throat of his attacker, "They have become too dependent on dar fancy flintlocks, which have almost no effect on us."

The dense cloud of smoke began to thin and Prometheus could see another legion of human soldiers running toward the battle line. He called out, "Captain Bartholomew, this may be a good opportunity to retreat."

Surrounded by soldiers, the two pirates fought feverishly back to back, fending off the living. The Captain yelled back, "It be too late for that. Me fear is that our ship may be in danger."

As the second wave of humans entered the battle, the undead became outnumbered two to one. The living used shotguns to blow the heads of the walking dead, sending brown and crimson brain matter over the block. The solders closed their ranks and completely encircled the zombies. Prometheus asked, "Captain, what do we do now?"

"We be fighting to da bitter end."

Patricia replied, "You were always too willing to run from a fight." She glanced at Bartholomew. "As long as I have a sword in my hand, this is not over."

Behind the human solders, a wave of screams and moans, echoed off the buildings. The Greek man glanced up to see the anti-human clan storm through the streets with spears, swords and axes. Attacking from the flanks, they caught the living off guard. Prometheus called out in excitement, "Titus' soldiers have come to our aid. The humans are the ones who are surrounded now."

A helicopter crashed on the street behind the battle, spreading a wall of flames down the block, which barricaded the soldiers and prevented their escape. Two of the crewman ran from the wreckage covered in flames. The anti-human clan fought, viciously slashing and disemboweling the living, with almost no regard to feeding on their bodies. Bartholomew asked Prometheus, "If Titus is dead, who be leading his people?"

The Athenian stood on the hood of a wrecked car for a better view of the battle. "I cannot tell who leads them, but they do fight as a well organized army."

He watched from atop the car as the battle continued. A small relief unit arrived to help the livings, but the large number of undead quickly overtook them. As the human numbers decreased, their demise accelerated. When the last soldier disappeared under a swarm of zombies, Prometheus scanned the battlefield. Both gray skinned and modern undead feasted on torsos and scattered body parts for several blocks. The few dead bodies that remained whole reanimated and stood up with trance-like stares. They staggered around in confusion, as Ravens and Turkey Vultures shared in the feast with the re-ans.

A tall woman, with long brown hair, a shapely athletic build and a bullet wound in her chest, stepped up to Prometheus. She wore a military jacket over her black cocktail dress and carried a long double-sided axe over her shoulder. "Are you the ancient man, Prometheus, I have heard about?"

"Yes, my new sister. I am Prometheus. What is your name and from where-"

The lovely dead woman cut him off. "Yeah, from where do I hail? I've heard all about you. My name is Hellion and I used to live right here. I fought for your rights and all it got me was a new life in the modern day Hades."

"Gratitude on your good fight for our honor. I hope this means, you do not share the thoughts of my old friend Titus?"

"I not only share his thoughts, I'm keeping them alive. His tribe here," she motioned her head to the gathering undead behind her, "voted me their new leader. You see, I fought to get the humans to accept you and allow you to live.

Now that I'm one of you, I realized the humans are the ones who no longer deserve this world."

"Perhaps, if we sit down and have a debate, I may be able to persuade you in a different direction with your thoughts."

"Sorry, Gramps, the Titus camp is no longer passive. As of tonight, we will take the fight to the weak humans. Do not misjudge our arrival here as an act of friendship. We came only for the chance to fight the livings. This first assault was payback for the death of Titus. There will be more to come."

* * *

In the makeshift sandbag bunker in the parking lot of the stadium, General Brown watched a video screen of the re-an battle a half mile from his position. The overhead shot, taken from a helicopter, showed the clouds of smoke loft above the streets for several blocks. As the haze dissipated, he saw a line of his troops advance on a wave of zombies, and surround them on the street. In the distance, he could hear the gunfire and explosions of the battle echo off the buildings. He reached into his pocket, pulled out his flask, unscrewed the cap and took a swig. "Finally, these civvies are starting to look like legit soldiers."

His clerk walked into the bunker with several pages of printouts in his hand. The thin young man wore glasses with duct tape holding the arms to the lenses. Brown turned to him and said, "What now?"

Shuffling through the papers, the civilian turned soldier replied, "If it can clear the re-an blockade in Kansas, our next shipment of diesel should be here late tomorrow. The civilian food and fresh water stations are reporting some of their shipments are not arriving and the missing supplies are not showing up on the black market. And with the latest hits to the grid, power rationing to the civilian population needs to be cut in half. The nuclear plant in Arizona, is providing all the power to the southwest."

"Send someone to the distribution warehouse and tell them to start handing out the water filters, so the civilians can take water from the rivers," Brown replied and quickly took another sip from his flask. "Tell the courier to ride one of the horses. Our fuel reserves are running low. In fact, send out the word that horses are now the primary source of transportation. If someone wants to take a truck, they have to clear it through me."

"Okay." The clerk sorted to another page in the stack. "Let's see, France and Germany want to know if we can send troops of any branch of the military to help them out at their front lines. Uhmm… Oh, and Brazil has gone dark. It appears the re-ans greatly outnumber the living and there have been no communications transmitted out of their country for over a week."

Brown took a longer swig from his flask. "I don't know why Europe thinks we have excess men. We were all hit with the same EMP and all of us lost troops with the re-an breakout." He glanced over at the video screen and saw his second wave of soldiers move toward the front line. "This looks like we finally might start to turn the tables on these walking road kill."

At the top of the screen in an area too dark to show details, he saw a large group of people move through the streets toward the battle. He pointed to the screen and asked, "Who are these people? Is this another civilian militia?"

The picture began to shake and spin. It flashed between the buildings, the street, and the sky right before the screen went black. Brown kicked his chair across the bunker. "Aww crap! Off in the distance of the downtown skyscrapers, he saw the wall of flames from the downed copter shoot down a street. A lieutenant ran into the bunker and called out, "Sir, we just lost our last bird to an RPG."

"Yeah, I'm aware of that, Lieutenant."

From the radio on the table in front of him, came the voice of a soldier in the battle. "Echo One, Echo One, this is Lima Two. We are surrounded on all sides and we have lost air support. Requesting immediate evac."

The large General picked up the radio mic and said, "We have no one left to come get you, son. Gather your men and make a run for the Platte River. Re-ans are skittish about crossing water. That should give you enough of an opening to get out of there."

He waited for a response, but heard nothing. Again, he put the microphone to his mouth. "Lima Two, pull back to the river. Do you copy?" No response. "Lima Two, do you copy?"

Through the radio speaker, he heard the moaning sounds of a re-an, which caused him to throw the mic at the radio with a sidearm pitch. "Damn it!"

He went to take another swig from his flask, but it was empty. He turned it upside down over his mouth with only one drop falling from the rim. Annoyed, he threw the flask across the bunker, reached into a trunk filled with supplies, and pulled out a full bottle of whiskey. Spinning off the cap, he chugged three large gulps. When he lowered the bottle and turned toward his two men in the bunker with him, he saw them slowly step back away from him, with wide eyed looks of fear on their faces."

He put the bottle on the table. "What? You've seen me drink way more than that and I've had far worse tantrums than this."

The two men continued to back step toward the front entrance of the bunker. Brown yelled, "What is it?"

One of the men pointed to the General's face. Brown touched his cheek with his fingertips and patted his way to his upper lip. Right below his nose, he felt something wet and sticky. In the low light from the single bulb overhead, he saw his fingers covered in blood. As the two men ran out of the bunker, the Lieutenant called, "The General has the Omega Virus!"

Brown rubbed his palm across the bottom of his nose and saw even more blood. Wiping the blood off on his shirt, he picked up the bottle of whiskey and said, "It looks like I don't have much time left. I better finish this now."

He inverted the bottle over his mouth and poured the liquor down his throat.

* * *

With the scattered fires leftover from the battle lighting the area, Captain Bartholomew sat on a piece of wreckage from one of the downed helicopters. He pulled out a rag and wiped the blood off his sword. Around him, a few remaining humans tried to escape, but were quickly pounced on by the undead. Their screams dissipated, as they bounced off the rubble remains of the buildings while they were eaten alive.

Patricia walked up and stood in front of him, still in the waitress uniform, and with her weapon on her hip. "That was some fine sword work you showed."

He glanced up from polishing his blade. "Aye, and I can say da same about you."

The lady pirate adjusted her sword so she could sit down next to him. "It is a shame we spent our years in confrontation with each other. We work well together."

Still cleaning his sword, he replied, "Aye."

"The descendants have pulled their forces back. Our territory has grown. The new arrival, Hellion has her soldiers stationed on the new front line."

"Aye, this be how it goes in this war. They attack, we eat them, or they run."

Pointing to a slash on his arm, Patricia said, "You have a wound. I shall help you get a dressing on it."

With a quick glance at his arm, Bartholomew said, "Tis be a scratch. Besides, I be dead. No use in tending ta something which do me no harm."

She slid closer and snuggled up to him. "What I would do for a bottle of rum right now."

Chapter 15

Prometheus walked along the dark street with several of other undead. Smoke continued to cling in the air from the earlier fight with the military forces. Ravens and Turkey Vultures scavenged the remains of the body parts, which littered the street. The occasional screams of the remaining living humans echoed off the buildings as they were eaten alive. Midnight, still wearing her silky blue nightgown, strolled alongside him and asked, "How often do we get involved in these battles?"

"I don't really know, my new friend. I only recently came back to this world. All of my memories are from the early days of this apocalypse, when the descendants greatly outnumbered us. Our confrontations in those days consisted mostly of small skirmishes. It appears as their numbers diminish, they are more willing to fight."

Greg, who had exchanged his business suit for a black canvas kilt and leather motorcycle vest, pointed to the front entrance of a building on their left. During a previous altercation with the humans, an explosion had blown the charred doors off their hinges. Broken glass and rubble lined the sidewalk of the dark structure. He said, "The last time we fought on this street, the descendants fought with much honor to keep us from entering this place. We never did break their lines of defense. Perhaps, we should investigate the interior to see what was so important for them to put up such an impenetrable barrier."

Prometheus gazed at the burnt out building. The smoke scars and blast holes told the story of the fierce battle that once took place on this spot. He replied, "Yes, perhaps this dwelling will give us information that could help us in our cause."

Walking inside the dark corridor, over the rubble of what remained of the transit, Greg led the others with his sword drawn and held in front of him. They all cautiously walked over the crumbled remains of the walls and ceiling, which lay on top of the once brilliant marble floors. Electrical fixtures hung free dangling by their wires and burn marks etched anything still standing.

John, wearing a long red ball gown marred with tears and scorch marks, said, "By the looks of this equipment scattered around, I would say this was some kind of research lab."

Greg replied, "But we have attacked these labs before. Why would they protect this one with more exuberance?" He pointed to a large silver door and asked, "What is past that grand threshold?"

John glanced at the door and said, "It's a walk-in freezer."

"Perhaps the object behind their fight is stored inside the room you call a freezer."

John stepped over some toppled shelves and pulled the freezer door open. The white interior light illuminated the room as a frosty mist rolled out across the floor. "It's empty, but it still has power. It must still be connected to one of the live main lines."

From the dark end of the lab, Prometheus heard the muffled words, "Kill me." He turned his head to listen to see if the words would repeat. He stopped and asked, "Did any of you hear that? I thought I heard someone speak to us."

"Do you think it's a human trapped in the rubble?" John asked.

Greg stepped away from the freezer and turned his head toward the darkness. "It can't be one of the living, because this voice spoke in our language. It would have to be one of our brothers or sisters."

The group quickly moved through the darkness until they came to a second room with two large heavy wooden doors hanging crooked on their hinges. Cautiously, Greg pushed the structures aside and led the other re-ans into the lightless room. From somewhere in the darkness, they heard a voice once again whisper, "Kill me. Whoever it may be entering this room, please kill me."

Nemi pulled out a flashlight from his backpack and scanned through the interior. The light reflected off metal autopsy tables and more overturned lab equipment. At the far end of the room, underneath some large chunks of fallen drywall and some support beams, they saw the source of the voice. A zombie strapped to a table called out, "Help me. Let Odin have mercy upon my soul and please kill me."

Prometheus and the others quickly moved across the room and unburied their brother. With the light illuminating his face, Prometheus recognized the trapped undead person. "My brother, Gunnar Benwa."

Gunnar lay naked on the table. His body was covered with round bruises and each one had notes of human scribble written on his skin next to the marks. One of his legs had been amputated with the bone and desiccated muscle still exposed. He ran his tongue over his dried cracked lips and with sadness on his face, he said, "It has felt as though many lifetimes have passed since I last heard my name spoken. My eyes have forgotten whom they see. I do not recognize you, but you remember me. Please, help my failed memory and tell me the name of the person who has come to my rescue."

As the others untied the leather straps, the Athenian grabbed his friend's hand. "It is me, Prometheus. I was killed shortly after our last discussion. For some reason, the gods felt the need to send me back and I returned in a new body."

"Prometheus, my brother," Gunner made a partial attempt to force his mouth into a smile. "I have thought about you and our talks. As I have laid here, unable to move for these many years, I replayed our conversations to keep my mind sane." He gazed up at his friend. "I see your eyes are still green. You have not been feeding enough to change them to blue."

"I have made the effort, but my feeding on human flesh has not yet elevated me to the final level of our quest."

Greg slid his sword back into its sheath and asked, "What happened to you, my brother? For years, we presumed you to be dead."

"I was captured by the descendants and placed on this table, so they could conduct experiments on me. They started by cutting off my leg and injecting it with all kinds of magic potions. In time, they eventually burned my leg and gave their evil concoctions directly to me. I believe they have tried to kill my soul, but Odin will not allow me to leave the world in such a way."

Midnight placed her hand on his chest, focused her eyes, scanned his body and said, "He has some kind of sickness in him. I can see it, but I do not recognize this type malady. It is a blackness, which travels through his blood and into his muscles. Unlike all other afflictions, I have seen, this one appears as though it is alive."

With the straps removed, Gunnar continued to lie on the table. "Yes, the descendants have experimented on me, all these years. This potion in my body causes me great pain as if it flows though me like fire. I once longed to remember what it would be like to feel again, but now I beg you to help me end my suffering."

John examined many of the vials and around the room. Holding one in the beam of the flashlight, he said, "I can't read this, but it sure looks like they have been working on an anti-virus. They must have been injecting this into him."

"There have been others who have been given the potion." Gunnar relied. "I have seen them die shortly after the injection. They screamed out in pain until the suffering ended. Their skin turned colors making them look like the livings."

Gunnar squeezed Prometheus' hand. "I have lain on this table in this corner for years, while they injected me with this fire. I have been motionless here all these years only able to see this same spot on the ceiling and limited parts of this room. No longer am I able to move. Please brother, end my suffering."

"Tell me what you need."

The Viking motioned for the Greek man to move closer and he whispered his wishes to his friend.

* * *

On the bank of the lake in the center of the city park, Prometheus and his crew stood around a small rowboat partially in the water. Inside, Gunnar lay motionless as they covered him with dead branches and leaves. The Viking looked at his Greek friend and said, "Thank you for this. I hope I will finally get my journey to Valhalla where I will walk along side my father once again."

Patting him on the shoulder, right before the last of the branches filled the boat, Prometheus said, "You will be there soon, my brother. If you do not return in another body as I did, we will know you are in the land of honored warriors."

With only his face showing through the branches, the Viking replied, "And I hope you can soon give your gifts to the descendants and bring this apocalypse to an end."

John ignited a road flare and threw it into the boat. The dried wood quickly took to a blaze as the group pushed the vessel from the bank. Flames rose higher reflecting on the water and lit up the whole body of water as the boat coasted to the center. The flickering light attracted more zombies as hundreds staggered from the darkness and gathered around edge of the entire lake.

* * *

John Colton stood in the stadium parking lot talking to two soldiers. From the distant skeletons of the skyscrapers, small trickles of smoke continued to snake into the air from the previous night's battle. A bonfire made of dead bodies burned on the edge of the lot, as soldiers and vehicles moved about without interest. The smoke drifted upwards and merged with the smoke from other distant fires turning the sky gray.

The civilian police officer, now in charge of the local military unit, spoke to the soldiers in front of him. "What did they do?"

The soldier who acted as the clerk to the General said, "About three in the morning, this large group of re-ans set a boat on fire and pushed it into the center of Ferril Lake, over in City Park. The scientists said it has to be some kind of territorial ceremony. The re-ans are claiming the park as their dominion."

Colton ran his fingers through his hair. "Why didn't you burn the General's body last night? There's been a standing order for both the military and civilians to cremate dead bodies immediately after death."

The young lieutenant quickly glanced at the burning pile of bodies, back to the officer and he replied, "When we saw General Brown bleeding from his nose and ears, we ran to get the bio team. By the time we came back, he had already died and turned into a zombie."

The other young soldier next to him continued, "All the flame throwers were being used in the battle downtown and all the diesel is in the vehicles until we get that reserve shipment. The only thing we could do was let him stagger away."

Colton shook his head. "Great, that's all we need is a giant yeti-like zombie with all of our military intelligence fighting against us." He tilted towards the remains of downtown Denver. "Where did he go?"

The lieutenant pointed to the east and said, "He wandered off toward the red zone."

Throwing his hands in the air, John said, "Fantastic. He's probably already the new leader of the horde. I'm sure without his flask of booze, he's one cranky zombie."

* * *

General Brown sat on the curb in front of the library drinking from a bottle of whiskey. His new body was that of a thin, somewhat short young man, with a bullet hole under his chin and a large exit wound in the back of his head. The bullet hole caused the whiskey to drip from his jaw. Vic, from Chicago, walked up to him and said, "Yo leaking guy, you're doing it all wrong."

Angry, the General yelled back, "Back off re-an, or I'll kick your decayed ass back across town."

Vic stood his ground. "Hey butthead, I'm trying to help you. Besides, you're dripping the booze all over yourself. You're going to go up in flames the next time the humans launch an attack."

Brown stood up, still holding the whiskey bottle and said, "That's it, I'm gonna-" He paused, as he scanned the dead man in front of him, paying particular attention to the top of his head. "There's something wrong."

"What's that?"

"You're taller than me. Nobody's taller than me."

Vic replied, "Yeah, welcome to your new body, get used to it." He pointed to the bottle in the General's hand. "I know what you're trying to do and you're doing it wrong."

Brown looked at the whiskey and said, "What? I have quiet an extensive history of drinking. It's the one thing, I know how to do rather well."

"If you want to get drunk, you can't do it with booze."

"Then what should I drink?"

"Coffee. Only, if you keep letting it drip out of your chin, you'll have to drink twice as much." Vic told him.

"Coffee? What?"

"Yeah, coffee. Follow me, I'll show you." As they walked together across the street, Vic asked, "So what's your name?"

"General…Chris. I was Chris Brown."

"Great, in your new life, we'll call you General Drips-a-lot."

* * *

Inside the remains of what used to be a coffee shop, undead filled the room, staggering around with ceramic mugs and various other vessels. It wasn't their usual zombie stagger, but more of a drunken nature. Overturned tables and broken chairs mixed with broken glass and pieces of sheetrock. Behind the counter, zombies crowded around two large coffee makers, pouring the beverage into their cups. Vic led the General across the room. "This is our pub and the coffee maker is our version of a still. It's not like we get thirsty or need to stay awake. For some reason, the caffeine gives us a pretty good buzz. Our dead bodies soak the stuff up like a sponge. Considering, we can no longer feel anything with our senses, the ability to get drunk becomes a great pleasure."

Brown quickly held out his whiskey bottle as another living dead filled it with java. Vic pointed to the power cable behind the coffee maker. "We ran a line to the next building where there happens to be one live circuit. Nobody even considered using the power for electrical lighting, especially when booze is at stake. I imagine, if the humans knew we still had power, they would cut it off so we protect this place quite fiercely."

The General took a swig from his bottle. He leaned his head back as a few drips fell from his chin. A smile of relaxation and enjoyment spread across his face. "Yeah, that's what I was looking for."

Chapter 16

The full moon lit up the streets with an eerie gray light. Hundreds of ravens scattered on the sidewalks and streets searched for scraps of food. A few small fires glowed inside some of the empty homes. An unusual silence filled the streets with no military actions against the walking dead this night. A brisk chill hung in the air, causing Daniel and Wendy to pull their heavy coats close to stay warm. He said to his wife, "I had hoped the cold temperatures would have taken away that awful rotting meat smell that blows around the city."

Wendy pulled her knitted wool hat farther down around her face. "I remember how people would complain when the smells from the stockyards blew across town. Compared to the smell of the re-ans, the stockyards seem like fresh flowers." She cautiously glanced at the black birds gathered on the street and turned to her husband. "Are you sure this is still a safe place to walk? I thought the green line moved back to Federal. We're at least three or four blocks into the quarantine zone."

"That green line was moved to keep the population a safe distance from the front lines of the re-an zone, way down in LoDo." Daniel pointed toward the abandon downtown buildings off in the distance. "I talked to the military two days ago and they told me I might be able to move back into my lab on Wyncoop next week, because they're pushing the re-ans out of downtown. We're safe here, because there are military units all around us."

She scanned the area and blew warm air on her hands, while rubbing them together. "I don't see any soldiers."

He smiled. "That's because they're holding the re-ans back all the way over on Larimer Street right now. Besides, this shortcut takes three miles off the walk home. You're too weak to travel that far every night after your treatment."

Clouds blew across the dark sky and covered the bright moon turning the street in front of them dark. Shadows stretched into black areas of unknown. With the absence of light, each minuscule sound became a possible threat.

Wendy said with an edge of caution in her voice, "I have a bad feeling about this area. I think I can walk the extra miles if we stay in the green zone. Look around, we're the only one's here."

They came to the corner of the block. Daniel pointed to the large three-story building, which had stood since the early 20th century, and said, "Look, all we have to do is cut across the North High School campus and we'll be one block from the green zone and four more blocks from home."

As they approached the old red stone building topped with a bell tower, flocks of ravens blanketed the open ground with several large vultures mixed in the population. Daniel looped his arm through his wife's and helped her pick up the speed of her walk. The sporadic sound of crunched leaves or the crack of a stick made his nerves slightly jolt with fear, but he tried not to show it so he wouldn't worry his wife. He wondered if there could be re-ans just out of sight hiding in the darkness, but he kept his focus on the illuminated streetlights several blocks away. They indicated the edge of the green zone, which meant their home and safety.

As they rounded the north side of the building in the parking lot, he saw several vultures feeding off the remains of a dead body. Ravens fought for space between the giant birds as they picked the bones clean. As they pecked and tore at the dried decayed flesh, the carcass would flinch as if it tried to come back to life. Still trying to keep his wife calm, with a nervous tone in his voice, he said, "Maybe we should pick up the pace a little more. I'm sure you're just as eager to get out of this cold air as I am."

Walking around the corner of the building, they came face-to-face with six re-ans. The living dead, with gray deteriorated skin and dried blood stained clothes, pinned them against the building. Daniel stepped in front of his wife trying to shield her from the demons. A zombie with stringy dark hair in a waitress uniform, pulled out a sword from around her waist and held the tip against the scientist's throat. Another undead, wearing a canvas kilt and leather vest with a sword strapped across his back, held his hand up and moaned in their strange language. The waitress lowered her sword with a hiss and they all groaned and tightened the circle around their human prey.

Wendy asked, "What are they doing? Why aren't they trying to eat us?"

A dead woman in a blue nightgown, moved close to her and scanned her body with her grayish-white haze covered eyes. Wendy shook with terror and tried not to move as the dead woman sized her up with curiosity expressed on her dead face. The zombie reached out and jerked the knit hat off the human woman's head, revealing her bald head, which caused the dead to moan even louder intermixed with hisses. Wendy screamed to her husband, "What are they doing?"

Daniel pushed the nightgown undead back and the waitress pressed the tip of her sword into his chest moving him a few steps away from his wife. A dead young soldier with bright green eyes, decayed gray skin and dried blood around his mouth, slowly staggered toward Wendy, who could no longer move out of fear. The zombie let out a deep moan and stood inches from the cancer victim. He raked his bony fingertips down her shoulder, across her chest and stopped at her abdomen. She began to cry with her body trembling, while trying to hold back screams of panic. Her husband tried to come to her aid, but two of the other undead held him back. He yelled, "Leave her alone, you bastard!"

The soldier clamped his cold dry hand around Wendy's wrist and brought her arm up to his mouth. Still crying, she pounded his chest and shoulder with her free arm. Unaffected, the dead man with the green eyes, opened his mouth revealing the decayed, blood stained, blackened teeth and bit into her forearm. He didn't take a mouthful of flesh. He only punctured her skin and then he released her.

Wendy looked at her bleeding arm and the round bite mark. "No. I don't want to become one of them." The zombies released Daniel and he wrapped his arms around his wife. She continued through the tears, "Don't let me become a re-an. If I start to turn, decapitate me, or burn my body, do something. Promise me, I won't become one of them."

He held her tight as tears streamed down his cheeks. "You're not going to become one of them. You're not going to die from this. It's nothing but a scratch. We can take care of this. I've seen much worse."

They both slid their backs down the wall of the building onto the cold concrete. Wendy sat in front of her husband wrapped inside his arms. The zombies slowly turned and staggered away, as if their mission was simply to recruit a new member. They disappeared into the dark shadows surrounding the building.

Wendy squeezed her hand over her wound and said through the tears. "I was barely holding onto life before this. With my immune system fried from the chemo, I know this is going to hit me fast." She gazed up at the sky. "Cremate my body. I don't want those birds eating me. Spread my ashes on a warm beach somewhere. When all of this is over, you can come visit me. You'll finally get to relax and read a book without me constantly pestering you to get in the water with me."

Daniel replied, "I have the initial batch of the antivirus in my lab. It's sitting in the vials ready to go. I'll give you the first dose. We have some volunteers coming in next week for the primary round of testing, but you can be the first. I know it will work."

His wife didn't say anything.

"Who knows, this anti-virus might even attack your cancer. In a few weeks, this re-an uprising will be over. You'll be strong and we can go to that warm place together. You can pester me all you want about going in the water."

She still said nothing. He noticed his wife had stopped crying. "Wendy, did you hear me. I'll get the military to take us back to my lab and you can have the antivirus. We can do it tonight. All I have to do is find the closest unit."

His wife's body went limp in his arms. He jostled her and said, "Wendy."

Loosening his grip, her body slumped over onto the ground. While crying, Daniel lay down next to her and placed his arm over her body. "Don't worry, when the sun rises, we'll wake up and go to my lab. You'll see; it will all be okay."

Daniel cried next to his dead wife through the cold night. As the first glimmer of sunlight appeared on the horizon, he felt Wendy's arm nudge. He sat up and placed his hands on her shoulder and hip. Her hand slowly closed and opened again. "That's it, Wendy. I knew you would pull through. I'll find some soldiers who can take us to my lab. By this afternoon, we'll be sitting in the dining room, drinking wine."

She bent her legs and moved her head as her bones cracked from stiffness. Daniel let go of her and stood up. Ravens moved closer, almost as if they tried to surround him. He lunged toward them to scare the birds away. "Get away from her! She's not dead."

He reached down and grabbed her hand to help her stand up. "That's it, sweetie, you can do it. You're doing great."

With an emotionless white face, Wendy slowly and awkwardly stood. Daniel smiled and said, "I'm so glad you made it through the night. Everything is going to be just fine, you'll see. I'll get you to my lab and we'll-"

His wife moaned and grabbed his shoulder. Confused he asked, "What are you doing?"

She tried to pull him closer, trying to bite him. Daniel pushed her away and backpedaled. He watched her stagger toward him with her hand outstretched, while groaning and hissing at him. The bite wound on her arm had turned purple and black. Her skin sagged on her bones. Daniel said, "I'm sorry, I can't kill you. Please forgive me." He turned and ran away.

* * *

Prometheus, along with Greg, Patricia, Princess Rachel and Midnight wandered across the abandoned remains of a high school campus on their way back to the library in downtown Denver. A large flock of ravens bounced along the ground behind them, as hundreds more blanketed the open ground around the building. The moon provided just enough light for them to make their way through the night. Midnight asked, "How hard is it to find these supplies in the abandoned areas of the city? What kind of items are we looking for?"

Greg answered, "When the descendants depart a new area, they leave behind many items, we can use to provide light, use as weapons or clothing. About the time, we pick an area clean, they seem to vacate another area."

Staggering out of the shadows of the building, they saw another living dead move toward them. As he came into the moonlight, they saw a tall deceased man with a clean-shaven head and Van Dyke beard. The new zombie called out, "Can you help me? I do not know where I am or why I am in this body."

Prometheus replied, "You must have recently died and have been brought to this life by the gods."

Walking closer, the dried blood from his mouth and nose became visible. "Is this heaven? I never put much thought into it before, but this is…so…not what I expected."

Greg told him, "Far from it, my friend. You have been sent to an evil place to perform an important mission."

Prometheus asked, "What is your name, my new friend?"

The man stopped in front of the group. "My name's Jason. I was at the airport helping the Air Force prep the passenger planes for military use. This Airbus suddenly dropped out of the clouds in a nosedive, right on top of our location. We all ran, but I'm guessing I didn't make it far enough away, because now I'm in this strange body, wandering around the quarantined zone, wondering why it doesn't feel so cold."

"Yes, brother," the Greek man responded, "we have all been placed in bodies, which do not belong to us."

"But the owner of this body, I don't understand why he would do this."

Midnight asked, "What are you talking about."

"The metal ring you put through the nose of an angry bull so you can control him. There is one of those rings through his man part."

Greg blurted out, "Itaiyo!" as he cringed and grabbed his groin.

"What did you say?" Midnight asked.

Patricia responded, "I believe he said ouch in his native tongue of Japanese."

Prometheus patted the man on the back. "Come with us, friend. We will explain this and many other parts of this strange world."

As the group came to the end of the building, two living humans walked around the corner. The man and woman were caught off guard, just as much as the undead. They pressed themselves against the red stonewall with terror across their faces. Patricia pulled her sword from its sheath and said, "We shall feed on these two and add to our strings of life. I will cut them to pieces so we can eat like civilized demons."

The two livings screamed out in their strange language of moans and hissing. It was clear without any translation, they begged for mercy. Before she could cut into the humans, Princess Rachel stopped her. "Wait, this human looks familiar." She turned to the others. "Where have we seen him before?"

"You're right." Greg said as he threw his hand in the air. We have seen this living before. He is the apothecary where they tortured our brother Gunnar. We should avenge the punishment they placed upon him."

Patricia lowered her sword and said, "I give the honor to you and your blade. You had fought next to the Viking."

Midnight stepped foreword, scanned the woman behind the man. "There is something wrong with this woman. I see a disease through her body. It's black and it is eating her on the inside. I think she has the cancer." She reached up and pulled the knit hat off, revealing the woman's baldhead.

Princess Rachel responded, "Brother Prometheus, don't you carry the cure for this plague called cancer?"

"Yes, the strings of life that I carry are for this affliction."

"Even though you do not have the blue eyes, perhaps the green eyes can still help her. If this man with her is the apothecary searching for the reason we are walking dead souls, he may understand our purpose for being."

Prometheus examined the woman and reached out with his hand. He gently ran his fingertips across the front of her body trying to figure out how he can help. "How can I give her my strings of life?"

The Princess pointed to the woman's arm. "Perhaps if you bite her, but do not eat her flesh. If your saliva touches her blood it will attack her illness."

"I will give it a try."

The Greek man in the soldier's body, held the woman's wrist while she pounded on his chest, with her free arm trying to get him to release his grip. Listening to her screams, he slowly bit into her forearm. The taste of her blood gave him a quick intoxication, which made him want to take large mouthfuls of her flesh. He fought against those urges and released his bite after his teeth had pierced her skin. He savored the fresh blood by licking it off his teeth and from around his lips.

"You have great discipline, my friend." Greg told him. "I would have not been able to stop myself from eating her entire arm."

The human man swept his arms around the woman as the two livings slid down the wall and sat on the concrete. Prometheus turned to his friends. "We should leave them be. If our plan works, we should see them again, as they will seek us out to find why my bite held the cure for the cancer."

The living dead turned and staggered off in the darkness, leaving the humans holding each other next to the building.

Chapter 17

Living dead staggered through the remains of the library, with the early morning sun streaming down on them. Through the broken windows, across the remains of the city center, smoke from the previous night's fires continued to loft through the air under a gray sky. The nightly battles with the military had reduced the business district from a forest of shining skyscrapers to the desolate ruins of a ghost town. Black and gray scorch mark, twisted metal, broken glass, and concrete fragments with protruding rebar dominated the landscape in all directions. Blast holes filled the streets and exposed the portions of the steam vents which once brought heat to the older buildings. The original red bricks, which formed the first roads and had been paved over for the past century, once came to the surface.

Prometheus stood at the large table listening to the morning gathering of the council. Captain Bartholomew pointed to the two new arrivals who both wore hunting attire with gunshot wounds to the chest and head. "We be having here Rainart and Isaiah who have journeyed here all da way from a land called Texas. They be bringing us news from other clans."

Rainart, who wore a blaze orange hunting vest over a brown t-shirt with a shotgun hole blasted through his chest, stepped up to the table and explained, "Many of our clans across this land and those beyond the great sea have been eliminated. The livings have come up with a potion which will eliminate our souls from these bodies and send them on to another world." He looked at the large wound in his chest. "I guess they will be killing us more dead than we already are in this world. We have heard from many of our brother clans their numbers are no longer on the increase. In some areas the returned souls have been eliminated entirely and the humans have reclaimed their land once occupied by re-ans."

Patricia replied, "But this may not be such a bad situation as it be our purpose to help our descendants survive, not eliminate them. This increase in population must mean they are no longer dying from the Omega plague."

Isaiah interjected, "Their deaths from the Omega virus continue to rise.

Our numbers are declining because if we try to feed on livings, who have ingested this potion, our soul will leave this body in a most painful way. We have watched many of our brothers regain the ability to feel pain only to experience the most torturous suffering imaginable. It is giving the livings the opportunity to collect more soldiers and build their armies up to greater numbers."

Bartholomew pointed to the city map stretched out on the table. The area in the city, which they occupied, had been circled. "Aye, me men, tell me the living soldiers have pushed their ranks all the way up to this river. They be having more troops and more machines which belch out the black smoke and make the ground rumble." He pointed to an area north of the train station. "Over here, they have spotted two of those demon dragons the moderns call tanks. With our armory in short supply, we will have hard luck storming those beasts with mere side arms and swords. It be more fierce an opponent than any Spanish man-o-war I ever done battle with on da sea."

Greg polished the blade of his sword with a scrap of leather while scanning the map and said, "Clan Titus, led by the warrior woman Hellion, still has a good supply of modern munitions. Many of their weapons can cause great damage to these beasts. We used many of these to bring down the metal flying dragons. I have not seen any in the air for many days and nights. It may be possible we have hunted them into extinction which only benefits both or our clans. Perhaps we can talk to Hellion and make some kind of trade."

"Ever since that she devil took to be leader of that village, they are no longer interested in siding with the likes of us." Bartholomew replied.

"The only way we be getting weapons from their clan would be to take them in battle." Patricia said as she placed her hand on the pommel of her sword.

Greg checked the faces of those at the table. "I do not wish to fight against our brothers even if they disagree with our purpose for this world. We must find another way to defend ourselves against these metal wyverns."

An explosion across the street rocked the library and sent glass and debris flying across the room. Those in attendance, staggered and tried to keep their balance as a cloud of dust and smoke rolled through the building. A gray skin zombie ran into the room and announced from the doorway, "The heavy dragons are here and they are belching out the fire and thunder."

As another explosion shook the ground from just outside the entrance to the building, Vic ran toward the door carrying bottles filled with gasoline and rags protruding from the tops. "Follow me my friends, I'll show you how we fight these bastards."

Captain Bartholomew followed behind the man from Chicago and asked, "How we be fighting these dragons with these little lanterns?"

"Trust me these will work. It's how the Russian people fought off German tanks during World War II."

In the bright sun, outside the library, an M1 Abrams tank sat one block down the street and rotated it's turret toward the library. The gray colored heavy machinery had been completely blanketed with living dead like ants on sugar. They all tried with no success to stop the enormous piece of metal pounding it with axes and clubs. The side streets filled with so many undead trying to join the fight, it looked like a parade.

Vic used a cigarette lighter to light the end of a Molotov cocktail and ran toward the vehicle. With a massive muzzle flash, the huge cannon fired a round, which penetrated the second floor of the library and detonated inside spraying glass and concrete down on the street and adding to the brown dust and smoke cloud enveloping the battle scene. Vic continued his charge, as an explosion on the street corner, immediately followed the second muzzle flash, where Vic had recently stood. As the smoke cleared, only a small crater remained.

A line of soldiers brandishing flamethrowers moved in front of the tank, laying down a wall of fire torching the hundreds of zombies who tried to surround the living army. Bartholomew grabbed Prometheus' arm and said, "Come me friend. This battle be already lost. We must pull our crew back to the underground bunker so we may continue our fight another time."

* * *

In an abandon high school surrounded by sandbag bunkers and patrolling soldiers keeping watch, Daniel closed up his laptop and stuffed it into an olive green military rucksack. The sound of diesel generators chugged in the background. Heavy electrical cables ran across the floor to all the equipment like black vines on the jungle floor. The only computer in the room was constructed from scavenged electronics. The monitor consisted of a laptop screen connected to an old smart phone as the processor and memory storage. Most of the glass test tubes and beakers had been replaced with plastic water bottles and pieces of scrap metal pounded into the shape of cups and bowls.

At the opposite end of the makeshift, primitive lab, three re-ans stood inside tight vertical steel cages. The bars were made from welded re-bar with rust spots showing signs of age and wear. Even though there was no room for them to move, their hands and legs had been chained to the ground with heavy metal riveted restraints and with leatherhead straps immobilizing them. The way Daniel and Lisa argued over the hiss and screeches of their prisoners, they had become immune the sounds.

Lisa placed several ampules of vaccine into a padded case taking extreme care of the valuable contents almost as if she handled nitroglycerin. "You can't leave the project at this point especially after all we have done to get here. We still have distribution logistics and follow up with the other cities. The military is going to fly us to Germany for the meeting with the European team. Berlin is said to be 75% clear of re-ans as of last week. When this is all over, there's going to be all the post trial analysis and data collection. We're going to have foundations and governments throwing grants at us for the rest of our lives."

"I don't give a damn about this anymore. I'm done helping my fellow man for the greater cause." Daniel cinched the top of his pack closed. "We came up with the cure. You can take all the glory for all I care. All I want to do is destroy those bastards and send them back to hell where they belong."

"But we have so much more important work. We have to collaborate with Dr. Becotte in Seattle on the Omega virus. It doesn't matter if we eliminate the re-ans if we are going to be wiped out by this next plague." She swept her hand in front of her, drawing attention the room. "As primitive as this may be, we are still one of the most advance labs in operation, today. We are in the best position to stop the outbreak."

Throwing the bag over his shoulder, he replied, "I have full faith in you and Dr. Becotte saving the world. You can have my Nobel and use it as a doorstop if you want. I've already talked to John Colton who heads the civilian brigade here in Denver. His unit is going to be made full-fledged soldiers, in a few weeks, which means they get to use the big guns…for as long as we still have guns. I have to report to him in the morning, and his camp is in the trees on the edge of the red zone by Sloan's Lake."

Lisa stepped up to him, placed her hand on his chest, and said, "Look, I'm sorry about Wendy. I feel just as guilty as you do, but it's time to move on now. When this is all over, it will be a new world for all of us. We are all going to be different people; a new society will exist across the world. You and I can start new lives together. How can we go through all of this and not be together in the end?"

"You want to see how I've changed. You want to see why we can't be together anymore?" Daniel gently pushed her aside and grabbed a syringe and an ampule with the vaccine. He filled the syringe and stepped up to the nearest caged re-an and jabbed the needle into her neck and pressed the plunger down.

The naked decayed gray-skinned woman with the rotted teeth and partially exposed ribcage shook violently, while she let out a high-pitched scream, similar to the squeal of a hog being slaughtered. The undead woman in the next cage, shook with apparent anger groaning, hissing and spitting toward the two scientists.

Lisa called out, "What are you doing? You can't inject the vaccine directly into a re-an. You know that's going to-"

Daniel interrupted, "I'm well aware of what's going to happen. I'm glad it's going to happen and I would do it personally to all the meat bags if I could."

The female re-an injected with the vaccine continued to shake, hiss and spit up blood. Slowly, color returned to her skin changing it from gray to the peachy flesh tone of the living. Her white hazed over eyes cleared to show her brown pupils and her lips went from black to red as she changed back into a person. The excruciating high-pitched scream took on a deeper tone, sounding more human. Coughing up large amounts of blood, the dead woman turned her head toward Daniel and said the human words, "Kill me."

The angry scientist stood, watching her shake and suffer from the effects of coming back to life in a rotted body. As she finally quieted her screams and went limp inside her constraints, it seemed to send a message of fear into the other two re-ans as their moans and hissing intensified. They fought against their chains as their cages shook and rattled. Daniel turned back toward Lisa and said, "You're right about a new world. The only people left will be the survivors, and the strong. I promise you, the strong will show no mercy to these creatures."

Chapter 18

An orange glow from the fires scattered around the city reflected off the low clouds in the night sky. Occasional gunfire and distant explosions filled the background as the ongoing battle with the humans continued. General Brown sat on the cracked and broken concrete sidewalk, with his back against the only wall still standing in the remains of the old train station. He drank black coffee from a thermos with much of it dripping out of the bullet hole under his chin. Prometheus stood a few feet away and asked, "Can you really feel intoxicated from that strange brew?"

"I can't feel the numbness, but I'm aware of all the effects. Things get blurry, I get all dizzy, and then I stop caring about the stresses of all this mess." Brown flicked his wrist out at the street and crumbled buildings.

A young soldier with a five-inch hole through his chest walked up to him with an empty metal cup. "Hey Drips, can I get some of your Joe?"

Brown stretched his arm out and poured some coffee into the dead man's cup. As he poured, he spotted through the chest hole, his former body stagger around the corner. He stood and shoved the thermos into the soldier's hands and quickly walked toward the corner. "Hey, that's my body and I want it back."

The large living dead person, still wearing the General's uniform, stopped and gave him a quizzical stare. Brown closed the distance and shouted, "Give me back my body before I have to beat you out of it."

As he drew close, he saw the dried blood around his body's mouth and nose which brought back the sensations he had when he died.

The soul inside the large former general replied, "And how do you propose we switch bodies?"

"I don't give a damn how, it just better happen. I'll give you three seconds before I open a can of whoop-ass on you."

His body stared back with the same type of tempestuous expression he often gave to those who annoyed him. "I don't think so."

Brown reached his former self and gave him a push to the chest which did nothing to move the giant zombie. "This is my body and I'm taking it back."

His former self gazed down on Brown, and said, "I was 5' 4" and spent my entire life looking up to everybody. I had to stand, on my toes to reach anything. Women would not even give me a second glance. Even though I'm stuck in this hell," he waved his hand around at the surrounding buildings under the orange sky, "it's nice to finally be tall. I think I'm going to find a basketball court so I can finally see what it feels like to dunk a ball."

"That's it; I'm going to kick your butt, which happens to be my butt."

Brown threw a punch which landed in the center of his old chest and didn't even phase the tall undead. With much ease and only one hand, the man pushed him to the ground. Drunk from the coffee, his legs shook as the former general stood and took another swing at the large zombie in front of him. Before his fist came close to landing on its target, the large body smacked him on the side of the head, and sent him staggering into the street. As he turned back toward his former self, a grenade exploded and ripped the left arm off of his old body.

Prometheus saw several living move around the corner with flamethrowers. They laid down a wall of flames while more grenades arched over and landed, in the street, blowing chunks of asphalt into the air. Through the clearing smoke, a human charged Brown waving a Calvary sword. The old general picked up his former left arm off the ground, and with a backhand swing, he hit the man in the head, sending him to the pavement.

Captain Bartholomew and his troops spread throughout the block and engaged in hand to hand, fighting as the humans crawled out of the shadows to join the fight. Zombies poured out from under manhole covers and storm drains to match and eventually outnumber the living. As the wall of fire evaporated, Prometheus saw the sight of undead feasting on the soldiers, who operated the flamethrowers. Men screamed as the broken and decayed teeth of the dead army ripped off parts of their bodies.

Two more waves of humans quickly appeared out of the darkness. They swung axes and swords cutting off the heads of the zombies who feasted on their comrades. Bartholomew glanced up at the nearest building and waved his arm over his head. From the rooftop, a storm of arrows rained down. The deadly projectiles hit both the living and living dead. The undead only continued to fight with the arrows protruding from their backs looking like porcupines. More humans fell, and were feasted upon. Streams of blood trickled through the streets meandering around various pieces of bodies and building rubble.

Prometheus saw a young human charge at him with a sword. He backed up against the wall and had no other route of escape. As the man closed in with his blade, Patricia appeared in his view, and she decapitated the human with one clean swipe of her sword. As other humans charged, she easily fended them off. While slashing at two and three at a time, she quickly turned her head back to Prometheus and said, "Hey green eyes, you need to get to safety."

The Greek man hurried along the wall and through the fragments of a doorway. Inside the ruins of the former train station, he saw a tunnel which led to the underground. Thinking this would offer him the best security, he walked into the dark concourse. Muffled sounds of explosions and clashing metal from battle on the street above vibrated through the walls. Dripping water and the creaking sounds of stress on the passageway, echoed in the darkness, as he cautiously made his way to the end of the burrow which eventually opened into a large room. The ceiling above had gaping battle holes and light flickered in from the fires and fighting along with smoke and dust snaking down through the cracks.

In the center of the room, the remains of a large model train scene sat underneath the debris. Prometheus walked over, touched one of the small train cars, and gazed at the miniature scene of mountains and lakes rolling down to what looked like a happy town. Staring at the joyful place with tiny plastic people, he realized the descendants did at one time have a peaceful world. He touched the model Ferris wheel and watched it turn. As it rotated, it turned a music box and released a happy tune.

A shadow streaked across the model and he glanced up to see three livings walk toward him with axes and swords. They carried the weapons low, letting them drag on the ground. They appeared to be regular civilians rather that military. It had been a very long time since had seen a human not dressed in a soldier's uniform. He turned to escape back up the tunnel only to find four more humans blocking his exit. These men all wore ragged and dirty clothes which had not seen the likes of soap and water in months. They appeared to be civilians who formed into a lynch mob.

All of the living closed the circle on the Athenian. Prometheus backed up against the table with model train and scanned back and forth between the two sets of men who continued to move closer. They didn't have the usual look of fear the descendants had when they saw him. Their expressions were more of anger as they let out their evil sounding hisses and moans. He saw one of them swing an axe toward his head and all went silent and black.

Chapter 19

Prometheus opened his eyes and stared up at a dark orange sky with patches of black clouds fading into a gray haze hanging in the air. He heard the familiar sounds of explosions, clashing metal and screams of the livings, as the undead feasted on them. The ancient man tried to stand, but found a sword stuck through his chest had pinned him down. A soldier with two five-inch holes clean through his chest and abdomen walked up grabbed the handle of the sword and said, "Let me help you out my brother." He pulled the sword out and helped the Greek man to his feet.

Scanning his surroundings, he saw nothing but smoldering ruins and rubble of what used to be downtown Denver. Rusted skeletal frames of cars and burned remains of tanks were scattered between the large mounds of broken bricks and concrete. With no more tall buildings to block his view, Prometheus saw this repeated scene for as far as his eyes would carry. Peppered across this landscape undead Ravens and Turkey Vultures with rotted beaks, missing wings and feathers searched the ground for scraps to scavenge between the various small fires adding to the apocalyptic scene.

The soldier who helped him to his feet said, "You have the green eyes. This must not be your first trip to the Village of Dead Souls."

"Yes brother, this is my third journey to this futuristic and horrible land our descendants have created." Prometheus said as he noticed a long cylindrical iron furnace. The smoke emanating from the contraption merged with haze which continuously hung in the air.

Glancing over his shoulder, the soldier explained to the Greek man, "The humans built thousands of these emergency crematoriums. They try to burn the bodies, as fast as possible to keep them from returning as one of us. I don't know if it really matters anymore. Their numbers are not as great as they were a few years ago. We outnumber them in significant proportions."

Taking in the devastating world around him, the Athenian asked, "I wonder how long I've been gone this time?"

"What is the last thing you remember before your journey almost ended?"

"I was in the basement of what the descendants called a train station. I believe this is where I met my temporary demise."

"There hasn't been a train station around here for years." He glanced to his right and said, "Here's our commander. She's been here for a long time. Maybe she can help determine how long you've have been gone."

A tall woman, with long brown hair, a shapely athletic build, wearing a military jacket, and an old decayed bullet wound in her chest, walked up to the two dead men. She placed her sawed off shotgun in the holster, strapped across her back, and asked, "Who's the green eyes?"

The soldier with holes in his chest, replied, "I didn't get his name."

Bowing to the dead woman, the Athenian said, "Greetings my name is Prometheus and I-"

The woman cut him off. "You hail from ancient Greece. Yeah, I remember you."

"You have the advantage of remembering me, but may I get-"

Again, she interrupted. "I'm Hellion. Welcome back. It's been a while since I've heard your name mentioned. You'll find this world is much different now from the one you remember." Her eyes focused on something in the far distance. "We're on our way to take down a meat lab. Stick with me and I'll eventually get you back to your clan."

Several blocks later, they came to three olive green inflated Quonset huts. Undead grouped around the fallen soldiers who recently guarded the buildings and feasted on their bodies pulling out organs and flesh like a pack of hyenas. Another soldier, with a large hole punctured through the left side of his chest, walked up to Hellion. "Those two buildings are empty, just some tables and chairs." He pointed to the closest hut. "We heard some human moaning in this one, and formed a perimeter around it just like you instructed."

"Gather units blue and red to storm the place. Let's see what the humans were so intent on protecting."

The soldier waved his arm to signal five other dead soldiers to follow him. With a small explosion, blowing the metal door down, they ran inside through the small wall of smoke. Hellion motioned her hand for Prometheus to follow her.

Inside the dark building, she pulled out a flashlight. The beam gave glimpses of a makeshift laboratory. Metal autopsy tables with the carved up remains of former zombies, microscopes, Bunsen burners, and a few vertical glass coolers filled the room. At the far end, her soldiers had surrounded a human woman with shoulder length blonde hair. She wore a white lab coat and held in front of her the nozzle end of a flamethrower keeping her attackers away. She continued to yell out in her strange moans as a clear signal to stay back. Behind the lady scientist, stood five narrow cages, each with a single naked motionless zombie. Hellion said, "It's been a while since we captured a meat lab still in operation."

One of her soldiers asked, "What should we do?"

"Kill her and see if any those bodies still have a soul inside."

"But if we move closer, she's going to burn us."

Hellion pulled a knife from a sheath on her hip and threw it like a fastball. It landed right in the scientist's chest, causing her to release the flamethrower. She dropped to her knees, still babbling out long sentences of her untranslatable language. As blood oozed out from between her fingers, she pointed to Prometheus. Her eyes opened wide with a look of surprise on her face, giving the impression she recognized his body. She let out a few more groans and fell dead to the floor, as blood poured from her wound, and flowed across the ground.

The soldier with two holes in his chest stood near the cages. While poking at one of the bodies, he said, "It looks like these are all empty."

"Use that flamethrower to burn the bodies. This scientist lady probably injected them with the anti-virus. We don't want any of ours to come along and feed on them."

From the cage at the far end came a weak voice. "I'm not dead."

Turning her flashlight to the dark corner, they saw a naked dead woman holding the bars of her cage and staring back. She had long dark hair and smooth white skin, which showed almost no decay, except for the dried bullet hole in her chest over her heart. Hellion grabbed a set of keys from the dead scientist's pocket and tossed them to a soldier. "Let our sister out of the squirrel cage."

With the door open, the nude woman quickly stepped over to the dead scientist, pulled her lab coat off and slipped it on herself. As she buttoned the center button, she kicked the dead woman's body in the stomach. "How do you like that, bitch? I'm wearing your jacket. I bet that pisses you off." She reached over, grabbed a small bell from the nearby table, and rang it. "It's time for your medicine," she said, as she again kicked the dead woman in the stomach. Ringing the bell a second time, she yelled, "Pay attention. Your friends are going experience intense pain for the first time in years as they slowly die."

"I'm guessing it was bad." Hellion said, as she watched the lady continuously kick the dead woman.

The undead lady stopped her beating and tugged at her coat to straighten it out. "I've been in that cage for years. Watching her torture the other re-ans and waiting for the day it would be my turn. I must have been her control subject." She spit on the dead scientist. "Either that, or she had a crush on me."

"You referred to us as re-ans, so I'm guessing that you must be a modern."

Prometheus stepped forward and said, "Greetings. What is your name and from-"

Hellion pressed the palm of her hand into the Athenian's face cutting him off and pushing him back. She said, "I'm Hellion. I'm the leader of this rebel unit."

The lab coat lady finger combed her hair back and said, "I've heard of you. Some of my cellmates said they had fought with you. Name's Janel, but my friends call me Salsa."

"Salsa?"

"Yeah, that's my nickname. It went with my profession."

Hellion squinted her left eye and replied, "And that profession was?"

Salsa scanned the room and saw all the soldiers staring at her. "Pole dancer." She gave a quick glance to her figure. "I had a nice body before, but this one is smoking hot. I could have made so much more money with this bod."

As smiles crossed the faces of the undead men, Prometheus asked, "What is a pole dancer?"

Hellion replied, "I'll explain later."

Outside the building, the orange sky had turned black with smoke, blocking out the moon. Random rubble fires provided the only light. Hellion stood next to her two new arrivals as they watched the undead wandering aimlessly through the ruins of the city. Salsa mentioned, "Things sure have changed since I last stood outdoors. What city is this?"

Hellion replied, "It used to be Denver."

Another soldier with more holes in his chest, walked up to her and said, "We have some believers approaching."

"Great, a sermon right now is just what I need."

Prometheus turned and saw a small group of undead walking toward them. A smile came to his face as he recognized them. "Captain Bartholomew, the fair lady Patricia and the good Egyptian Nemi."

The pirate captain, now sporting an eye patch, stopped a few feet away and said, "Madam Hellion, We be hearing you captured a meat lab. Did ya be finding anyone?"

Hellion motioned her head toward Salsa. "This chick was one of their test rats." She placed her hand on Prometheus' back. "Green eyes here happens to be one of your lost puppies. I think you'll want him back."

Patricia stepped close to the young soldier's body and studied his eyes. "No. It can't be." She gave him a hug. "Brother Prometheus. It has been three long years since we have seen you last."

"Blimey, just when I thought there be nothing about dis world dat would surprise me. The Greek man be coming back again."

"Are you the pirate captains that I've heard about?" Salsa asked.

"Aye, we be the only pirates in these parts."

She faced Hellion. "I'm grateful and indebted to you for rescuing me, but I really want to hang with these guys for a while. I guess, I'm leaning more toward their cause than yours."

Hellion motioned her head toward the pirate captain. "Go ahead. You will not be much of a soldier if you don't want to be here."

As Prometheus and Salsa walked away with the pirates, he mentioned, "This world has changed rather dramatically since I last walked this ground."

Patricia replied, "Yes, the descendant's numbers have decreased to the point their society has collapsed. When we last spoke, it was a civil war between the living and the dead. The war evolved into a true apocalypse of the dead. As one of those walking dead, I fear for what may become of this world."

Bartholomew continued, "Even our clan be having nightly debates about us continuing to collect the strings of life. There be so few living left, we don't know if we can save them anymore."

Prometheus asked, "Why do you continue this war if it is killing those we intend to save?"

"We be not killing da living as fast as the plague."

"What plague?"

Salsa joined in the conversation. "It's called the Omega virus. It began spreading around the globe back at the start of this re-an uprising. Nobody paid attention to it at first. Bodies rising from the dead got more attention than a few people coughing up blood did. Once the health community realized what they had on their hands, there were not enough scientists and labs left to find a cure. A few years back when I died, the virus was killing more people than the re-ans."

Prometheus glanced toward the lady pirate. "The fair Patricia. Do you not carry the gift of a remedy for this plague?"

"Yes, this is my job to pass a cure for the Omega plague on to our descendants. Unfortunately, we still have no idea how to pass this to them, and they are still intent on wiping, us from the surface of this planet."

* * *

Daniel Cronsworth placed another lit candle under the little iron boiler of a miniature tabletop model steam engine. The heated gas from the tank shot through narrow twisted copper tubes into the cylinder, which pushed the piston back and forth. The piston turned a wheel connected to a small generator with wires running to a single light bulb. The dim yellow light flickered across the map spread out on a piece of scrap plywood, set atop a few cinderblocks. Several men in the civilian militia stood around the makeshift table and studied the parchment.

John Colton placed himself on the opposite side of the map. He wore a tattered brown canvas jacket covered with splattered blood and burn marks. Underneath the coat, his black shirt no longer showed signs it was once a police officer uniform. He asked, "How are we doing on fuel for the flamethrower?"

"We're down to one tank."

"Shotgun shells?"

"We have ten. Six are reloads with gravel."

Colton rubbed his chin and replied, "Let's save those in case we are overrun. We'll make axes and blades our primary weapons." He glanced over at the doctor. "Daniel, how's our food rations?"

"We're low on bread and dried fruits. There's thirty cases of canned beans and eight pounds of dried noodles. The military gave us twenty pounds of rice, but we gave half of that to a caravan of folks headed to the coast in exchange for fixing our main generator."

"It looks like we'll be eating a lot of beans for a while. How's the greenhouse looking? What about the fresh vegetables?"

"We have guards posted night and day at the greenhouse. So far, there hasn't been any trouble, but it's pretty well hidden. The corn, tomatoes, green beans, squash and spinach are all starting to grow. If we can keep the boiler running, they should be ready for harvest in two months. We're working on making a trade with the Boulder militia for some watermelon seeds."

"What about the horses? How are they doing?"

"The horses are doing fine. They are grazing out in the fields and drinking from the river. They have it better than us."

Colton brought his attention back to the map. "Okay, I talked to East Arapahoe and they gave me the details of the offensive tomorrow. Every remaining civilian militia in North America, combined with local military units is going to launch a blitz on all re-an tribes within reach. It's our version of a zombie Tet Offensive. We've been assigned to move on the Lodo tribe around the old Union Station." He pointed to the spot on the map. "The regular soldiers are going to lead the show. We're going to hang back and cover their flanks."

Daniel asked, "When do we move?"

"The re-ans are more active at night. If we hit them right around dusk, we can catch them at the time they are most vulnerable."

* * *

Standing on the second and highest floor in the skeletal remains of what used to be a skyscraper, Colton raised a pair of binoculars to his eyes. A quarter mile away, he saw the thirty to forty re-ans staggering aimlessly around the scattered rubble. The walking partially decomposed corpses wore ragged and torn clothes, which covered their gray rotted skin. Mixed among them, undead coyotes sniffed the ground in their search for something living. A hundred yards away, sixty soldiers hid behind piles of shattered concrete, burnt out tanks, and inside blast craters waiting for their orders to attack. Between them and the living dead, lay an open field of dirt, which once used to be the heart of the downtown nightclub district.

Colton lowered the field glasses and quietly said to Daniel, "The regulars are in place. Those walking meat bags are going get mowed down before they get the chance to drool on themselves."

One of the soldiers closest to the open field, waved his hand to the men next to him, signaling it was time for them to move. All ten men sprang up, jumped over the dirt mound in front of them and ran across the field with shotguns in-hand. The re-ans didn't react. They only continued their directionless wandering.

Remaining in tight formation, the ten soldiers closed to within thirty yards and raised their shotguns to their shoulders. Around twenty-five yards, the ground beneath them gave way and they all fell into a deep concealed pit. Three foot long, sharpened wooden spikes, five inches in diameter, lined the entire bottom of the hole. The soldiers all became impaled as the several stilettos pierced through their bodies and killed them instantly.

The aimless walking of the re-ans turned into a coordinated charge toward the second wave of soldiers who carried flamethrowers and laid down a wall of flames. Through the wall of fire, burning zombies staggered toward the soldiers, grabbing them in a death hug, which spread the fire causing their fuel tanks to explode.

Attacking from both flanks, the remaining soldiers moved in launching grenades into the center of the battle. The explosions tore re-ans apart, but the upper portions of their decomposed bodies continued to crawl and roll toward their enemy.

Hundreds of re-ans emerged from the sewers, dark shadows of building ruins, and the side streets. They had all the regulars surrounded and closed in the circle. Daniel asked, "Do we move now?"

Colton raised his hand and yelled, "We need to get down there and clear a hole in this wave of re-ans so the regulars can pull back." Throwing his arm forward, he said, "Let's go!"

The former police officer led the charge with Daniel and the other men close behind. Coming in contact with the first wave of zombies, they quickly swung their modified axes with serrated blades, and makeshift swords made from scrap metal, and they sliced the heads, arms, and legs off the undead.

They opened a small clearing in the rear wave of zombies as hundreds more continued to pour in from below ground and the dark corners of the crumbled buildings. One of the regular soldiers called out, "Pull back!" and they made their way through the small opening as it closed tighter. Several of the soldiers, who were killed in the pit, crawled out with glassy eyes and staggered around in a confused state. Several of the wounded soldiers tried to crawl toward safety, but the dead coyotes pounced on them, finishing the job.

Colton helped the last soldier through the opening and gave a quick scan to see if there were any more men alive in the midst of the horde. He turned back toward his retreating men and stepped on a hidden bear leg spring trap. The steel contraption clamped down on his lower shin, shattering his bones as the large sharp teeth dug in deep. He fell to the ground and heard the crack and crunch of his ankle. Looking down on the trap, he saw his foot turned backwards pointing the opposite way of his knee.

Trying to pry the vise open, he only managed to cut up his fingers and hands. A quick glance at his men, and he saw them all with their backs turned, still retreating to safe ground. Turning back to his mangled foot, he saw a pair of leather boots standing next to the trap. Slowly, his eyes followed up the legs inside those boots, until he saw a tall female re-an wearing a tattered camouflage jacket, with a sawed off shotgun strapped to her back. Her stringy long brown hair hung down to her shoulder and helped hide her sickly gray skin. Parts of her jawbone were visible through the open decayed holes in the side of her face.

Colton knew he was done. He lay back on the ground and watched the dead woman pull her weapon off her back. She pointed the barrel directly at his face and held it inches away.

The former police officer thought about the time he came home with a new puppy. His five-year-old son came running out the front door of their house with a smile spread from ear to ear. His wife stood on the porch, with her arms crossed in front of her, watching their son grasp the little dog under a clear blue sky. The air smelled like fresh cut grass. His son rolled on the lawn, as the puppy licked his face. As he turned toward his wife, all went silent and black.

Chapter 20

Hundreds of candles, placed throughout the tunnel, provided the only light in the underground cavern. The flickering yellow glow, which faded off and disappeared in the distant darkness, cast shadows on the old rock and brick structure. Tiny bits of mortar and dirt flaked off the arched roof and left thin streams of dust like strings hanging from the ceiling. The dripping sounds echoed through the passageway, while small patches of water oozed through the sections of the old worn brick walls. Prometheus and Itaiyo walked past two undead working a forge while a third hammered red hot metal on an anvil.

"There's a big advantage to having all of you ancients. Blacksmithing and sword making has been a lost art with all of us moderns," Itaiyo commented, as he watched the red glowing sparks fly from the metal and bounce along the ground.

Prometheus responded, "Considering all of the magnificence this world has to offer, it is odd as to how the skills from my place in history, seem to have become the necessities for our survival."

With the metal works in the distant end of the tunnel, the two living dead approached a table with Captain Bartholomew, Patricia, Salsa and several others. More candles lit the area with a yellow flicker. Spread out in front of them was a hand drawn map of the city with areas marked as descendants and dead. Remembering their last meeting held in the former library, Prometheus scanned his surroundings and asked with some confusion, "What is this cavern where we stand? Why do we not gather in that grand building called a library?"

Itaiyo replied, "The library's gone. The army kept blowing up any buildings where we gathered. There's not much left on the surface for us or the humans to occupy." He waved his hand over his head at the bricks above him. "These tunnels were built under the city back in the late 1800's. They ran between the upscale hotels and the brothels, so the socialites could get there and back without being seen. Because of the powerful people using these passages to get to the hookers, the city didn't exactly brag about their existence. As the decades passed, and the brothels closed down, people forgot these things existed. Apparently, these don't show up on any current charts used by the army, so we're somewhat safe down here."

Bartholomew pointed to the map spread out on the table and said, "Dis be our position here. Da soldiers be holed up in these spots here, here, and along here. If we still be trying to collect da strings of life, there be no more livings in what da moderns call downtown. We be needing to send our gathering parties out further beyond the soldier encampments." He glanced over at General Brown, who sat along the wall holding his thermos filled with coffee and staring blankly at the opposite wall. "What do you have ta say, army man? They be telling me you once served in dis military with all the fancy guns and sky ships."

While he continued to stare at the wet ground in front of him, Brown answered, "You're going to find the majority of livings along the rivers. They need the water and most have built waterwheels to turn generators for electric light and radios. Only these river colonies are most likely to have been vaccinated, so we can't use their flesh." He took a sip from his thermos and some of the brown liquid dripped out of the bullet hole under his chin. "The ones you want are further back in the trees. They're trying to isolate themselves from what's left of society. Most of them are too afraid to get vaccinated."

Bartholomew asked, "How we be finding these tree dwellers, if they don't be wanting to be found?"

"Simple, they build fires for cooking and to keep warm. Just look for the smoke rising from the trees during the day and the fire light after dark."

Prometheus studied the map and pointed to the four corners of the dead area. "What if we break off into four new villages placed at the edge of our land. We would have less distance to travel in our ventures to these tree clans. It would also split up the descendant's army. Instead of focusing their strengths on one large group of us undead, they would have to confront the four different villages spread out in four different areas. It should give us a better chance of one clan gathering the required strings of life."

Nemi, the Egyptian, responded, "Like the Clan Titus led by the Valkyrie, Hellion, I have doubts about us collecting these strings for the god's purpose." He pointed to Prometheus. "Look at our brother. He has worn the green eyes for many years and has yet to graduate to the blue. What comes of the final level, if we cannot tell the descendants for what purpose we exist, and how we are here to help?"

"Why don't we just tell them or write a note on the ground?" Salsa asked, as she stepped out of the shadows and into the candle light.

The others around the table turned to her with confusion expressed on their lifeless faces. Patricia answered, "Have you not heard the screeching and hissing they use to speak. Their written words are nothing more than scribble and non-sense. We have no way of communicating our message to them."

Prometheus added, "Without the ability to speak in a common language, we are permanently cut apart."

As if she had no idea what they just told her, Salsa responded, "All we need to do is write the message down. I know they can't understand us when we speak, but they should be able to read our writing." She glanced around at the confused faces around her and realized that she needed to clarify her point. "When I was in that cage, being tortured by that witch, I tried so many times to take her clipboard away so I could simply write down a message."

Patricia said, "Our writing appears to them, the same as theirs appears to us. It comes across as nothing but scribble."

Throwing her hands in the air, Salsa replied, "I have no idea what you guys are talking about."

Bartholomew tapped his finger on the map. "We be discussing this at a later time. For now, we must concentrate our efforts. I believe our friend Prometheus may have a good plan."

As the pirate captain continued to talk, Itaiyo glanced over at Salsa and asked, "If you got your hands on that lady's clipboard, what were you going to write?"

"The first thing I wanted to tell her was to stop calling me Subject 143." Salsa answered in a low voice, so she wouldn't disrupt the conversation. "I'm sure that would have been followed with something along the lines of; take your hands off me, you damn dirty ape."

Itaiyo gave a bit of smirk at the humor in her message. His face quickly changed to serious, as he realized what she just said, while the rest of the conversation trickled off to silence as the attention focused back on her. Salsa glanced at the undead around her with their faces partially shadowed with the flicker of the candle flames. "What…what did I say?" Her voice echoed down the dark tunnel as another chip of mortar fell from the ancient structure and dripping water filled the temporary silent void.

Bartholomew stood up straight and placed his hand on the pommel of his sword strapped to his hip. He squinted his one good eye while staring at her. "Da you mean ta say ya can understand da speak of da living?"

"Yeah, that's the gift I'm supposed to give to them. I can understand all languages. I thought we all had one of these super power things we would pass along, so they could survive another million years or something like that."

Nemi asked, "You can understand what they are saying?"

"Yes, I can understand what they are saying and what they are writing. I thought all of you could do that."

Patricia responded, "Only you have the ability to hear their voices. Can they understand you?"

"I tried for years to reason with that bitch that held me in a cage. If she could understand me, she kept it to herself. I don't know if they could read my writing. I figured they could, because I could read theirs."

Bartholomew handed her a piece of charcoal and said, "Write some words on this map. If it looks like the scratch of the descendants we may be able to speak with them."

Salsa took the charcoal and wrote, "Greetings, take me to your leader." The rest of the undead around the table gave out a sigh of disappointment as they read the message. Nemi said, "This places us back to our position of the all the years we have occupied these bodies. We will never be able to speak our intentions and this war will continue. This is a never ending circle of tragedy."

Prometheus stared into Salsa's eyes and came to a realization. "We do not feed on the living to sustain our bodies. We only do it to collect the strings of life. If we concentrate all the strings on the fair Salsa, she may be able to reach the level of blue eyes and we would have our bridge allowing us to speak to the descendants. This could end the war and allow us to work together on passing our gifts. Hopefully, the gods will see we have completed our mission and they will let us continue our journey to the afterlife in peace."

While he pondered the plan, Bartholomew twisted his sword back and forth in its sheath, causing the leather to creak. He studied Salsa, who still wore only the white lab coat stained with the scientist's blood, and replied, "You be having a point, me friend. With the limited amount of living who do not carry da fire, if we be giving our sister all the good bites of meat, she can become da town crier carrying da message between all tribes."

Prometheus asked, "What is the fire?"

Patricia told him, "Some of the descendants have been injected with something called the anti-virus. If anyone tries to collect strings of life from one who carries the fire inside them, they will burn from the inside and cease to exist in this world."

Itaiyo interjected, "This makes sense then. If we choose Salsa as the one who gets all the good DNA, she should be able to carry our message to the living, she would be able to speak to them and eventually pass her abilities so they can talk to us."

Hearing these words brought the ancient Greek man to a sudden realization. "That's it!" Prometheus blurted out." The others turned to him, looking for an answer to his outburst. He smiled and pointed toward her. "Our sister, Salsa, she is the chosen one."

Bartholomew asked, "What do you mean by the chosen one?"

"The prophecy, KC from Golden, her mission was to teach us the prophecy. It revolved around the chosen one."

Patricia asked, "What is this prophecy?"

"I have forgotten the words in the exact order we were to remember them."

A few feet down the tunnel, Princess Rachel in the body of the Harajuku girl, stepped into the light. "I remember the words. It was important that we never forget them." She thought for a moment, and then recited, "The soft colored song will carry the words of the chosen one. These words will be held silent for 100 years until the one who holds the spark of the flame, gives them to the children of the descendants."

Itaiyo said, "So if she can translate human and zombie-speak, Salsa must be the chosen one. The rest of it doesn't make sense, but I think she's the key to ending this war."

* * *

Daniel stood by the fire and stared at the flames as they danced into the air. He thought about how primitive his life had become and how something as simple as a fire became a luxury in these types of living conditions. Memories of living in a house with running water and a home theater seemed like some other distant life.

Another citizen militia approached with a modified battle-axe strapped to his hip like a sword. His tattered brown canvas jacket showed years of confrontations with the re-ans, as did his weathered face and the long scare down his cheek. He held his leathered hands out to warm them in the flames, as the cool air settled down around them in the final hour of sunlight for the day. He glanced at the scientist and asked, "You new?"

"I joined up a few weeks back." Daniel answered.

The man with the axe stuck his hand out and said, "Name's Larski, Jeremy Larski."

Returning the handshake, Daniel replied, "Daniel Cronsworth."

Jeremy thought for a moment as he gazed at the new man. "Cronsworth, aren't you that scientist who came up with the re-an vaccination? I remember seeing you on the news, before the all the broadcasts stopped a few years ago. In fact, it was probably the last thing I ever saw on television."

"I was one of several researchers who collaborated on the vaccine." He scanned Jeremy's clothes and saw his sun-damaged face with the deep scar across his left cheek. "You look like you've been in this unit for a long time. Your scar is deep. It appears to have healed a long time ago."

A crack of a twig caught Jeremy's attention for a second, as he slightly turned his head toward the trees where the sound originated. "I joined up back at the beginning, when we were the crazies who shouldn't be taking the law into our own hands. Now, what's left of the population looks to us as the only remaining fragments of order and law."

"What did you do back before the uprising?"

Larski brought his attention back to the fire and continued warming his hands. "I sat behind a desk all day staring at a computer monitor as a data analyst. I spent my days dreaming of a time when I wouldn't have to look at a screen." He gazed to the top of the fire with a distant stare. "It's been eight years since I've touched a computer. It's been four years since I saw one in working condition."

"What made you join up?"

"Same as all the others, back then I lost my family. Those demon scums ambushed us as we came home. We had heard about the re-ans, but only saw them on the news. After the first couple of weeks, they weren't even the top story at night. I figured there was no way they would spread out to the suburbs. We never saw a need to change our life for something that would go away in a few months. They got to my wife as I tried to find a weapon in the garage. I held her in my arms through the night as she turned. Before I could destroy her body, she bit the kids." He glanced up from the fire at Daniel. "Why'd you join up? You must've had it good. As one of the Government VIP's, you probably had a steady supply of food, hours of electricity every day, a roof over your head, clean water, hot showers and military protection. Not many people would leave those luxuries for the caveman life."

Out in the trees, another crack of a twig caught the attention of both men. As the sound dissipated into the breeze through the brush, Daniel answered, "There's not much Government left these days. Even the military is starting to ration supplies between the compounds," he paused for a moment, and then continued. "I lost my wife days before the vaccine went public. I also held her in my arms as she transformed into a re-an. After that, I didn't want to fight from behind a microscope any more."

"Still, you were close to what's left of a government. What news did you hear about the outside world? I'm sure you had access to a radio."

"There's all kinds of reports coming in from all over, but I learned the real news is what you didn't hear. China, Greece, and the entire continent of Africa have gone dark. As soon as information, broadcasts, or curriers stop coming from a country, they are crossed off the map. Nobody tries to send help or find out what the situation is, just act as though the country no longer exists."

"I knew about Greece, but not Africa." Jeremy went back to warming his hands. "What about the elections? I heard the government was going to hold elections this year. There's even going to be new positions for people to hold. Stuff like Minister of Food Supply and Secretary of Electricity Rations."

Daniel shook his head and brought his gaze down to his feet. "There's not going to be any elections or any new jobs. That's just something they leaked to the public to raise hopes. With all the areas that have gone dark just in the States, it's hard to consider us one continuous country anymore. Eighteen states no longer exist and three more are on their way out. The only power on the grid is coming from the three remaining nuclear plants."

"What about Hawaii? There're rumors they were never affected by the uprising. If you can make it out there, it's life as it used to be."

Daniel shook his head in despair. "No, Hawaii was the first state to go black."

Another dried stick snap in the trees, drawing their attention. The crack turned into soft footsteps, which soon developed into several sets of feet. Daniel grabbed an old steel fencepost that had been sharpened into a sword, and he held it toward the source of the sound. Jeremy kept one hand on his axe, and gently waved the palm of his other hand toward the scientist, wanting him to lower the weapon.

Through the trees, Daniel saw two more civilian militia men appear at the other side of the fire. One had a sawed off shotgun in his hand and the other carried a modified battle axe. Between the two men, they held the arms of a woman wearing an olive green jacket, shirt and pants. The standard issue clothing the military had been handing out to civilians. She kept her face down so the others could not see her. One of the men said to Jeremy, "We found her out by the farm. She said she wants to join our cause."

Larski glanced at the woman and turned his attention back to the fire. As he rubbed his hands, he said, "Okay, take her to the compound. Olivia said she could use some help in the med tent."

The man standing next to the mysterious woman replied, "I tried to take her there, but she said she has some kind of special intel and skills we might find useful on the front lines." He hesitated for a moment and cleared his throat. "I think you need to hear who she is."

Jeremy lowered his hands, turned to her and said, "We really don't have any standards here as to who gets to fight, so if you want to be on the frontlines, it's your call. What's your name and who are you that I need to approve whether you get to join our cause?"

The lady with the reddish-brown hair turned her head up and let the light of the fire illuminate her face. "I think you might know me by the name of Pink."

Chapter 21

The low clouds in the night sky continued to glow orange from the many bonfires scattered across the Front Range and they cast a dim glow on the land. Smoke from numerous makeshift crematoriums maintained a constant haze hanging in the air. Through the trees, distant fires flickered like single candles flames. Prometheus stood behind a tree watching the narrow dirt road for any movement. Midnight waited next to him, staring in the opposite direction. Dispersed through the forest, he could see glimpses of his fellow undead, all waiting for something living to come down the road.

Midnight spoke in a low voice and asked the Athenian, "Seeing how you are from ancient Greece, you should be able to confirm or deny one of the biggest mysteries of your time."

With a bit of interest in her question, he slightly turned from his post toward her. "What is this great mystery?"

"Did Atlantis really exist?"

The question slightly confused him. He briefly took his eyes off the road and glanced at the former dancehall girl. "Of course, Atlantis really existed. Why would anyone consider this to be a mystery?"

"During my lifetime, which was a little over a hundred years ago, no one could find the city. Maybe they've found it since then, but I haven't seen a newspaper in a very long time." Midnight brought her attention back to the road. "The only written record of it existed in Homer's, *Odyssey,* and that was a work of fiction."

"Of course, Atlantis existed. I visited the fine city many times." Hearing her speak of his time in such a way, slightly angered the normally gentle man. "What do you mean; the *Odyssey* was a work of fiction? It was considered one of the greatest plays of our time. If you are familiar with it, this would indicate it lasted through the centuries."

"He did speak of actual cities and islands, but Homer also wrote about a giant Cyclops and witches turning men into pigs. Did you ever see a Cyclops? Did you ever meet a witch?"

"I…" Prometheus thought back and realized that, even though he never doubted their existence, he never did see such a beast. "I may have never seen such a creature, but many a good man saw and engaged in battle with the giants. If witches did not exist, then why would so many men speak of them?"

"Did you personally know someone who fought a Cyclops or was it a friend of a friend situation?"

The question made him again realize all his knowledge of the legend were based on stories passed down through the generations, and he had taken them as fact, with no other basis than to believe his elders. "I may have never met such a warrior, but so many men have claimed to have battled the beasts, how could they all be speaking non-truths?"

Captain Bartholomew and Patricia quietly walked up to the Greek man, causing him to halt his argument. Midnight tilted toward the pair and said, "Speaking of fiction, this is something that I never would have believed unless I saw it for myself."

Patricia asked, "What did you need to see?"

"If someone had told me, while I was alive, that I would one day join a band of rebels led by a pair of undead lovebird pirates, I would have considered them to be gale-minded."

Both of the pirates gave slight smirks as they glanced toward each other. Bartholomew replied, "I would have thought da same thing. Hearing such demented words would cause me ta run such a person through with me sword to rid them of da dementia." He glanced at Patricia and squeezed her hand.

Human voices emanating from the darkness at the far end of the road, stopped their conversation, as they all turned toward the source of the sound. Bartholomew and Patricia stepped up to the edge of the shadows bordering the road to gain a better view. Prometheus noticed how their hands automatically pressed down on the pommel of their swords, as if they prepared to board a merchant ship. Soft footsteps on the rocks and dirt, blended with the hiss and moans of the living voices as they rose in volume indicating they drew closer.

Through a sliver of gray light strapped across the road, the small band of humans appeared briefly before vanishing back into the darkness. Bartholomew whispered, "They didn't look like soldiers."

Patricia answered, "They might still have weapons. The glimpse we had was too brief to see if they are armed."

The voices and footsteps grew louder as the group of living came within view inside the gray light. They did not appear to be military and showed no signs of weapons. It looked to be several families searching for a safe location. They carried large backpacks stuffed to capacity with additional gear attached to the outside. Their clothes looked to be mismatched items, showing many years of wear and they hung loosely on their bodies. A few of them pulled wagons overflowing with bundles of supplies. The humans became too involved in their own conversation to notice three undead stepping onto the road and following behind them. As one of the re-ans shuffled a foot on the gravel, a young woman in the group of livings noticed and casually turned her head to check the source of the sound.

Spotting the zombies in the distance, she quickly alerted the others and they immediately ran down the road to escape the danger. As they entered a shadowed section of the road, twenty more re-ans sprang out of the trees and pounced on them, like lions on prey.

The humans screeched and howled in fear, as they tried to fight off the dead who were armed with swords and pikes. The men circled around the women trying to protect them. They pulled out baseball bats and heavy wood clubs, swinging wildly at their attackers. The primitive weapons would make contact with the living dead, but would not do more than knock them down. Using swords and pikes, the re-ans impaled several men and slashed across some of the women. Blood sprayed and spurted across the group as several of the humans fell to the ground with their intestines spilling out onto the road.

One of the human males stepped out of the group and smashed one of the older grays with a bat. The impact was so intense that it crushed the re-ans head like a melon. Another zombie jumped on the man's back, and bit into the lower part of his neck, where it joined with the shoulder. Lifting his head, the undead attacker pulled a large chunk of flesh out, between his teeth, with blood gushing from the wound and pouring out of the dead soul's mouth. Bartholomew ran his sword through the man's stomach and partially into the re-an still on livings back. The man fell to the ground with the zombie still on top of him. The living person went silent, as the undead assailant frantically rolled around on the ground, screaming in pain, grabbing his head and pulling at his skin. He even tore pieces of his own flesh off as if it were the cause his agony.

The other living dead, surrounding the pile of humans, quickly turned to watch their fellow clan member on the ground. Most of the humans lay dead, while the others who remained partially alive slowly tried to crawl away from the pile, releasing low moans interjected with some hissing.

Watching the zombie convulse with pain, Prometheus asked, "Why does he thrash about in such pain?"

Bartholomew shook his head in despair, and answered, "He bit the flesh of a human who has the fire." He swung his sword across the screaming re-an's throat, severing his head and silencing his screams.

Midnight walked around the pile of living victims scanning each individual body. "All of these livings have been injected with the antivirus." She pointed to a woman drenched with blood, who had a gash cut down her front, and she was missing part of one arm from the elbow down. The human used her intact arm, trying to pull herself along the ground and leaving a wide trail of crimson mud. "This one here does not have the black inside her. I don't think she's been injected."

The pirate captain took out his dagger from his belt, stepped over to the woman, bent over her and carved out a handful of flesh from the human's shoulder. The woman screamed and hissed as she tried to hammer the undead man with her good arm. Bartholomew dismissed her efforts to fight back and tossed the chunk of flesh to one of the re-ans circled around the pile of humans. "Here ya go. Ya be testing this to see if it be holding the fire."

The zombie, who caught the piece of shoulder muscle, took a large bite and chewed it up with blood oozing down the corners of his mouth. The others watched in silence to see if he would fall to the ground in pain. A few seconds passed and the re-an shoved the remaining piece of flesh into his mouth with no ill effects.

"It be seeming she is clean of da fire." Bartholomew said as he reached down and cut a large square from the woman's leg while she continued to scream and roll on the ground. He tossed the piece of leg muscle to Salsa. "This be for you, me lady."

The former dancer, now wearing universal camouflage clothing, caught the piece of flesh and quickly bit into it. Blood dripped down her military jacket, as she used her palm to force the large raw meat into her mouth. As the pirate stepped away from the woman, who was still clinging by a thread to life, the other undead pounced on her like a flock of vultures on a fresh kill. It took another minute, before the ear piercing screams and moans from the woman buried at the bottom of re-ans, ceased.

* * *

Daniel struck his knife against the piece of flint, sending white sparks into the dry kindling, igniting a fire underneath the small still constructed from scavenged parts. The main pot was an old pressure cooker with the handle broken off. It sat on top of two rocks with the fire between them. A copper tube connected to the steam vent ran into the lid of an insulated sports bottle. A second tube carried the steam out of the container through a long coiled section with the condensed alcohol dripping into a plastic Sponge Bob Square Pants cup.

He blew on the embers to heat it up and then turned back to Pink, who sat in front of the main fire warming her hands. As he sat down, he explained,

"We need the alcohol to sterilize cuts and wounds. If the military comes through with the two hundred pounds of corn, they promised us, we can build a larger still and make enough to power the generators. Maybe we can even get one of the vehicles running." Daniel said as he walked away from the boiler and sat next to her on the log.

Pink continued to stare at the fire and replied, "We're not in the real world any more. You don't have to rationalize it."

With a quizzical expression, he glanced at her and replied, "I don't understand."

"This isn't the society where we grew up and lived. There are no more rules here other than to survive. If you want to sip some moonshine, get a buzz going, and forget about our fate for a while, nobody's going to arrest you, judge you, or even care. The morality we once used as our measurement of decency no longer exists in this caveman world."

The scientist reached into his backpack lying next to the log and pulled out a plastic bottle labeled carpet cleaner. Unscrewing the cap, he tilted it up and took a swig. Offering it to Pink, he said, "I made this last week. I found a Juniper tree with just enough berries to make a batch. It has a little more flavor than the rice moonshine."

Pink took a swig from the bottle and handed it back to him with little reaction to the taste or the strength. "You need a bigger bump keg and longer condensation coil. You're getting some methanol bleed through and losing some alcohol from evaporation."

Daniel glanced at the plastic bottle. "You got all that from one sip?"

"All these years, you've been distilling in your fancy lab. You had clean conditions, controlled temperatures and cultured yeast. You were doing it for research purposes, but I'm sure you occasionally thought you were so bad when you sneaked a sip. Out here," Pink waved her hand at the surrounding forest, "we've been mashing in caves and bunkers for our survival. We learned that once you light that pot, you have to post guards. If the smell didn't draw nomads and wanderers set on hijacking your stash, it would bring the Ravens, which meant the re-ans would be close behind." She turned toward the scientist. "We had to make the decision to use potato for food or shine. You would think it would be a no brainer and food would always win, but it's been years since I've eaten a potato. So yeah, I could tell all that from one sip. When we made our shine, we had to do it quickly and we had to do it right. "

"Great. We should put you in charge of distilling. There really is a need to use the alcohol for first aid and fuel."

She brought her attention back to the fire as the light in the dark orange and gray sky continued to grow dim. "That's not why I'm here. If I wanted to make booze, I could have stayed out there."

A crack from the trees put Daniel on guard, and he reached for his machete. Pink remained calm and stared at the flames dancing into the air. As the scientist calmed his alert, he relaxed and asked, "Why are you here?"

"I heard you had joined the cause and wanted to talk you out of it."

Daniel shook his head in disbelief. "I thought we were on the same side with the same goal. You don't still consider these creatures to be," he paused to think, "What did you call them back then, 'Second Lifers.'"

"We do have the same goal." She replied with a condescending tone. "I'm well aware of what these demons are. You are of no use out here."

"I want to fight until this planet is rid of these demons." Daniel turned back to the fire.

"As do I. But, we are never going to win with brute force. Look at us." She circled her hands at their small camp. "We're down to fighting with sticks and rocks. Every time we lose a soldier, they gain one more. The battle was lost on the first day and we just didn't see it."

"It sounds like you've given up."

"No, you gave up. We need you back in your lab, making a stronger anti-virus. It won't be long until the re-ans adapt to this strain and make it useless."

"There's plenty of labs making anti-virus. I'm taking my fight to the front lines. I'm not going to hide behind test tubes any longer."

"No, that's how we are going to lose this war. Think about it. How are we being wiped out? Look at the damage the Omega virus did to our population. The re-ans are killing us with their cells. This is a war where the front lines are on a microscopic level."

Three civilian militiamen appeared through the dark shadows of the trees in the dimming light of dusk and shouldered their scrap metal swords. The man with a bushy red beard stepped forward and said, "We were down by the road when we smelled your mash. You wouldn't have any extra? Our med kit is out of antiseptic." He gave a slight smile, indicating he didn't really think they would believe that he wanted it for medical reasons.

Pink rolled her eyes and continued her conversation with Daniel. "Think about how fast the Omega virus killed off China and Eastern Europe. We can do the same to the re-ans. If you and the other lab geeks can get our remaining population vaccinated, by this time next year, we will be rebuilding our society. We'll have electricity and hot showers, instead of hiding in the trees."

Bushy Red Beard chimed in and said, "Ah, guys?"

Daniel glanced up and saw the man pointing to the ground at the edge of the fire light. He stood up to see over the fire and saw the rotted body of a dead Raven bound into the clearing. It pecked at the ground, and then looked up at the humans. It had one eye missing and a decayed hole in its chest with small broken ribs protruding. Daniel grabbed his battle-axe and stood ready to fight. The three militia soldiers held out their swords and stepped back to back, watching all points of the clearing. Pink remained sitting on the log, warming her hands showing little concern over the possibility of an attack.

From the trees, behind the Raven, came the low moaning sounds of the re-ans. The men formed a wall in front of Pink. Daniel saw movement in the shadows of the tree and said, "There they are."

Six re-ans slowly emerged from the darkness into the light of the fire. Their torn clothing was encrusted with dried blood and it covered their decayed gray skin. The smell of rotten meat swept through the camp as they staggered closer to the fire. Their moans mixed with hissing gave an eerie chill to the already cold air. Blood mixed with saliva dripped from their black and broken teeth. One of them held out his hand with bones showing through the dead skin as he screeched.

Bushy Red Beard said, "We need to move around and encircle them. That's our best chance of not getting bitten. You two go to the left. Me and this guy will-"

Pink stood up and cut him off. "You idiots." She reached into Daniels backpack and pulled out the bottle of moonshine. "Stand back!" she barked out at the soldiers, who parted, giving her clear line of sight to the undead.

The men took a few steps back from the fire as the demons closed the distance. Pink, unscrewed the top of the bottle and threw the contents at the re-ans. As the alcohol flew over the top of the fire, it ignited and landed on the undead. The zombies burst into flames as their screeches intensified. They staggered into each other and fell to the ground with their dried clothing sending colored flames into the darkness. As their movement ceased, Daniel saw their blackened charred bodies continue to boil from the small amounts of burning fat left under their skin.

Pink reached into her pack and pulled out a sawed-off shotgun. She turned away from the fire toward the dark forest behind her. "Those re-ans were the distraction. They wanted to draw our attention over there, so they could sneak up behind us."

Two more zombies staggered out of the darkness into the light. She walked right up to their rotted bodies, placed the end of the barrel against the face of the first undead and pulled the trigger. Its head exploded in a cloud of blood and brain matter. Bushy Red Beard swung his sword at the second re-an, decapitating it. Both dead torsos fell on top of each other at her feet. Pink turned back to Daniel and asked, "So how do you like fighting on the frontlines now?"

Chapter 22

Inside the sandbag bunker, Daniel listened to the young military man give his report on the latest statistics gathered from the various war zones. The smell of smoke from the nearby crematoriums lofted through the air with an unavoidable sickly sweet smell. Occasional sporadic gunshots echoed in the distance. Pink sat next to him with a navy blue wool hat pulled down tight around her face and a scarf bundled up high around her neck. Even though the majority of the current soldiers had no idea who she was, she wanted to be cautious about her identity. She sat low in the chair and kept her head down. The limited lighting offered by the kerosene lamps assisted in concealing her face.

The soldier at the end of the table wore a uniform, which appeared to be one size too big for his thin frame. The scuffed up stars on his collar sat crooked, indicating the 25 year old had only recently been promoted to General, and his brass had been handed down several times. He glanced at the small piece of dark slate with the numbers written in white chalk. "The latest counts are in. For the first time, since we started the re-an census, their numbers have dropped, not much, but they didn't increase which means our counter attack with the anti-virus might be working."

Daniel sat up and asked, "Could it be an error in the data sample? We went through a population decrease once before. It was followed by an explosion of re-ans in areas where we thought we had eliminated them."

"I don't think this is the case here." The young officer shook his head as he glanced at the chalkboard again. "This is a compilation of numbers from all over the country and a few sites in Canada. We haven't received any hard figures from Europe, but we hear they are finding the same thing in areas where the anti-virus has been distributed." The young General set the slate down on the table and addressed all those at the table. "It looks like the momentum is finally going our way." He quickly pointed to the scientist. "Thanks to Dr. Cronsworth and his colleagues, the anti-virus they developed is working."

Daniel responded, "However, the living are still taking a big hit from the Omega virus. Do you have any numbers on our total population?"

The young General rubbed the back of his neck and let out a sigh. With hesitation in his voice, he said, "These are all rough estimates of course, but I hear the population in the United States is somewhere around seventy million." Those around the table mumbled their surprise. "It's hard to get data out of Europe; so many countries have gone dark. The numbers I've heard are that England might be down to eight million and Germany is somewhere around ten million."

An officer with shoulder length dark hair, sitting at the table across from Pink asked, "What about France?"

"All indications right now are that France has gone dark. We haven't heard a thing from them in over two weeks. There are no more refugees coming out of the country and living animals have not been seen around the borders. This seems to be the final indication in most countries that they are off the grid."

A civilian man wearing a worn flannel shirt with a few torn holes and dirty jeans walked in the bunker and whispered something in the General's ear. The officer shook his head and brought his attention back to the table. "We've been experiencing some outbreaks of violence from civilians at some of the distribution points. We need to assign more men to the food rationing stations to help keep the crowds under control. Coronel Frank has asked if we can post some units along the highways. There are reports of pirates attacking refugee caravans along the Interstate routes. They're getting bold and not only going after civilians, they're attacking military trucks as well. A lot of our corn and sugar has been showing up on the black market. Its value for making alcohol appears to be greater than its value as food." He pointed to one of his officers at the far end of the table. "John, can you take care of that for me? We are losing enough men to the re-ans, we don't need to lose more from our own kind."

The older man with a gray beard nodded his head.

The young officer glanced down at his chalkboard and continued, "Here's something strange. There are reports from Texas, New York, Iowa, Oregon and even here in Colorado of re-ans attacking military food caravans and only stealing coffee. For some reason, the meat bags are attracted to the stuff. Some units have mentioned using the beans as bait to lure them into a trap, but nobody wants to give up any of their rations."

A soldier sitting next to Daniel said, "Coffee is one of the most valuable commodities right now. With Brazil going dark, it's going to be scarcer and we could even see it being used as the next form of currency. People are already using it as a bartering unit."

The general nodded his head in agreement and ended his meeting with, "That's all I have for now. Remember to tell your people to walk when possible and use horses if they have them. We need to conserve all the fuel we can."

As the people around the table stood to leave, the young officer said, "Dr. Cronsworth, I need to speak to you outside."

As she skirted past all the military men, Pink kept her head down and then ventured out of the entrance into the daylight.

Outside, under the gray sky and smoke filled air, the general stepped to the side of the bunker to pass on additional information. Nearby, a steam engine turned an electrical generator providing power to the radio tent. The coal fire under the boiler coughed out black smoke, which towered high into the atmosphere. Next to the corral of horses, mash was still cooking in a large pot, turning it into much needed alcohol fuel. At the far end of the camp, Daniel noticed a six foot high stack of dead bodies waiting to be placed in the crematorium, which had more smoke bellowing out the top. The General noticed the scientist stare at the corpses and said, "Those are the most recent nightly drops."

"What do you mean?" The scientist asked.

"Over there by the front gate to the compound where the fence lights can't reach." The young officer pointed to the razor wire fence next to the edge of the forest. "Those who have given up on this world come here at night to commit suicide so we will burn their bodies and keep them from turning re-an. During the day, we get some travelers who will drop off a few bodies. We try to torch them as quickly as we can, but in the morning when we go out to scoop up the drop-offs, some of them get up and stagger away."

Scanning the area to make sure no one was within hearing distance, he changed the subject. "I didn't want to get people's hopes up, especially when I don't even know what this means, if it means anything at all. Maybe you can do something with it."

Daniel glanced at Pink, trying to hide her face while standing over by one of the military horses. He turned back to the officer. "What up?"

"There's this strange report out of Florida in one of the areas that received the anti-virus a few weeks ago. Seventy some people were trapped in a building surrounded by re-ans. The damn meat bags tied the civilians down, while this dead park ranger went down the line biting each one in the arm. For some reason, he didn't eat them, he just bit them. Luckily, they all had been vaccinated. The zombie went into convulsions and expired within seconds after gnawing the last civilian. It must have scared the other meat bags, because they took off without feeding on their captured prey. The medicine did its job, because nobody died from the bite."

The doctor nodded his head. "Yes, it sounds like the serum worked well. We tested it thoroughly on captured test subjects. Our observations were that when the other re-ans saw one of their own die such a violent death, it terrified them."

"The effectiveness of your potion is not why I'm telling you this story. Here's the strange part." The general let out a deep breath, as if he didn't believe what he was about to say. "Remember, this is Florida. There's still a good population of older and elderly folks living there. The majority of these people who had been captured suffered from gout or some type of arthritis. They all reported to the soldiers who pulled them out of the building that the pain in their joints had disappeared. The swelling in their fingers, knuckles and knees had simply evaporated. They felt like they could go run a marathon." He shrugged his shoulders. "I thought you'd want to hear about one of the side effects of your drug."

Daniel pondered the information as he stared at the ground. "If it cured arthritis, we would have heard about it from people all over the world. There had to be something different about these people in Florida. Maybe it was their diet, or something they've been exposed to in the environment. It's possible there could have been a contamination in that particular batch of serum, which resulted in positive effects. It happens all the time in my line of work." He turned his attention back to the young officer. "Did the report mention anything else, anything unusual?"

"No, nothing out of the ordinary. The people who were captured did say this dead park ranger had full blue eyes, rather than the usual milky gray, but that was it."

Daniel noticed Pink, trying to wave him over without calling attention to herself. "Thanks, I'll keep it mind. When this is all over and we get our world back, I'll be in a better position to study the subsidiary effects of the drug. Who knows when this is all over and they start giving out Nobel awards again, maybe I'll get two."

* * *

With a sawed-off shotgun strapped to her back, heavy leather boots, and a full-length black duster, Hellion walked through the dark underground tunnel with two undead soldiers with holes pierced through their bodies caused by the pit traps she set up through the city. Water dripping from the old bricks echoed through the corridor lit only by the occasional candle. Along with her guardsmen, a short woman, wearing civilian issued olive green clothing, tagged along. As the group approached Bartholomew and the others gathered around a table, Prometheus stepped forward and said, "Our sister from Clan Titus has come to pay us a visit."

Hellion brought her attention to their leader. "Hey Captain, I have a new fish for your group. She's a believer just like you and quite scrappy. She'll make a good addition to your merry little bunch of do-gooders."

Prometheus opened his mouth to ask a question, but Hellion cut him off. "Save the ancient speak, Socrates." She placed her hand on the new arrival's shoulder. "Tell them your story, sister."

The new woman stepped out of the shadows into the flickering candle light. Her dirty clothes and matted shoulder length sandy hair showed what living condition must be like for the humans. She had welder's goggles draped around her neck and wore scuffed motorcycle boots. The dried blood under her nose and ears indicated the former tenant of this body died from the Omega Virus. She said to the group as she scanned the tunnel, "So this is the legendary re-an lair. There were rumors, but not many believed it existed. I always pictured it a bit more sinister than this, with zombies feeding on body parts and humans trapped in cocoons for later consumption." She scanned the group in front of her and said, "My name's Cathy" She stuck her hand out to Bartholomew who appeared confused by the gesture.

General Brown explained, "She wants to shake your hand. It's common in this era for women to greet men in this fashion. They stopped doing the curtsy a hundred years ago."

Bartholomew slowly reached out and shook her hand. Cathy continued, "I've been told to explain my bio, because apparently, we are all from different centuries. I happen to have died only a few days ago, when Hellion and her mob raided my camp. I don't know why I had to come back in this lady's body when mine was so much nicer," she glanced at her clothes and ran her hand down her shirt, "but here I am, a full blown re-an. I guess it's time for me to learn all the secret passwords and why we seem to be obsessed with coffee. I'm not looking forward to eating people, but I guess that's what we do."

The pirate captain stared past the newcomer and asked Hellion, "Other than she be believing in our cause, why you be thinking she would make a good addition to me crew? I be getting fresh swabs every day."

Hellion motioned her head toward the new arrival. "Tell them what you were in the middle of doing when we raided your tent."

Cathy smirked a bit. "I was in the middle of a session with a client."

"These guys didn't understand when you wanted to shake their hand. You're going to have to be more specific with them." Hellion explained.

"I was in the middle of a torture session with a client." She noticed the blank expressions on the faces of those around her and added to her explanation. "There's still a need for my services, even in this world. People still have needs even after the collapse of society. I actually moved up higher on the social ladder and not just because I was rich," she hesitated and glanced at her surroundings, "at least by today's standards."

Hellion saw the bewildered expressions on the faces of the ancients and jumped in with more explanation, "She's a dominatrix."

A big smile spread across General Brown's face as he stepped closer to Cathy. "Hi, I'm Chris. We should go drink some coffee and talk about… whatever."

Bartholomew glanced at Cathy then to Hellion with a quizzical look. "I still not be understanding your line of work."

Brown continued his lines to Cathy, "Or if you feel I'm not talking enough, you can try to make me talk in whatever fashion you think is necessary. In my past life, I had all kinds of classified intel. Maybe you could get me to give up some of those secrets."

Trying to ignore the General, Hellion explained to the ancient pirate, "Men would pay her to torture them."

Cathy added, "I was right at the pinnacle of the session, when my client," she paused to choose her words, "asked me… to beat him harder."

Still confused, the pirate asked, "So, what I used to do to me captives as punishment, men be paying you to do for fun?" He threw his hands in the air. "This world be getting stranger every day."

Brown chimed in again, "If you have to beat me harder for intel, I don't care. Really, let's go get some coffee. Wait till you see what it does for you."

"That's the basics of what I do." Cathy put her hands on her hips. "And, I would like to say, I was well compensated. I never had to worry about food, electricity credits, clothes and I had enough coffee to have a cup every morning."

"Coffee!" Brown fell to his knees. "This is already torture. Please tell me you have some coffee with you."

Wearing leather chaps, an old bomber jacket, tall boots, and a suede top hat with brass gears attached to the band and welding goggles draped around her neck, Salsa moved into the flickering light from the shadows of the tunnel. Two dead soldiers acting as bodyguards stayed next to her as she moved through the group. She scanned Cathy while walking around the new arrival, keeping her hand on top of the pommel of her sword strapped to her hip. "You know," she spoke to Bartholomew, "little miss Beat Me Harder here, can be of some use to us, seeing as how she can make the humans talk, and I can understand what they're saying. We could be a nice pair."

Chapter 23

Prometheus walked with Patricia through the ruins and rubble of the city as though they strolled in the park on a Sunday afternoon. The always-present smoke and haze covered the sky turning the sun into a reddish orange glowing ball. Scattered re-ans staggered and wandered in and out of the shadows cast by the large piles of concrete, dirt and twisted metal. Small wisps of smoke swirled up from various impact craters created from the previous night's battle with the humans. Ravens peppered the landscape as they searched for scraps of human remains usually found on these battlefields. Prometheus continued with their conversation. "So in your time period it was common to sail between all the lands?"

Patricia stepped over a rotted severed leg. "All the nations and lands traded goods with each other. This drove the need to build ships to bring all these products across the seas. This also brought the rise of privateers and pirates, the occupation which I chose to join."

"Even though we didn't sail across," the Athenian paused for a moment, "or I should say around this world, we also had our share of pirates on the waters. I do not recall hearing of any female pirates."

Patricia replied, "Even in my day, there were very few woman sailors, let alone lady captains. I know of only three other women who commanded their own pirate ship as I did.

Prometheus glanced at Patricia's face. "I see we both share the trait of green eyes. How long have you had them?"

"A few nights ago, in the raids, I took a test bite out of one of the livings to see if he would be safe for Salsa to feed upon. Midnight said he appeared to be free of the fire. When I did not burn from the inside, Salsa and the others in her court feasted on him. The next morning, Bartholomew commented on my green eyes that even death could not hide their beauty." She glanced down and tried to hold back a slight smile.

"The complexities of emotions after one's death are far beyond anything I could have imagined during life."

Prometheus saw Greg and several others returning from the previous nights scavenging raids in the forest. Greg wore a heavy canvas kilt, and a martial arts ghee with the sleeves cut off. All the soldiers appeared worn and scarred from a fierce night of battle. As she noticed Greg carrying Bartholomew's sword, Patricia ran toward the group. She stopped in front of the Samurai and quickly asked with fear in her voice, "Why do you carry the sword of our Captain?"

Greg lowered his head and replied with sadness. "We found a small group of non-soldiers traveling the road. As we made our attack, it turned out to be a trap set for us. The living poured out of the trees and surrounded us. We were outnumbered ten to one."

She noticed all the blood splattered on the sword sheath and grip. "What happened to the Captain?"

"He led us into the battle and became the first victim. The humans had spring traps hidden in the road. One grabbed his leg with its sharp metal teeth and kept him from moving. He bravely fought off many with his sword, but he soon became overrun and his body torn apart by several pikes. We had to retreat or suffer the same fate."

Patricia asked to see the sword. After Greg handed it to her, she strapped it around her waist and asked, "Where did this attack occur?"

Greg pointed to the south and replied, "A few miles from here. The place that the modern's call the town of Littleton. But, there is nothing left of his body, because the humans…"

Before he could finish, Patricia ran off to the south with the Captain's blade. Greg motioned to some of his soldiers. "We must go with her."

* * *

Patricia ran through the trees with her sword drawn as she entered the small clearing occupied by a band of humans. They sat around a fire laughing and drinking, so they were caught completely off guard. As the first person stood to confront her, she sprang off a rock, sailed through the air and rammed her sword through his chest as she landed in front of him. With smooth quick motions, she pulled the blade out and sliced across the throat of another living. A man charged with a long wooden pike, which impaled through her abdomen. She ran up the shaft toward the man and with a backhand swing of her sword, she decapitated her attacker.

Greg and the other living dead soldiers poured out of the trees and a full-fledged battle ensued. Patricia ran through the group of humans, wielding her blade, with each swing delivering a deathblow to the human at the receiving end. The fight only lasted a few minutes, as most of the livings lay mangled on the blood soaked ground. Arms, legs, and intestines littered the clearing as the few people still alive tried to crawl away. The undead lady pirate walked up to the slow moving foes, grabbed arms and legs and bit into them, taking out huge chunks of flesh and muscle.

Greg warned her, "You shouldn't do that. You don't know if they have the fire inside their bodies."

"I don't care." Patricia replied with blood pouring down the sides of her mouth.

Several of the dead bodies slowly stood from the ground, some missing arms, some with intestines spilling out of their midsections. They scanned the area with confused expressions and asked, "Where am I?"

"Whose body is this?"

"How did I get here?"

"We should get back. There are military patrols in this area. Our numbers are small and we would not fair well if surrounded." Greg said, as he circled his hand indicating to his soldiers that he wanted them to round up the new arrivals.

Patricia stared into the trees leading away from the city. "You go back. I have vengeance which needs to be satisfied." She said as she ran off into the trees.

* * *

Prometheus sat on top of a large section of concrete which used to be a floor to one of the skyscrapers which once proudly rose from the ground before the uprising. He took in the sight of the rising sun turning the smoke filled sky deep red. He wondered if the air felt cool or if it was humid and warm.

In the distance, he saw a lone figure walk toward him. As the light slowly increased, and the distance decreased, he saw it take the form of Patricia. He noticed the hole in her stomach from the pike and her dress soaked in fresh blood. Dried blood covered every inch of her skin and hair, along with her sword and scabbard. She walked up and stopped in front of the Athenian without saying a word. Prometheus scanned her entire body and broke the silence. "How did your vengeance go? How many descendants did you kill? You look as though you actually took a bath in blood."

"It had to be hundreds of livings. I must have fed on all the remaining humans who did not have the fire."

"Did you find peace with all this killing?"

Patricia glanced down at the hands and tried to rub the dried blood off. "No, I do not think that will ever happen in this macabre world. Maybe the next life will hold some happiness for me."

She turned up and looked at the Greek man. His eyes opened wide as he said, "My sister, your eyes have turned blue. You are ready to pass along your gift given to you by the gods. Perhaps your next life will arrive sooner than expected."

She picked up a piece of scrap metal and polished it with the only dry part of her dress. Gazing at her reflection she replied, "I no longer care about passing this needed string of life to the living. A cure for the Omega plague will not be enough to save them at this point. I feel we are witness to the end of our world."

Behind the lady pirate, in the distance, Prometheus saw new arrivals stagger through the rubble. With his attention toward the distant undead, he said, "It looks like your converts have followed you home."

She turned her head and quickly glanced at her victims. "Yes, the humans who I fed on trailed behind me all night. I think many are ancients who will need to be given lessons to educate them on their place in this netherworld."

Chapter 24

Prometheus lit candles placed in crevices throughout the tunnel. The voices of the night's scavenging party echoed from the far end in the shadows. He turned in the opposite direction and cast his voice into the darkness where the candle flames did not reach. "My good sister, Salsa, it sounds like they have returned from their night of hunting."

Salsa emerged from the shadows into the flickering light, which reflected off her bright green eyes. She walked across the muddy ground with the grace of royalty wearing a blue velvet Victorian era gown, leather wrist cuffs, and a black derby with welding goggles around the brim. The sword belt around her waist also contained two daggers and a 9mm Colt handgun.

Patricia arrived first and dumped her numerous swords, daggers and other primitive weapons on the map table. Her waitress uniform had turned dark brown from all the dried blood permeated into the fabric. The rest of the night's soldiers staggered in behind her. Salsa asked, "Did you have any luck finding fresh meat?"

Patricia glanced back at her people and said, "You can see for yourself."

Greg and General Brown carried into the light a human man in his mid thirties, with tattered clothing and fresh blood showing through some of the tears in his shirt. His arms were tied to a wooden pike across his shoulders giving him a crucified appearance. He let out the usual evil hissing and moans with anger expressed on his face. They hung the ends of the pike on two protruding bricks on the wall of the tunnel, which kept his feet inches off the ground. Salsa listened to the sounds from his mouth and explained, "Oh, he's mad at us. He's calling us all kinds of names." She tilted toward General Brown. "He's even questioning your gender."

Cathy moved her way through the crowd which had gathered around the man. She lowered her welding goggles from her eyes and took off the snowboarding helmet, which showed signs of battle scars. Sliding off her leather bomber jacket, she stood in front of the prisoner and said, "Do you want me to do my thing with this guy?"

Salsa replied with a simple nod.

The former dominatrix grabbed one of Patricia's daggers from the table. She placed the tip in the center of the man's armpit pressing hard enough to create a dent in his skin, but not draw blood. His demon sounds continued to spill from his mouth. Salsa translated, "He's still name calling. I think you need to take him from being mad to scared."

Cathy relocated the blade from under his arm to just below his right eye. Instead of talking, the human went silent.

"There you go." Salsa said. "I think we have his attention now."

Cathy set the dagger down on the table and said, "This always confuses them." She reached out and fluttered her fingertips up and down his side to tickle him. His moaning took on a tone of laughter. As she continued with no hesitation, his face turned red and he gasped to take in a breath.

"Stop." Salsa said as she raised her hand. "I think this is working."

In-between breaths, the human blurted out with more hissing and groaning sounds. Salsa filled in the gaps. "The insults have changed from the marital status of our parents to us being some kind of crazy freaks."

Cathy glanced around the room and pointed to one of the undead soldiers. "You, I need your help. Grab his leg, take his shoe off, and hold his foot up."

The assistant followed her instructions. She scanned the weapons set on the map table. Running her hand over the various blades and maces, she picked up a club made from the thin end of a baseball bat. Staring the prisoner in the eye, she pounded the bottom of his foot with one quick blow. The cracking sound came from his bone breaking and not from the bat. The ear-piercing screech that emanated out of his mouth did not need a translation. It was obvious that he screamed out in pain. Cathy brought the bat down on the top of his foot with it ending in another crack of bones. As she wound up for another swing, Salsa raised her hand and called out, "Stop"

She studied his face as she listened to his rant. "He stopped calling us names and moved on to threatening us." She continued to translate. "He's talking about the vaccine and how they are going to use it to wipe us out. They are going to start injecting us directly." She moved closer to the human. "The army has started operation Blow Dart in other parts of the country and has cleared re-ans from entire cities. He mumbled something about gassing us."

Salsa turned to the other living dead. Prometheus explained, "If we are to finish our mission to pass along our strings of life to the descendants, we must get our sister to the state of blue eyes, so we can communicate with them and end this war."

The Chosen One turned back to their prisoner and said, "I guess, I can start down that road with this guy here and put him out of his misery."

As she reached out to grab his arm, Midnight stepped up and stopped her. "Wait, I think he has the fire inside him. It doesn't look the same though." She studied the man who continued to groan and hiss. "This is a different kind of darkness. Maybe he has the Omega Plague."

Salsa shrugged her shoulders. "The Omega virus isn't going to hurt me"

With her mouth inches from taking a bite out the doomed victim, Prometheus stopped her. "Wait. Perhaps it would be better for me to test your food for poison before my sister takes her first bite."

She handed the arm over the Greek man, and she said, "Be my guest."

Prometheus took a bite out of the man's arm. The prisoner screamed even louder. With blood dripping down the sides of his mouth, the ancient man nodded his head to give the approval. As Salsa leaned down to take a bite, Prometheus fell to the ground screaming.

He yelled, "It burns! It feels like a fire is trying to escape from inside my body."

Staring up at the re-ans, who were helpless to assist him, his vision changed. The faces of his friends dissolved into gray decayed skin. Open wounds, which he had never seen before, appeared across their bodies, as did areas of missing flesh exposing bones and dried muscle and tendons. He saw Patricia lift her sword and bring it down on his throat.

* * *

Daniel sat in front of the fire under a night sky watching a group of civilians try to figure out how to set up their military issue tent in the dark. Drinking moonshine from his metal coffee mug, he saw several off duty soldiers standing on the edge of the light laughing and drinking. The military men, all in their early twenties, ventured outside the military compound and joined the civilians so they could drink. Pink sat down next to the scientist, pointed to his cup and said, "We need that for fuel. You can get in a lot of trouble if you're caught drinking it."

Dr. Cronsworth continued to watch the young soldiers. "You know I saw a group of families on their way to Arizona. They had kids with them that couldn't have been more than 5 or 6."

Pink gazed into the fire. "They were probably going to the Phoenix compound. I hear they built thirty-foot walls around the entire square mile, just like an old castle. It sounds like a safe place for families."

"Yeah, but that wasn't my point. They had young children with them."

"I think that's why they are called families."

"But, they were 6 years old. They were born after the uprising." He motioned his hand in a circle toward the forest. "This is the only world they know." He turned to Pink. "They've never slept in a bed. They've never watched television, seen a movie or used an indoor bathroom. They've probably never heard the term, indoor plumbing. For them, they will grow up in the futuristic world equivalent of tenth century."

Pink grabbed the mug full of booze from his hands and took a sip. "Nah, when this is all over, we'll get our world back. Sure, it will take a decade or more to rebuild it all. But, one day we'll be sitting on our front porch telling our grandkids stories about the uprising just like our elders talked about what life was like during the war."

Daniel took the moonshine back and gulped some down. "I don't know if that day will ever happen."

"Sure it will."

"It would be nice to see, but our population has a long way to go before we could recover. If you do the math, this looks like it might be our last stand. We're about to join the dinosaurs on the list of former tenants of this planet."

"I know it looks bad now, but your anti-virus is working. It should only take another year or so and the re-ans will only be a memory."

"As will I."

Pink took the mug back with a wrinkled brow of puzzlement. "What are you talking about?" She took a sip of moonshine.

"If the re-ans don't get us, the Omega virus will."

"I'm sure you and your colleagues will find a cure for the Omega." The crack of a branch from the darkness beyond the light caught her attention briefly. "Hell, you found a cure for zombies. I'd imagine any disease after that would be child's play."

The scientist stared at the fire with a blank emotionless face. "I've had a scratchy throat for a couple of days with a slight fever."

"So you can still get the flu even during a zombie apocalypse."

"I've had three nose bleeds today and some bleeding out of my ears. I have the early stages Omega. I won't see the new world. I won't see next week."

Pink stared at the mug of moonshine they had been sharing. "Maybe you could have started our conversation with this information before I started drinking your hooch."

He glanced at the mug in her hand. "The virus can't live in alcohol. You can only get infected from direct contact with your blood." Daniel held up his arm to reveal a small scratch near his elbow. "I got this last week climbing through what used to be Mercy Hospital west of here. It should have healed up by now." He placed his finger next to the wound. "See this swelling, that's the virus multiplying and growing."

"You don't know for sure if you're infected. We live in a dirty world. I'm sure some antibiotics should clear that up. With your connections, you should be able to get all the drugs you need."

"I've been on antibiotics for a few days. It's the Omega."

A raven landed on a rock near the family setting up the tent. The sight sent a cold rush of fear through the scientist. Pink stood up and whistled to get the attention of the young soldiers. They turned toward her and she pointed to the bird.

Re-ans armed with swords and battle-axes quickly emerged from the trees. The soldiers disappeared under the wave of undead with only their screams to indicate they were still alive. The demons seized the family members and dragged them into the darkness of the forest. Their screams slowly filtered off in the distance.

Pink grabbed a burning log from the fire, held it out toward the advancing dead and threw the moonshine through the flames at the zombies. "Come on, this way!" She said to Daniel as she waved her arm toward the compound and ran off.

A re-an wearing a leather kilt and carrying a samurai sword grabbed the scientist's arm and pulled him to the ground. The living dead pressed the tip of his sword into the Daniel's chest to keep him pinned down. He watched as Pink disappeared into the darkness, leaving him alone with the devils.

A female undead, with black stringy hair and dried blood around her rotted lips, walked up and appeared to stop the kilt wearing attacker from running his sword through the human's body. She stared at Cronsworth with her hazed white eyes. Her face and dried gray skin showed years of deterioration with muscle, bone and tendons showing through tears and holes in her body. She leaned closer with her dirt encrusted hair hanging down, while she moaned and screeched to the others in her group.

Another woman re-an approached, as the battle with the humans continued behind them. She wore a cutlass on her hip and a waitress uniform, which had turned dark brown from all the dried blood. The tension and fear became too much for Daniel to handle. "Do it! Get it over with! I knew this day would come. Finish me!" He called out to the kilt-wearing zombie with the sword. "I want to leave this world."

After he blurted out those words, his fear diminished. He knew the end had come and there was nothing left to cause him any fear.

The female living dead with the blue hazed eyes and cutlass pressed her hand on his chest and brought her face within inches of his. With her free hand, she pulled his mouth open and let her saliva drip into his mouth. He felt her cold bodily fluid slide down his throat. His immediate thought was not to accept it, but his reflexes kicked in and he swallowed the dead woman's spit.

An explosion and a flash of light in the trees indicated the military had arrived. The re-ans disappeared back into the darkness of the trees as quickly as they arrived. Daniel sat up and saw soldiers armed with battle swords and shotguns storm into the light of the fire. They attended to the remains of the young soldiers on the ground. Pink pushed her way from between two of the soldiers and ran to the aid of her friend.

Chapter 25

Prometheus opened his eyes and saw nothing in the blackness of his surroundings. He sat up and felt the wet cold ground with his fingertips. *Perhaps, I have finally left the future world and moved to a life with the gods.* He ran his hands down his body. *This body feels fit. These clothes do not feel to be in a state of decay.* Standing, he felt his way through the darkness along the solid brick wall. He called out, "Is anyone there?"

A pinpoint of light appeared in the distance. It grew in size as it moved closer. The sound of footsteps grew in volume and echoed off the walls. Transforming from a blur, the light became a lantern carried by a woman. The Greek man called out to the person, "Who approaches me and from where do you hail?"

The woman with the lantern stopped while she replied, "Prometheus? Is that you?" She continued walking until her face became visible.

"Patricia," he responded, "I see I have returned to the future world once again. How long have I been absent?"

The dead lady pirate, wearing thick leather gauntlets, tall black motorcycle boots, and welding goggles draped around her neck, set the lantern down and wrapped her hands around her old friend. "Prometheus, it is so good to have you back. There have been many changes in this world since we last spoke some six months ago."

They released their hug and she picked up her light. Prometheus glanced down at his new body, but could only see the green clothes issued by the military to civilians. "Without a reflection glass, I do not know what kind of body I occupy. Would you please describe how I look?"

Patricia scanned him in the dim light and said, "You are in the body of a young man, maybe late twenties, with shoulder length dark hair. The clothes would indicate he was from one of the compounds protected by the soldiers."

"Did he die from the Omega plague?"

"I doubt the plague is what brought his demise. In this new day, there are very few who are dying from the Omega. My guess is this young man came down here to take the poison and commit suicide. It seems suicides are about the only bodies left for us to inhabit. Why the livings come down here to die, I don't know." She picked up the light and waved her hand forward. "Come with me. We should get back to the others. It is not safe this far out."

As they walked through the darkness, Prometheus noticed at the edge of the light, decayed bodies lay on the edge of the underground tunnel. He realized he had not seen too many bodies in this world. He wondered why they did not transform into re-ans. Patricia noticed his interest in the dead and explained, "All these people had been injected with the fire, so when they died, they could not be re-inhabited. Some died in battles with us, but most came down here to take the poison."

"What is this poison which seems to be so popular with the descendants?"

"I don't know exactly what it is. The humans come down here, take a green pill, sit on the ground and eventually they fall over dead. For some erroneous reason, they chose this time to give up."

They rounded a corner and he saw a light in the distance with the silhouettes of other living dead gathered in the center. "What do you mean by 'this time'?"

The lady pirate glanced at him and said, "The humans are winning their war. Our numbers are on the decline."

They walked into the circle of light and she announced, "Look who I found in the suicide tunnel. It is our old friend Prometheus."

General Brown stepped up to the Greek man, slapped him on the shoulder and said, "Prometheus you old goat. Did you bring any coffee with you?"

On the other end of the group, he saw a woman emerge into the light from the shadows. She wore a full-length leather welding coat, tall hiking boots, a leather corset, a brown felt top hat and motorcycle goggles perched on her forehead. Two undead well-armed soldiers stood by her side. As she tilted her head up, the light reflected off her bright green eyes and she said, "Prometheus my old friend, it is good to have you back."

The Athenian smiled and replied, "I see you are still trying to attain your final strings of life, my good sister Salsa."

Brown interjected, "Yeah, it's hard to find humans who have not been vaccinated. A few times, we almost lost her in battle. So, we stopped taking her out on raids and adopted a safe house system. We move Salsa to a different location each night and bring the captured humans to her. Say, while you were gone and socializing with the gods, did they happen to tell you where we could find some coffee?"

Ignoring the question, Prometheus asked, "What is this I hear about our numbers on the decline?"

"In the months since we last saw you, the living have appeared to get the upper hand on the Omega Virus." Salsa answered. "We don't know if they found a cure or if it just ran its course. However, the vaccine has taken its toll on our population. They've turned it into a weapon. In some areas, it's used very effectively against us in a gas form. Even though, we don't breathe it in, it somehow permeates our skin and gets inside of us."

Patricia chimed in with, "Speaking of moving, Salsa, it is that time of night." She looked at Brown. "General, will you take her and her guards to the cavern below the old train station? Prometheus, why don't you come with the rest of us on our nightly search for a human without the fire?"

* * *

Patricia held her hand up, indicating she wanted the others to stop. Standing behind a boulder in the dark forest, Prometheus saw a group of humans sitting around a fire in the clearing. The lady pirate motioned for Midnight to join her at the front of the tree line. "Can you see anything from here?"

Midnight strained to view any disease in their bodies. "It is difficult to see from this distance, but the man over there in the dark shirt might be clean. I need to get closer to be sure."

Patricia gave silent hand signals, telling her soldiers to spread out, and surround the human camp. She moved her archers back into the shadows of the forest. Prometheus watched them move quietly through the trees to their positions and thought about how much their soldier training had advanced in his absence. With the band of living surrounded, Patricia led the charge.

She ran into the clearing, wielding her sword, as the others did the same from all directions. Caught off guard, the humans scrambled to find their weapons, but the dead quickly pounced on them. Midnight moved around the battle signaling who had the vaccine in their veins. Pointing to various humans she would say, "He has the fire…she has the fire…fire in his blood."

If she pointed to a human, it became their death sentence as they turned into a threat to the dead. The zombies would quickly run them through with a sword or pike killing them instantly. As she came to the man in the dark shirt and long blond hair, she held up her hand. "Stop." Midnight moved closer and scanned his body in detail. "This one does not have the fire."

Behind her, only a few humans remained alive and continued to fight. Two of the zombie soldiers began to tie up the descendant by his arms. He let out moans and hissing sounds, but it was clear he was afraid. Patricia grabbed one of her soldiers by the arm to give him instructions. "Take Midnight around to the remaining humans so she can-"

Before she could finish, a small red dart hit the zombie soldier in the neck. He immediately fell to the ground and went into convulsions as he screamed in pain. Another living dead fell to the ground screaming with a dart in his shoulder. More small red darts zipped through the air and hit trees and the ground. Soldiers with the human military poured out of the forest with blow darts and flamethrowers. Patricia grabbed Prometheus, pushed him toward Midnight and the captured human. "Take them back to the safe house. I'll stay and hold them off as long as I can."

As the Greek man stumbled forward, he said, "But how will you-"

The pirate cut him off. "No time for arguments. Go!"

Arrows flew from the shadows of the trees hitting the humans and taking them down. Prometheus, Midnight and the two zombie soldiers picked up the prisoner and carried him into the darkness of the trees as Patricia and her army fought off the living.

* * *

Daniel lifted his eyes from his microscope and noticed the higher than normal level of activity around the camp. He stepped out of his makeshift lab tent and watched as soldiers moved quickly to gather supplies. Pink walked past wearing dark sunglasses and her knit hat pulled low on her face. The scientist said to her, "You know you stand out more when you wear those sunglasses." She stopped and turned to him. "We haven't seen the sun in months. This gray cloud cover is the perfect light filter. With all the smoke haze in the air, I would think those dark glasses would only make it more difficult to see."

Pink took the sunglasses off and placed them in her pocket. He asked her, "Do you know what all the commotion is about?"

She stepped closer to keep their conversation quiet. "They're getting ready for some big raid. Scouts have found the re-ans are protecting some female. Speculation is she must be some kind of zombie queen or something, because of the way they move her around and keep bodyguards on her at all times."

"So they're going to capture their queen."

"Yeah, maybe she's the key to their reanimation. If we have her, we just might be able to bring all of this to an end."

"I'll talk to the General and see if I can study her when they bring her into camp."

Chapter 26

As fragments of dirt blasted past their bodies from the explosion, the dust cloud surrounded them. A magnesium flare floated above the battle scene casting a white light through the smoke filled air. Prometheus brought his head up from behind a large concrete boulder to see human soldiers quickly scatter from rubble pile to rubble pile. Greg called out to his archers to let their arrows rain down on the opposing army. Before the projectiles became airborne, the dead samurai led a charge with thirty of his fellow zombies. As they reached the humans and engaged them in hand-to-hand fighting, the arrows from the archers poured down. They pierced the bodies of both the humans and the living dead.

Many of the living soldiers tried to take cover under piles of debris, but most became victim to the projectiles. The dead samurai and his men looked like pin cushions, as they fought off the humans with the arrows protruding from all parts of their bodies.

General Brown stood from his covered position and called out to his small group of undead, "Let's get him underground." The re-ans carried their kidnapped human toward the entrance of the burrow. Brown grabbed Prometheus by the arm and said, "Hey, old man, we need to get out of here before their reinforcements arrive." He pointed to the three story skeletal remains of a former skyscraper. "They will try to flank us from over there and cut off our access to the tunnel. Let's move before that happens."

The Greek man quickly followed the General to a set of stairs hidden between two large mounds of rubble. The primitive steps carved into the dirt led downward into the tunnels. At the bottom of the staircase, Brown lit an oil lamp and handed it to Prometheus. "Here, you can be the front of the train."

With the lantern held out in front of him, Prometheus tried to envision what lay ahead in the darkness. Echoes of the human groans bounced off the brick from distant battles with re-ans. He carefully placed each step because he did not want to deliver their prize back to the military. As they drew closer to the underground battle, Brown placed his hand on the Athenian's shoulder to stop him. The General motioned his head to the right towards the partially caved-in entrance to a side passageway. Traveling down the smaller corridor, the sounds of the battle faded.

From the shadows of the tunnel, the ruined remains of an electronics store emerged in the dim light. As they carefully stepped over the debris, Prometheus asked, "This appears to be what is left of a modern day merchant. Why would such a business be underground?"

Brown helped the others carry the kidnap victim over a fallen steel I-beam. He explained, "In the early days of the war, an ordinance caused the store to fall into this tunnel. As the rest of the building collapsed, this store remained buried and hidden all these years."

Next to a cracked computer monitor, Prometheus saw a box with a picture of a video camera on the cover. He picked it up, studied it in the light, and said, "I remember this. The good teacher Jennifer felt we should have one. She even fought bravely and sacrificed herself so we could keep one of these."

Brown walked away from the human and grabbed the package. "A video cam." He opened the box and took out the glistening white camera. "I haven't seen one of these in years." Checking the contents of the box he continued, "It even has batteries. I wonder if they're still good."

He took the batteries out of the plastic bag and inserted them into the unit. The screen on the back lit up and displayed their dimly lit feet. He tilted up at Prometheus. "Why did this Jennifer chick say we needed this? Did it have something to do with that prophecy?"

The Greek man glanced at the camera and turned toward the passageway. "I don't remember. It did seem to be important to her and I gave my word we would keep one of these protected."

Brown placed the camera in his pocket and pointed into the dark tunnel. "I'll hang on to it for a while." He jerked his head toward the prisoner. "Let's get this guy back to our lair."

Lit with handmade candles, a wide section of the tunnel served as the safe house for the night. Brown held the human in front of him and called out to the re-ans who emerged from the shadows to see what the night's scavenging brought to them. "Where is she?"

Prometheus saw a figure come forth from a dark notch in the tunnel wall. Salsa in her long coat, top hat, and leather corset and pants walked with smooth grace through the crowd and stopped in front of the human. She placed the tip of her finger on the prisoner's lower lip, ran it down his face through his chest, and let it fall off his body. "Is he clean?"

Midnight stepped through the crowd and scanned the man who focused his evil sounds at her. She grabbed his lower jaw and stared into his eyes. "He looks clean. I don't see any trace of the fire."

Salsa glanced at a dead solder next to her and motioned her head toward the human. The re-an grabbed the man's arm and took a bite out of his bicep. The prisoner screamed out in pain as the zombie chewed up and swallowed the bloody flesh. Brown and his men struggled to keep him still with him fighting against his ropes.

All eyes focused on the undead soldier as he waited for the vaccine to take effect. With no reaction, he said, "He's clean."

Salsa took another step closer to the man. She grabbed the back of his head and pressed her lips against his, only she ended the long kiss by biting off his lower lip. Pulling her face back, blood poured out of his mouth, over his chin and down his chest. His evil moans of pain bounced off the brick walls of the tunnel. She ripped open the front of his shirt, exposed his skin and quickly bit into his shoulder, pulling off a large chunk of muscle with her teeth like a lion feasting on a kill. The human passed out from the loss of blood and fell to the ground.

With blood streaming down from her mouth onto her chest, Salsa swallowed the last of her meal. She glanced at the crowd around her and they all went silent. Prometheus said to her, "My good sister, your eyes have turned blue. We can now speak to the humans and end this war."

* * *

Flashlight beams pierced through the dust inside the ruins of what used to be Daniel's laboratory. Surrounded by soldiers, the scientist eyed his workplace with the same nostalgic feel he would have if it were the remains of his boyhood home. Gazing at his old filing cabinet, he listened to a soldier report to the squad leader. "Sir, all of our intel said they would move their Queen to this location on this night"

The squad leader replied, "It looks like our intel was wrong. We'll regroup and try again tomorrow night. Where are they expected to move her tomorrow?"

"Their pattern indicates she will be in the old high school."

A light glowed from beneath a pile of crumbled drywall and ceiling tiles. Two soldiers cleared the debris as Daniel walked toward them. Underneath the rubble, he saw his old specimen refrigerator still operating. A soldier turned to him and asked, "How is this thing still running?"

The scientist spotted the heavy electrical cord running into the unit. "It's connected to a live line. There's some hot lines running underground which are still connected to the grid." The soldier replied, "But there are no operating power plants left in the state."

"There's a plant in Arizona that has remained up and running through the uprising. As long as it stays connected to the grid, there will be live wires. The trick is finding the hot ones out of the thousands of dead lines."

Daniel pointed to the side of the room where the ceiling had collapsed. "Behind those beams, there's a walk-in freezer, which is still probably still working. Think about how much ice will go for on the black market during the summer."

He noticed some of his old Petri dishes sitting on the bottom of cooler. The dish with re-an scribble had spilled into another dish with a neon green gel. Where the two contents mixed, the colored gel turned clear. He opened the door and grabbed both dishes holding them in the light from a flashlight. The squad leader asked, "Hey, Doc, what's that?"

"The green indicates the presence of cancer cells. The clear area is where the two dishes contaminated each other, but killed the cancer cells."

"What's in the other dish?"

Daniel glanced at the label one more time. It still had the scribble when it had been placed there by the re-an. "It's zombie saliva."

"Are you saying saliva from a meat bag can cure cancer?"

The scientist stared at the soldier with hazed over expression. "It has that appearance."

Chapter 27

Salsa sat in the center of the stage on a throne, once used as a prop for school plays, inside the remains of the old North High School theatre and watched over the crowd of some one hundred living dead as they staggered and wandered through the auditorium. Several gray skins stood nearby waiting for her instructions. Their decayed bodies had been reinforced scrap parts scavenged from the city. Metal hinges placed on their joints, and brass gears and rods to aid their movement, made them look part like part dead human and part machine.

On the side stage, Cathy taught several of the undead the finer skills of using a leather bullwhip.

Salsa still wore the long coat, top hat and leather corset. She now bore a knee brace with additional gears connected to small door dampeners which helped her to move her leg mechanically. Candles placed throughout the large room cast a yellow light reflecting off the high ceiling with pockets of dark shadows along the wall. A commotion came from the hallway outside the heavy wooden doors. Salsa lowered her dark green welding goggles to see across the auditorium better. As the doors burst open, Prometheus turned toward the noise.

Patricia and her crew stormed into the theatre covered in fresh blood spray and black burn marks from their recent battle. As she walked down the isle toward the stage, she announced, "We got one."

Sitting on her throne, with the tone of royalty, Salsa asked, "Is she important? Will the living listen to her?"

Stepping onto the stage the lady pirate answered, "We caught her leaving one of the military camps. The way they fought to get her back, she must be of some value to the army. Even if she's not, the fact we captured her has certainly brought the interest of the livings."

Her crew carried their kidnap victim onto the stage. She had her feet and hands tied with heavy rope and a burlap bag covering her head. Fresh blood splatter covered the front of her olive green military issued clothes. Patricia continued, "Here she is. We don't have much time. General Brown and his men are stationed at the front of the building to fend off the soldiers who chased us here. It appears as though they have sent an entire legion and will soon break through our outer defenses."

Listening to the sounds emanating from the human under the bag, Salsa stood from her throne and approached the woman. "She's real mad at us…something about she is going to torch this place to the ground and watch us burn."

She yanked the bag off and the human stopped her rant with a startled expression on her face. The zombie queen asked, "What's your name?"

The human scanned the room and slowly reverted to her threats. Salsa glanced at Patricia and said to her, "I can understand her, but this will not work unless she can understand me. I have to transfer some DNA into her body."

She grabbed the woman by the back of her head and pressed her mouth against the human's lips. Silenced, the hostage struggled and squirmed to get her face away, but the former dancer held them close in a wet kiss. Pulling away, the hostage returned to her rant with undead saliva dripping from her lips. Salsa stepped back and said, "We'll let that settle in for a moment and see if it works."

The woman's tirade came to a sudden stop as her eyes opened wide and she glanced at the all re-ans around her. Patricia commented, "I think we have her attention."

Salsa translated the woman's groans. "She wants to know why she can suddenly understand us."

The lady pirated requested, "I would like to understand her language. Perhaps you should share your stings of life with some of us."

Salsa pressed her lips against the lady pirate and pulled her close. As they pulled apart, Patricia said, "I can understand the human."

The zombie queen with the blue eyes walked around the stage kissing the other living dead. After she smacked Prometheus on the lips, he heard the woman say, "Why is it you no longer look so dead and decayed? You almost look like you're still alive. What's happening to me? Have I transformed into a re-an?"

Salsa stepped in front of the woman and said, "Let's start with your name."

With astonishment cemented on her face, the woman cautiously said, "My name's Pink."

Reaching in one of the pockets on her long coat, Salsa pulled out the white video camera. She switched it on and handed it to Prometheus. "General Brown gave this to me. I would say if there was ever a time to update our Facebook status, it would be now."

The ancient Greek man shook his head in confusion. "I don't understand."

Salsa wrapped her hands around his to show him how to hold the electronic device. "Just hold this steady and keep this end pointed at me and our new friend. The camera will do the rest."

Pink called out, "What's going on? Why can I understand what you're saying? You're not groaning and hissing at me anymore. Have you always had the ability to speak? What are you going to do with me?"

"You are also no longer moaning and hissing at us, missy." Salsa said, as she strutted around her prisoner. "You have been chosen to bring our message to the world. Consider it an honor. You've made it into the history books. They are going to build statues of you in parks. You are going to be the key to human survival."

Holding her bound hands up, she replied, "Please let me go. I don't want to become one of you. Once, there was a time when I actually fought for your rights. I'm not the person you want for this plan."

Walking around the stage, Salsa explained, "See this man holding the camera, he's from ancient Greece. The man who grabbed you on the road is an ancient samurai warrior and the woman beside him sailed the world's oceans as a pirate during the eighteenth century. I walked the same streets as you. We probably stood in line for coffee together and we never knew it. You see, when we died, our souls were transferred to these bodies. It's the god's way of recycling."

"Your souls were transferred into dead bodies? Why?"

"We all carry new strands of DNA. Humans need these new genes to continue to evolve on this planet."

"How do you have new DNA? Why would we need this to continue our evolution? What gods sent you here?"

Continuing her performance, Salsa removed her top hat, held it out for one of her servants to take from her hand. "So many questions and so little time." She paused and the distant sounds of the battle filtered through the auditorium. "It's called gene fade and the human population has reached its end. Your gradual extinction has already begun. Without these new strands of life, you will go the way of the dinosaurs. Think of it as though the gods have given you the chance to start over."

"What are these new strands? How are they going to keep us from going extinct? What gods are you talking about?"

"We carry all kinds of goodies. As you probably guessed, I have the ability to understand all languages. When I kissed you and transferred my saliva into your mouth, you acquired this trait when you ingested my DNA."

Pink glanced around the stage at the other undead. "What other abilities do the other re-ans have?"

Salsa placed one finger on Prometheus' shoulder. "Our Greek friend here has the ability to cure all cancers. I'm sure the drug companies are going to hate that." She walked to the stage and pointed to various zombies. "We have the cure for diabetes, immunity to poisons, vision in new light spectrums, the Omega virus and pretty much any thing mentioned in all of the medical journals."

"So you have the cures for all diseases and all we have to do is ingest some of your DNA and we will continue to evolve? We will be free of disease and all other maladies which have plagued us throughout time."

Salsa stopped her strut in front of her prisoner. "It's a little more complicated than that, but you have the basic idea."

An explosion tore through the heavy wooden doors at the entrance to the theatre. Soldiers poured through the settling smoke with flamethrowers. Zombies caught in the streams of fire ran toward the attackers. They wrapped their fiery bodies around the soldiers, causing the flamethrower units to explode into massive fireballs.

General Brown and his men burst into the auditorium behind the soldiers engaged in battle with the humans. The clang of metal swords echoed off the walls. Several grenades went off in different parts of the room. As the smoke cleared, the large number of living dead had surrounded the few remaining soldiers. Gathered in a circle in the center of the theatre, a soldier pulled a grenade out of his side pouch. As the other soldiers placed their hands on the explosive, Prometheus heard him yell, "If we're done, we're taking as many of you bastards with us as possible."

Salsa screamed from the stage, "No! Wait!"

The grenade detonated and shredded both the humans and undead spraying their body parts throughout the room. While the debris fell to the ground and the smoke settled, General Brown slowly stood from underneath a mound of crumbled drywall and said, "We don't have much time before their reinforcements arrive. We need to get Salsa out of here." He glanced up at the front of the room as fear and excitement spread across his face. He ran and jumped up on the stage where Patricia and Salsa kneeled over their human captive.

Brown stood over them and called out, "Pink! Is it really you?"

Still holding the video camera, Prometheus pointed it toward the human lady who had a wooden shard from the shredded front doors, sticking out of her chest. Blood oozed out of the wound as she struggled to breathe. The former military leader dropped to one knee, lifted her head gently in his hand

and said, "Hold on we'll get you some help." He couldn't understand her response and asked, "What's she saying?"

Salsa grabbed the back of his head and kissed him. With his eyes refocused on Pink he said, "You can't die, not now. I'll get you to a mobile hospital. They'll get this little splinter out of you and you'll be as good as new."

With blood trickling out of the corner of her mouth, Pink responded, "Who are you?"

"It's me Chris. I know it doesn't look like me. When I died, my soul was placed in this strange body, but I promise I'm the same person who's had a pathetic schoolboy crush on you for years."

"You had a crush on me?" She managed to form a slight smile through the pain. "Why didn't you ask me out on a date? You would have liked my answer."

"The general and the tree hugger named Pink. What an odd couple we would have made. Plus, I was two feet taller than you were. Dancing would have been a problem."

Pink tried to bring a smile to her face through all the pain. "I think we would have been a great team."

He wiped some of the blood away from her mouth. "I always wanted to ask, how did you get the name Pink? It couldn't be the name your parents gave you."

"It's comes from my last name, Rosasingen. In German, it means pink song. So, all my friends started calling me Pink."

"What's your real name?"

Before she could answer, Pink closed her eyes and passed away in his arms. Brown lowered his head in sorrow. Salsa grabbed the video camera from Prometheus, turned it off, and placed in Pink's front pants pocket. She pointed to two of her bodyguards. "You guys need to take her to that lab where you found me. The one we sometimes use as a safe house. There's a freezer in the back that's still operational. We'll place her body inside to keep it preserved. After we spread our message to the rest of the humans, they can give her a decent burial. Maybe she can be the first human buried as a symbol the war is over."

The undead bodyguards lifted her from the stage floor and carried toward the back entrance to the theater. Prometheus spoke up, "I'll go with them to help place her at peace." As Salsa glanced up at him with fright in her eyes, he felt a sharp pain in his neck. He slapped his hand on the source and found a small red dart. The concussion from an explosion caused his ears to go deaf while he fell to the ground. He saw more re-ans fall with red darts in various parts of their bodies. His body felt as though it burned from the inside.

Salsa pulled out a handgun tucked it in her waistband, and fired it into the auditorium as an explosion erupted behind her. The giant red curtain fell from the rafters. A zombie engulfed in flames ran across the stage in a silent macabre scene as Prometheus slowly closed his eye while darkness and silence fell upon him.

Chapter 28

Prometheus opened his eyes and saw a mat of intertwined green vines covering the ceiling. They ran down the decayed curved walls and spread out on the dirt floor. Sunlight lit the area from the large opening to the tunnel a few feet away. Beyond the entrance, blue sky stretched all the way to the horizon, as fresh clean smelling air lofted through the tunnel. He sat up and saw himself surrounded by people draped in animal skins. Judging by the grayness of their skin and the stringiness of their hair, he knew they had to be re-ans.

One of the undead touched the Greek man's face and said, "It worked. The song of dead and this body brought one of our ancestors back to us and he has the legendary blue eyes. I told you the song is more important than the dance." He turned toward the Athenian. "Please tell us where you are from."

Prometheus swung his legs to the side of the table and tried to clear his mind. He did not know if he had returned to the same world or if the gods had placed him in a new domain. "I am from Athens many centuries ago. What is your name?"

"My name is General and I am of the Douglas tribe."

The Greek man scanned the remains of the tunnel covered in live growth. It had been years since he had seen green foliage. "Is the war over?" He looked down at his primitive brown soft leather shirt and pants made from deer hide.

The undead around him stepped back with astonishment. Their leader said, "Do you know of the war between the humans and the Rans?"

"Yes, I was there at the beginning and many of its years thereafter. Is it over? Did the humans take the strings of life?"

General said to him, "The war has been over for a little more than one hundred years. We only know of it from stories told to us by the elders." He paused and brought his glance downward. "That is the stories our elders told us when we were still alive."

The Athenian slid off the crude wooden table and walked out of the tunnel entrance. Outside, for the first time in years, he saw a clear sky, trees filled with green leaves, and heard the songs of birds with no ravens to be seen anywhere. The ground was void of war debris, demolished building, and only carpeted with various green grasses and colorful flowers. "Where are we? This does not look like the future world where we fought the livings."

"We are standing outside one of the dark tunnels. When we were human children, our parents often told us to stay away from these caverns, because Rans lived in them. As we grew older, we thought Rans were just a myth told to us so we would not stray from our village. No one had seen a Ran since the time of our grandparents and they were thought to have died out many years ago. But, after I drowned in the river, I found myself here, living with a tribe of the exact creatures of the legend. We have many stories of the humans attacking us with an unseen fire, so we keep ourselves hidden."

While staring in amazement at the landscape Prometheus asked, "If the war is over, why are we still here?"

General wrinkled his brow with puzzlement across his face. "We are here to pass our stings of life to the living. Only, we do not know how."

"We haven't passed our gifts to the humans?"

"If you fought in the war, would you not understand this as our mission?"

He turned to General with a bit of anger building up in his voice. "Where's Salsa?"

"Who?"

"Midnight? Patricia the lady pirate? General Brown? Greg the samurai warrior, are they still here?"

Dan glanced with confusion at the other primitively dressed members of his undead clan. "We have never heard of such people."

Prometheus suddenly realized something. "Wait, where is the old laboratory?"

"What is a laboratory?"

"Never mind. Where is the old city center?"

"Do you mean the ancient ruins? We have been told never to go there, because evil lurks in the darkness and shadows."

The Athenian grabbed Dan by the shoulders. "Why, why can't you go there? What evil is in the ruins?"

"The warning has been passed down for all these years to stay away. We do not remember the reason, only that evil is in the darkness."

"We need to go to these ruins. I must see if the laboratory is still in place."

* * *

Prometheus and the animal skin re-ans approached what was left of the ancient city of Denver. Only the bare skeletal frames of a few buildings remained no higher than the first floor. They had been completely encased in green vines and the trees covered them to the point where they were difficult to see from a distance. The grounds which once bore the black asphalt streets and concrete sidewalks lay blanketed in a carpet of tall green grass which swayed in the wind, giving the illusion of ocean waves. Scanning the area to get a sense of where they were, Prometheus spotted a mound covered in bushes, in front of the remains of a brick corner section of a building. He pointed and said, "There, that has to be it."

As they walked toward the mound, General asked, "Tell me Prometheus from the Athens tribe, why are we in the forbidden grounds? I do not like being here as our elders warned us to stay away. It will not serve us well if we anger the gods."

"Your elders warned you to stay away, because this is where the dead lived.' He turned to his new friend. "You are one of the dead." He brought his attention back to the section of the building. "We are here to complete the prophecy."

"What prophecy?"

Walking around the mound, he saw the edge of a staircase leading into the ground hidden under a large rock. Pushing against the obstacle, he said, "Help me move this. The laboratory is down below.

With the rock out of the way, Prometheus answered General's question as they walked down the remains of the stairs. "At the beginning of the uprising, the K.C. from Golden brought us the prophecy from the Gods. I believe the final piece needed to fulfill it is down here." They carefully made their way through the dark cavern of rocks, tree roots, and scattered lab equipment covered with a century of dust and dirt. "It went like this; the soft colored song will carry the words of the chosen one. These words will be held silent for 100 years, until the one who holds the spark of the flame gives them to the children of the descendants."

As Prometheus pulled aside a curtain of roots and unveiled the stainless steel door to the walk-in freezer, General said, "I don't understand what this means."

"My good sister Salsa was the chosen one who could communicate with the humans. Her words were given to the soft colored song to hold for one hundred years." He pulled the door open and the interior light illuminated the room. General and his re-ans gasped at their first sight of white artificial light. A frosty mist rolled out of the freezer as Prometheus invited the others inside.

The re-ans wearing animal skin shivered and held their arms to their shoulders. General said, "It is like the days of white in here."

In the back of the freezer, the Athenian saw the frost covered frozen body of Pink. He pointed to her and said, "This lady is the soft colored song. Her name is Pink." He reached into her pocket, pulled out the video camera and held it up. "These are the words she held for one hundred years. We must take this to the humans."

* * *

Walking across the grassy meadow, under a bright clear sky, General and the others stopped while Prometheus continued toward the village. The sight of the living dead caused the villagers to scramble in a panic, between their grass and adobe huts. Mothers grabbed their children to keep them away from harm and the men gathered hunting spears and bows.

Entering a dirt path leading to the edge of the settlement, Prometheus held the video camera out in front of him. The men of the village formed a line across the entrance and held their spear tips out to stop the monster. A few feet from the trembling guards, he placed the camera on the ground, with the viewing screen toward the men, and then he pressed the power button.

Slowly backing away into the meadow, he heard Salsa's voice say, "Just keep it steady and point this end at our friend."

The men's eyes lit up, as they cautiously lowered their spears. One man slowly stepped toward the camera and picked it up. Prometheus backed away from the men and let them watch the video.

As the humans listened to Pink translate the moaning sounds of the re-ans, they relaxed their guard. At the end of the video, one of the village men cautiously walked away from the village entrance and approached Prometheus. Standing ten feet away he asked, "Can you understand me?"

"Yes."

The re-an's answer startled the all the men guarding the entrance. Even though it sounded like a zombie moan to them, they understood the reply. Slowly, the man closest to the Athenian stepped forward and gently touched his shoulder. When the zombie did not attack or try to bite him, he asked, "So are you really here to help us?"

Prometheus nodded his head and smiled.

* * *

In the field outside the village, Prometheus and the zombies gathered with the villagers. The humans cautiously touched the re-ans who no longer appeared as monsters. Two of the men approached the Athenian escorting a woman from the village. They held up the video camera and played the section where Salsa kissed General Brown so he could understand the human language. One of the men asked, "If you do this with one of our women, would she understand your words and be able to pass the ability to the rest of us?"

Knowing they wouldn't be able to understand his verbal answer, he simply replied with a nod. He reached out his hand motioning for the woman to come closer. With hesitation in her steps, she moved toward the undead coerced slightly by the men. Expressing fear and extreme dislike, she closed her eyes tight and puckered her lips and face. Prometheus gently moved in and placed his dead lips against hers. The woman slightly relaxed her lips and allowed some of the dead man's saliva into her mouth. Not able to tolerate it any more, she pushed the re-an away.

Prometheus asked, "Can you understand my words?"

The woman's eyes opened wide with astonishment as she said, "I can understand the demon's speech."

With a smile, he replied, "My name is Prometheus and I lived a very long time ago."

* * *

As the humans kissed and passed the ability to speak all languages to each other, they happily engaged in conversations with the dead souls from the various time periods. Some of the more recent dead were able to talk to their families again. The gathering took on the atmosphere of a celebration.

General walked up to Prometheus and asked, "So they heard those words from your magic box and we will finally get to pass our life strings to them?"

"Yes, the end has finally come. The mission bestowed upon us by the gods has finally come to the final stage. Salsa showed us we could exchange this DNA by kissing. By the looks of our new friends, it appears possible for us to collect the strings in the same manner."

Prometheus saw a young woman dressed in the same type of clothing as the villagers, wandering through the meadow with the appearance of being lost. He left the gathering to walk out to her and asked, "Greetings, what is your name and from where…what do you remember last?"

The young woman with long sandy colored hair tilted toward him with a bit of a quizzical stare. "I was standing at the fountain to gather a jar of water when the Spartans attacked. A brave man came to my defense, but sadly, he met his demise at the end of sword trying to protect my life. The soldiers pulled me away from him and he ran me through with a blade. After a brief and confusing talk with Zeus, I found myself here. It was only moments ago that I stood at the fountain. How can I be in another land so quickly?"

A smile spread across Prometheus' face. "And, what is your name?"

"I am Gia."

He wrapped his hand around her forearm in the traditional Greek manner. "My name is Prometheus and I have a quite story to tell you."

9 780996 086783